"How to Drive a Man Wild."

Steele read the title then looked down at Taylor and chuckled. Her face flamed with embarrassment, and she was sure her discomfort showed on her face.

"You don't learn this from reading, you learn it from doing." His voice lowered an octave, "If you need a practice partner..."

"I was looking at the other book. I thought it might be a good resource since I don't have a background in criminal law," Taylor said.

His grin broadened as he read the other title. *Killers Without a Conscience.* He shook his head. "Not likely."

"You never know, I may even learn enough to teach you a thing or two," she said, taking refuge in haughtiness.

"I'm sure you could," Steele said. At the husky note in his voice, Taylor looked up at him and wished she hadn't. The way he was looking at her made her feel as if she'd just stepped in front of a raging fire.

Dear Reader,

The verdict is in: legal thrillers are a hit! In response to your demands, we're thrilled to continue with our ongoing program of "Legal Thrillers"—stories of secret scandals and crimes of passion. Of legal eagles who battle the system and undeniable desire.

Maggie Ferguson is one woman who knows her way around a courtroom. She's a lawyer from Springfield, Illinois. Maggie's debut book, *Looks Are Deceiving*, made her an instant reader favorite.

Be sure to look for the "Legal Thriller" flash for the best in romantic suspense!

Regards,

Debra Matteucci
Senior Editor and Editorial Coodinator
Harlequin Books
300 East 42nd Street, Sixth Floor
New York, New York 10017

Crime of
Passion

Maggie Ferguson

Harlequin Books

TORONTO • NEW YORK • LONDON
AMSTERDAM • PARIS • SYDNEY • HAMBURG
STOCKHOLM • ATHENS • TOKYO • MILAN
MADRID • WARSAW • BUDAPEST • AUCKLAND

To my sisters, Juanita and Margaret.
Thanks for your support.

ISBN 0-373-22347-1

CRIME OF PASSION

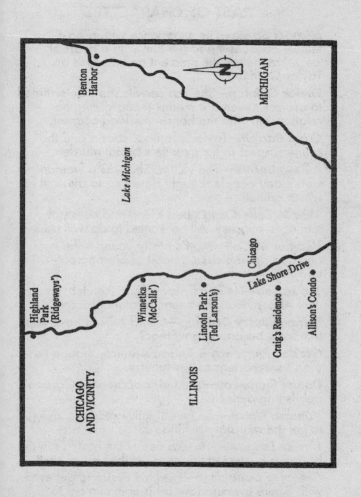

CHICAGO AND VICINITY

ILLINOIS

Highland Park
(Ridgeways')

Winnetka
(McCalls')

Lincoln Park
(Ted Larson's)

Craig's Residence

Allison's Condo

Chicago

Lake Shore Drive

Lake Michigan

Benton Harbor

MICHIGAN

N

CAST OF CHARACTERS

Michael Steele—His experience with a past female cocounsel had left him with a heart of ice...that melted the moment he laid eyes on Taylor Quinlan.

Taylor Quinlan—She has secrets she's determined to protect...even if it means jeopardizing her relationship with the handsome lead counsel.

Craig Barrett—Taylor's famous cousin and the prime suspect in his ex-wife's brutal murder.

Allison Barrett—The victim. She was a woman who many people thought deserved to die, but for which crime?

Matt McCall—Craig's best friend and personal manager–attorney. All he wanted to do was help.

Heather McCall—Matt's pretty young wife. She had an unpleasant habit of blurting out unwelcome truths.

Ted Larson—He usually loved 'em, then left 'em... until Allison. Had she been his fatal attraction?

Senator Barry Denning—Could Allison have kept him from becoming governor?

Gordon Ridgeway—Allison's fiancé, though he didn't shed a tear at her funeral.

Daniel Ridgeway—The heir apparent to Gordon's publishing dynasty.

Vanessa Norris—An investigative reporter, *dying* to get the real story behind Allison's murder.

Hawke Longtree—He was one of the best PI's in the business, but would this case get the best of him?

Detective Donaldson—Had his desire to get even with Steele overshadowed his commitment to uphold the law?

Chapter One

"She was dead before she hit the ground...."

Taylor Quinlan shuddered at Deputy Coroner Dr. James Kingsley's cold recitation of the facts of the murder. From the grim expressions on the faces of Matt and Heather McCall and her cousin Craig, who were seated with her on the courtroom pew, she knew they were similarly affected by the deputy coroner's words.

It was still hard to believe that Allison Barrett was dead. It was even harder to believe that Craig was the prime suspect in her brutal murder. He sat next to her now, staring straight ahead, ramrod stiff. His mahogany-brown-skinned face had a grayish cast, and his brown-black eyes were overbright with unshed tears. Even with everything that had happened between Allison and him, he'd loved her—perhaps obsessively so.

Giving herself a mental shake, Taylor leaned over and squeezed Craig's hand. It was icy cold.

She exchanged a brief look with the stocky, bearded man who sat on the other side of Craig. Matt McCall was Craig's best friend. *Best friend.* She turned the phrase over in her mind. It was such an inadequate description of the relationship the men shared. They couldn't have been closer if they'd been related by blood. Normally Matt's tobacco-brown-skinned face was animated and his black eyes twinkled with merriment, but like Craig, the strain he'd been under since Allison's murder almost a week ago was beginning to show. Now he looked tired and haggard and every one of his thirty-seven years. Taylor hoped he could keep himself emotionally intact through all this; she was counting on him to take her place on Craig's legal defense team—to get her out of this nightmare.

As if he'd read her troubled thoughts, Matt gave her an almost imperceptible thumbs-up sign. She forced a wan smile. She was glad one of them was confident. That was just like him, she thought, seeing the silver lining in a bad situation. But then, he had an advantage. Unlike her, he thought they would be able to get Craig out of this mess.

She was hard-pressed to feel any semblance of confidence as she glanced around the crowded courtroom. It was packed, standing room only, filled with gaping on-lookers, as well as a horde of reporters representing all the media. After all, this was the coroner's inquest into the death of Allison Jane Barrett, estranged wife of popular daytime television talk-show host Craig Barrett. It was a media event.

Unlike other legal proceedings, the coroner's inquest was presided over by the county coroner and was usually conducted in the coroner's office. Due to overwhelming public interest in Allison's death, this inquest was being held in Judge Witherspoon's courtroom. Even though the purpose of the inquest was not to determine guilt or innocence, but rather the cause of the decedent's death and whether foul play was involved, it was still the last place Taylor wanted to be. She was in way over her head. She had no business representing Craig. She had no idea what she'd do if he was called to testify. Her stomach knotted at just the thought. She should have put her foot down when Craig had told her of his plans to attend.

All of this flashed through her mind as Dr. Kingsley paused in his testimony and scanned his notes. "Oh, yes, here it is," he mumbled before peering nearsightedly at Cook County Coroner Barbara Oliver. "I arrived at the crime scene at approximately 1:15 a.m. The body was still warm. The victim's skin had a waxy blue-gray appearance. The lips and nails were pale, and rigor mortis had not set in. Based on the police reports and the temperature of the body when I arrived, I believe death occurred sometime between 10:30 and 11:30 p.m. on the night of Tuesday, July 3.''

The deputy coroner's voice droned on as he responded to a series of technical questions: the position of the body when he arrived, whether the body had been moved, the direction of the blows and whether there was evidence of sexual assault or the presence of drugs or alcohol in Allison's system. He concluded with a brief statement on the general condition of her health.

Next to testify was a young Hispanic police officer, who took his place in the witness seat. The knot in Taylor's stomach got even tighter as she waited for his testimony to begin.

"What time did you discover the body?" the coroner asked.

Officer Gonzales cleared his throat. "The 911 call came in at about eleven-thirty. We were dispatched to the Barrett residence about five minutes later. My partner and I were cruising east on Ontario at about the three-hundred block. I was driving. I cut south on Michigan to Lake Shore Drive. It only took us about three minutes to get over there, but it took us another five minutes to get inside."

"Is that because the house was locked?"

"Yes, ma'am. We ran around back. The curtains at the French doors off the patio were slightly parted, allowing us to see inside. We could see Mrs. Barrett lying on her back in a pool of blood. We smashed a windowpane in one of the French doors and unlocked the door. She was dead, but the body was still warm. I would guess that she had been dead no more than thirty minutes."

"Did you search the premises?" Coroner Oliver asked.

"Yes, ma'am. First we disarmed the security system, which had gone off when we broke the window. Then we conducted a thorough check of the place but didn't find anyone, but we did note that the tape from the surveillance camera outside the condo was missing. It must have been about 12:15 a.m. when we notified homicide and the coroner's office.''

"Thank you, Officer Gonzales. You may step down." The coroner turned to gesture at another officer. "Detective Donaldson, please take the stand."

Taylor watched as a reed-thin redheaded man was sworn in and then took the seat adjacent to the coroner's bench. Coroner Oliver began by asking several preliminary questions: the detective's full name, number of years on the force, nature of his job. From there the questions moved to more substantive matters. "What time did you arrive at the Barrett residence?"

"It was about twelve-thirty."

"Tell us what you found."

"Officers Gonzales and Meeker let us in. They told us that the house had been locked and the security system armed when they arrived. That told me right away that whoever killed Mrs. Barrett knew her well enough to be familiar with her security system. However, the perpetrator obviously left in a big hurry."

"What do you mean?"

"The place was a wreck," Detective Donaldson said, leaning forward slightly. "Books thrown on the floor. Plants strewn about. The contents of Mrs. Barrett's purse dumped on the floor. The scene looked staged to me, though. I think the killer was trying to make it look like she'd walked in on a break-in, but something spooked him before he could finish setting things up."

"So you don't think Mrs. Barrett was killed during the commission of a burglary?"

Detective Donaldson shook his head. "Definitely not. There was no signs of a break-in. Besides, a burglar wouldn't pass up a fourteen-carat-gold-and-diamond bracelet and other expensive jewelry like Mrs. Barrett was wearing in favor of a few dollars from her purse."

"What about physical evidence? Did you find any at the crime scene?"

Detective Donaldson shifted in his seat as if he wasn't entirely comfortable with the question, but Taylor sensed he was playing to the reporters in back—drawing things out, heightening the tension. It was certainly working with her, she thought. Anxiety gnawed in her gut as she waited for his answer.

"Mrs. Barrett was beaten to death with a blunt object," Donaldson said finally. "A fireplace poker was missing, and I think that could have been the murder weapon." He shrugged his stooped shoulders. "Then again, it could have been a large paperweight or candlestick or something of that nature. Whatever the murder weapon was, we didn't find it at the scene. The killer must have taken it with him." Donaldson's face darkened. "There was a lot of blood at the scene, but at this point we don't know if any of it was the killer's. Forensics is still doing DNA testing. The only prints in the room were those of Mrs. Barrett and her husband."

"Did you question the neighbor who called 911?" the coroner asked.

Detective Donaldson nodded. "Yeah, we questioned him." He consulted his notes. "Mr. Lee Trebeck. He said he heard what appeared to be a violent argument coming from the Barrett condo about an hour before he called 911. He wanted to go over, but his wife refused to allow it. By the time he convinced her to let him go over, things had quieted down. When the argument started again, he called the police and watched the Barrett house. He said he saw no one leave, but that isn't too surprising since the front door of the Barrett house is hidden from the Trebecks' by a large hedge." Donaldson paused to glance at Craig, then added, "Mr. Trebeck reported seeing a man cross the street halfway down the block, just before the patrol car arrived."

Taylor closed her eyes. Donaldson's revelation couldn't have been more explosive if he'd said the neighbor had ID'ed Craig. The courtroom buzzed.

"Barrett, it had to be Barrett! Who else would have access to the security code?"

"Did you get the neighbor's name?"

"Phone... I got to get to a phone!"

"Order in the court!" the coroner called out sternly, pounding her gavel. "Order in the court!" The ruckus died down instantly. Coroner Oliver turned back to the witness and nodded. "Please continue, Detective Donaldson."

"As I said, Mr. Trebeck saw this man. Unfortunately it was dark out, and the man was too far away for Mr. Trebeck to get a good look at him. All he could say was that the man was tall, about six feet, with a lean, muscular build."

What was left unsaid, Taylor thought bleakly, was that the neighbor's description roughly matched Craig. Before she could dwell on the significance of that, the coroner's next question commanded her full attention.

"Did you question relatives and friends of the deceased to determine if they were aware of any problems Mrs. Barrett might have been having, or if anyone had a vendetta against her?"

Detective Donaldson nodded. "We questioned a number of Mrs. Barrett's friends. A couple of people reported that a while back she'd had some problems with Ted Larson, a former boyfriend. Nothing serious. The only problem Mrs. Barrett was currently having was with her estranged husband." Donaldson shifted in his chair. "Mr. Barrett admitted that things had been turbulent between them during the marriage and for a period after they separated, but he said that in recent months they'd talked of a reconciliation." Taylor could hear the *but* coming as Donaldson speared Craig with a hard look, then added, "Friends of the deceased verified that what he said was true, but they also said that in recent weeks things had cooled between the couple."

"Did they offer a reason for that?"

The detective nodded. "Mrs. Barrett had begun seeing another man, and that had led to several violent arguments between Barrett and his wife. The day before she was murdered, several people reported hearing Mr. Barrett say something to the effect, 'If I can't have you, then no one will.'"

Taylor's spirits plummeted. Donaldson might as well have said Craig had killed his wife.

The courtroom erupted.

"I knew it!"

"What a story!"

Several reporters raced out of the courtroom to call in this latest development immediately.

"Order in the court! Order in the court!" Coroner Oliver shouted, pounding her gavel as pandemonium reigned. When calm was once again restored, she looked angrily about the courtroom before her gaze came to rest on the reporters in back. "If there are any more outbursts, I'll have the clerk clear the courtroom." Turning back to Donaldson, she asked, "You said Mr. Barrett threatened his wife?"

"That's correct."

"Did you check into his whereabouts on the night of the murder?"

"Yeah, we checked him out." Donaldson's voice was laced with open skepticism. "A female friend of Mr. Barrett, a Pamela Olsen, said he came by her place around ten-thirty and they were together all evening in her apartment."

"What about Mr. Larson?"

Donaldson shook his head. "We checked him out, but he also had an alibi."

"So where are you in the investigation?"

Donaldson shifted uncomfortably in his seat. "At this point we're not ruling anybody in or out. We haven't charged anyone for the murder. We have our suspicions, but nothing concrete that we can act on at this time. Our investigation is still ongoing."

Coroner Oliver excused Detective Donaldson. Taylor's heart jumped in her throat when the coroner looked briefly at Craig, but thankfully he was not called to testify. A stream of witnesses followed: the neighbor, Lee

Trebeck, several friends, police officers and police experts.

When all the testimony had been heard, the coroner briefly addressed the six-person jury before they convened to begin deliberations. To the surprise of no one, they were back in fifteen minutes to present their finding.

"We have heard the testimony of witnesses, police officers and police experts," the jury foreman began. "It is our finding that Allison Jane Barrett met her death at the hands of person or persons unknown. We therefore recommend that this case be referred to the State's Attorney for further investigation as a homicide."

The coroner thanked the jury and discharged them, and people began streaming out of the courtroom. As Taylor had expected, a fairly large contingent of reporters milled around the exit doors in back. No doubt even more were posted in the hallway outside waiting to attack. To avoid the impending onslaught, the clerk ushered Matt, Taylor, Heather and Craig out of the courtroom through a side door and into the elevator used to transport prisoners.

"I told you it would be all right," Matt said as the elevator came to a quiet whoosh on the ground floor. Then he sighed. "But man, I'm glad it's over."

"So am I," Taylor agreed. She looked quickly over her shoulder to make sure none of the reporters had followed them. "Looks like we lost that bunch of gossipmongers, but let's not hang around here to find out."

"I'm with you," Craig said. "I won't be able to relax until we're out of here."

Taylor quickly led the group down a narrow corridor and opened the door leading outside. Instantly several dozen reporters descended upon them like a swarm of angry locusts. Cameras flashed, minicams rolled and microphones pounced.

"Craig, is it true the station is planning to pull your show off the air until the police clear you of any involvement in your wife's murder?"

"It is being reported in a number of papers that in addition to Ms. Quinlan, you've retained Michael Steele to represent you. Is that because you believe the state will be bringing charges against you in connection with your wife's death?"

"What do you think of Howard Dunlap's allegation that Allison was going after half your assets in the divorce action?"

The questions came fast and furious. Taylor and Matt moved quickly, placing themselves between Craig and the media. "No comment," Taylor shouted. "No comment." Out of the corner of her eye, she saw Matt hustling Craig through the mob as Heather scurried behind. When Taylor turned to follow, a woman stepped in front of her, blocking her path. She was in her thirties, very slender, with short blond hair, a toothpaste smile and blue eyes that gleamed with a faintly predatory light. Vanessa Norris, the reigning queen of tabloid television. Taylor issued a silent groan; that was all they needed. Before she could step aside, a microphone was shoved under her nose.

"Ms. Quinlan, why didn't your cousin testify at the inquest? Don't you think the public might construe his failure to speak out against the charges being leveled against him as a sign of guilt?"

"No comment," Taylor said, elbowing Norris out of the way. Ahead of her, Matt quickly maneuvered Craig through the hordes of reporters into a waiting limousine. Taylor followed, slamming the car door after her. She plopped into the seat beside Craig while Heather and Matt took the seat opposite them.

In seconds the car engine roared to life. A horn honked, warning all to get out of the way, then they were moving. Like the parting of the Red Sea, reporters dove to the right and left of the car. It picked up speed, moving fast, faster—leaving minicams and reporters behind.

"I've never been so scared in my life," Heather said, straightening her perfectly coiffed auburn hair that had been slightly mussed during the melee. "They were like

a mob! For a moment there, I thought we might not
make it. Do I look all right?''

Only Heather McCall would ask such a question at a
time like this, Taylor thought. It wasn't that the brown-
eyed, honey-colored beauty was shallow, exactly. *Self-
absorbed* was a more apt description. Actually Taylor
had been amazed that Heather wanted to accompany
them to the inquest. It wasn't as if she and Allison were
close. But that was just like her; one minute you thought
you had her all figured out, and then she'd turn around
and do something totally unexpected.

Regardless of the kind of woman she was, it was clear
that Matt loved her dearly. A sad smile touched Taylor's
lips as she watched Matt put a protective arm around his
wife of ten months and whisper something to her. How
she wished she could have that kind of close, loving relationship with someone. A husband, children...the
whole nine yards.

It was not to be for her, though, and she'd accepted
that long ago. Mental illness. Two little words. Words
that she had attached little meaning to until the year she
turned sixteen. Losing her parents at the age of ten,
moving to another state to live with her Uncle Bob and
Aunt Ida, their subsequent divorce and later Uncle Bob's
suicide had made her a quiet, withdrawn child. It had
taken time, but with Aunt Ida's loving guidance she'd finally come out of her shell.

The school year had started off wonderfully: she and
her best friend, Sally, were in the same homeroom; she'd
made the cheerleader squad; and topping things off, Ken
Parker, the most popular boy in high school, had asked
her out. She'd been on cloud nine and couldn't wait to tell
her aunt the good news, but instead of being happy for
her, a strange expression had crossed Aunt Ida's face,
followed by an even stranger statement that she should
not take him too seriously.

Naturally Taylor had questioned her about the cryptic
comment. That was when she'd broken down and told
Taylor the secret she'd borne alone for so many years. A

secret that she had not even been able to share with her own son, Craig. A secret that would change Taylor's life forever. Aunt Ida had tearfully explained that the Barretts had a bad gene, a gene that left them predisposed to mental illness. The evidence was irrefutable. Grandpa Barrett, her uncle and her mother had all been its victims.

The picture she presented of Taylor's mother and Uncle Bob was of two people given to bouts of depression, irrational, sometimes even violent behavior that had ended in suicide and murder. She'd explained in detail the lengths she and Taylor's father had gone to hide the true state of their spouses' mental condition from her and Craig and the outside world. But sadly they had been unable to halt the progression of the disease, and it had first robbed them of their faculties and ultimately taken their lives.

If Taylor lived to be a hundred, she'd always remember the horror she'd felt at hearing how her parents had really died, as well as what the future held for her. It had been like a death sentence. It didn't matter that the doctors couldn't say whether she and Craig would in fact suffer the same fate as their parents. In her young mind, life as she knew it was over. Frightened and confused, she'd refused to heed her aunt's warnings about not saying anything to anyone, and confided in her best friend, Sally. The moment the words were out, she'd wished she could take them back. She'd seen revulsion and then fear in Sally's eyes, and that was the end of their friendship. After that she'd needed no further prompting about not saying anything to anyone.

As she'd gotten older and came to understand what life had been like for her father and aunt with their respective spouses, she'd known that marriage and children were out of the question. She wouldn't bring anyone else into her nightmare. That was why she had steered clear of personal entanglements, focusing instead on her legal career.

And that was also why she was now racked with un-
certainty about Craig's innocence. God, she didn't want
to believe he could hurt anyone, least of all Allison, but
with their family history, she had to face the fact that it
was possible. Under the circumstances, was it really fair
or even ethical for her to represent him? Yet she couldn't
tell anyone how she was feeling. She was backed into a
corner.

"Taylor?"

Craig's voice slowly penetrated her troubled thoughts.

"I'm sorry, Craig," she said, pulling herself together.
"What did you say?"

"I want to thank you for coming with us today." He
cleared his throat. "I know we haven't been close in recent years, and we've had our differences, but..." His
voice trailed off.

Taylor nodded vaguely. "Forget it. I want to help."
She knew the words sounded inadequate. She wished she
could say something more encouraging, but the words
caught in her throat.

"What happens next?" Heather asked, looking from
Matt to Taylor. "Do you think the State's Attorney will
pursue the matter?"

She groaned inwardly. That was the last thing she
wanted to discuss in front of Craig. From the look Matt
threw her, she knew that he felt the same way.

"We'll have to wait and see," she said. Then, in an effort to steer the conversation in a different direction, she
asked, "Did you see Vanessa Norris out there?"

"Yeah, no doubt trying to see what other dirt she
could stir up," Matt said, following her lead. He looked
at Craig. "Man, I couldn't believe it when I flipped on
the set this morning and there was Howard Dunlap being interviewed by Norris. He should be strung up by his
thumbs. For Pete's sake, the guy's your personal assistant."

"*Ex*-assistant," Craig corrected with a sigh.

"Whatever," Matt said with a dismissive wave of his
hand. "But Dunlap is supposed to be your friend. He

knows better than to talk to that barracuda. The woman is the queen of slime.''

Taylor nodded. ''I know that and you know that, but a lot of the viewing public don't. Because of her stint as an investigative reporter with the *Washington Times,* people think she's a fair and objective reporter.''

''That's the problem,'' Matt said, warming to the subject. ''A lot of people believe her. After this morning's show, a large segment of the public probably believe that Craig killed Allison because she was bleeding him dry.''

''Don't forget yesterday's show,'' Craig added, his voice laced with pain. ''According to police sources, I killed Allison in a jealous rage.''

''No one who knows you could possibly believe that,'' Heather soothed.

''Oh, God, I keep thinking this is just a nightmare and I'm going to wake up,'' Craig muttered. He turned his head to the side and stared bleakly out the car window. The early afternoon sun beamed into the car, casting light and dark shadow on the high cheekbones of his face. With his shaved head and long, slender neck, he looked desolate and utterly vulnerable.

Taylor swallowed hard and bit back tears. If only she'd been able to convince Aunt Ida to tell him about his possible medical condition, maybe they wouldn't be facing this problem today.

A strained silence settled over the car's occupants and was finally broken by Matt as he leaned over and gave his friend's arm a reassuring squeeze. ''Sorry, buddy, but you're news and news spells ratings. I'm afraid things are going to get a whole lot rougher before they get better.'' He gave Craig a faint smile. ''But you know, Heather and I are here for you. And Taylor is meeting with Michael Steele later this afternoon. We're going to get you out of this.''

''Why are we being so pessimistic?'' Heather asked. ''Maybe it will all blow over. Isn't that why you're paying Michael Steele a small fortune to make sure it does?''

"We're being realistic," Taylor said cautiously. "We're hoping for the best, but we have to be prepared for the worst. That's why I thought we should bring in a criminal defense attorney now. We have to be prepared for anything that happens."

"You sure you don't want me to sit in at the meeting with Steele?" Craig asked.

Taylor shook her head. "This first meeting should be with just the lawyers." She tried to sound confident and upbeat. "We need to talk procedural stuff."

"Translated, she's going to try to convince Steele to let me take her place," Matt said.

"I—I think it would be for the best," Taylor added quickly.

Craig gave Matt a wan smile. "I'm sorry Steele wasn't amenable to both of you helping with the case. At first he insisted on working alone. When he finally agreed to let Taylor act as co-counsel, I let it go. I didn't press too hard because I didn't want him to refuse to take the case."

Matt issued a weary sigh. "We really shouldn't have been surprised. He does have a reputation for being a lone wolf."

Craig's eyes moved from Taylor to Matt. "Then I guess we scored something of a victory that Steele even agreed to let Taylor assist."

Lucky me, Taylor thought miserably.

Heather's pretty, heart-shaped face puckered into a frown. "I still don't understand why he selected you. Matt has practiced more than a dozen years and he's handled several criminal cases, while..." She gave Taylor a tight little smile. "Well, you're just twenty-eight. You've only been out of law school four years and you've never even handled a criminal case. No offense, but Matt is infinitely better qualified than you."

Taylor shrugged. "I couldn't agree with you more. Frankly I don't understand it, either. Steele didn't give Craig any reason, but he did make it clear that he would only need my help for a few weeks at the most."

"I hope that means he thinks no charges will be brought against Craig," Matt said.

"God, I hope that's the case," Craig said, his voice heavy with emotion.

Me, too, thought Taylor. *Me, too.*

A few minutes later the car pulled up to the curb in front of a tall downtown office building.

"Do you really have to go into the office?" Heather asked her husband, pouting prettily.

Matt gave her an indulgent smile. "'Fraid so, but I'll be home early. Taylor is meeting with Steele in—" he glanced at his watch "—fifteen minutes. I want to hang around just in case Steele goes along with the substitution or will at least let me help with procedural matters." He paused, then looked at Craig. "I want you to go home with Heather. When our meeting is over, I'll run by your place and pick up a few things for you. We'll bring Steele by later this evening."

Craig frowned. "I can't impose on you—"

"Nonsense. You're not imposing. You're my best friend, and I want to help. Besides, the number of reporters camped outside your house has probably doubled now that Allison's death has been officially ruled a homicide."

Craig ran a hand over his shaved head in frustration. "Once they figure out I'm at your place, they'll just camp out there. I can't do that to you."

"You're going to stay with Heather and me, and that's final." Matt's voice brooked no argument.

Heather offered Craig a warm smile. "We're family," she said, taking his hand in hers. "Families stick together, especially at a time like this."

Craig's mouth curved into a slight smile. "Thanks."

"Now that that's settled, Taylor and I had better get going," Matt said. He gave Heather a quick kiss.

"See you in a few hours," Taylor said, alighting from the limousine.

Matt fell into step beside her as they entered the thirty-story office building and crossed to the bank of elevators. "It looks bad," he murmured.

Taylor nodded. "I know. I didn't want to say anything in front of Craig, but Donaldson all but said he thought Craig was the killer."

The elevator doors opened and they got on with several other businessmen, effectively cutting off further conversation until they were in Matt's office. There he began to pace back and forth like a caged tiger. Taylor took the chair across from his desk.

"What really galls me is Donaldson's talk about looking at the evidence and other people. That's just so much bunk." Matt emphasized his statement with a flick of his hand. "We all know that the only person the cops are looking at is Craig. Oh, I know the boyfriend or spouse of a murdered victim is the first person the police look at, but I thought they would move beyond that, that they would at least follow up on other leads."

Taylor nodded in agreement. "I read the statement Craig gave the police. There's nothing really incriminating in it."

Matt slumped wearily into a leather chair next to his oak desk. "I didn't see anything, either. I hope we haven't overlooked something." For a moment Matt remained silent, staring down at his hands. When he looked up, his expression was bleak. "I just wish he hadn't said anything at all. I should have tied him down. Knocked him out. Done something . . . *anything* to stop him from going to the police."

Taylor sighed. "Don't blame yourself. You did what you could. You know how bullheaded Craig can be. He wouldn't listen to you or me."

"But I'm his lawyer—"

"You're his *manager* and *entertainment* lawyer," Taylor corrected. "Neither you nor I have a background in criminal law. That's why we agreed that we needed to bring in someone who does." She chewed her lower lip.

"I wish he'd gone with Leonard Friedman instead of Michael Steele."

He gave her a sharp look. "Are you having second thoughts?"

She shook her head. "Not about the need for a criminal lawyer. Just about Steele."

"Steele's the best there is. We were darn lucky to get him."

"I know," Taylor hedged. How could she explain that ever since she'd heard that Steele was taking the case, she'd had an uneasy feeling about him. They had never met, but she sensed that Steele would not be as malleable as Friedman would have been. And damn, that was what she needed...someone who wouldn't probe too deeply her reason for not wanting to represent Craig. She felt as if she was drowning in quicksand; the harder she fought, the deeper she sank.

"Taylor? Is everything all right?" Matt asked. His face searched hers, concerned.

She offered him a faint smile. "It's just nerves." She glanced at her watch. "By the way, it's one-thirty. Where is our esteemed attorney?"

AT THAT VERY MOMENT, Michael Steele was sprinting along LaSalle Street. "Damn," he muttered as his hazel eyes quickly scanned the building addresses. Where the hell was that building? He checked his watch again. One-thirty.

He realized now that he should have taken a cab from the hotel. After spending the past four days cooped up in his office until all hours of the night trying to clear his calendar before leaving for Chicago, he had felt the need to stretch his legs and get some fresh air. Last night had been especially grueling. He'd worked late into the night to finish several projects, including an appellate brief for a client currently serving a twenty-year prison term. When he'd finally gotten home in the wee hours of the morning, he'd fallen into bed and promptly overslept, missing his early-morning flight out of Washington-

Dulles. He'd had to scramble to get a seat on a later flight.

He'd looked forward to relaxing once he reached his hotel, but that was not to be. Instead, a bombshell had been dropped on him: Gavin Walker, one of his senior attorneys, would not be able to assist him on the Barrett case after all. If Steele hadn't already committed himself, he would've dropped it right then and there. The case was problematic as it was, and this would only make the situation worse. He already had two major criminal cases going; now he was trying to juggle a third.

He issued a weary sigh. He was definitely getting too old for this kind of juggling act. That thought made him sigh again. If the truth be known, he was tired of that and a whole lot of things—like coming home every night to an empty house.

Lately Steele had caught himself wondering what it would be like to have a private life, to have more than a fleeting liaison with a member of the opposite sex, to have a real home—a wife, children. Unfortunately he never seemed to get much further than wondering. After his disastrous relationship with Daphne Brooks, he'd found it hard to trust anyone. It was easier to submerge himself in work. That wasn't much of a hardship; law was in his blood.

Which was the reason why, at one forty-five that afternoon, Steele found himself charging up the steps of a prestigious LaSalle Street office building on his way to a meeting with Craig Barrett's attorney. He needed another criminal case like he needed a hole in the head. Yet the moment he'd read Gavin's preliminary write-up of the case, he'd known he was going to take it.

It was the kind of case that had gotten Steele involved in law in the first place—a case in which all the signs pointed to a man headed to prison for a crime he hadn't committed. Most of Steele's clients were poor, and he handled many of those cases for free. That was one reason why he was willing to take the occasional high-profile, large-fee-generating case like Barrett's—to support those cases that generated no fee at all. He smiled wryly. Hell, he'd take any case where he thought a miscarriage of justice was about to take place.

His eyes narrowed as he stepped into the elevator. Something wasn't right about the Barrett case. He couldn't put his finger on it, but something pulled at the back of his mind. He had a bad feeling about Taylor Quinlan, and now he found himself being saddled with her—not for just a few weeks as he'd originally thought, but for the duration of the case. If he had his druthers, he wouldn't let her within a mile of it.

Unfortunately he didn't have a choice. He was already stretched to the limit, and the only way he could take this case on would be with the assistance of other counsel. In the past, when he'd found himself in this kind of bind, Gavin Walker had been there to pick up the slack. Not this time. Gavin couldn't do it, and he couldn't bring in anyone else. The press had already gotten wind of Quinlan's involvement in the case. If he dropped her now, they would put the worst possible interpretation on it. He was stuck with her. But he was going to make damn sure he got some answers before they went any further.

Steele shook off these thoughts as he stepped off the elevator on the twenty-seventh floor and looked around the luxurious reception area of the law firm of Haraman, Giusto, McCall and Williams. The walls were adorned with original art, the carpeting was thick and plush and the furnishings had cost more than most people earned in a year. He was sure it was meant to drive home to prospective clients a single, unassailable fact: they were getting the best legal minds that money could buy.

As he approached, he saw that the large oak reception desk in the center of the room was empty. Several office doors off the lobby were also closed.

He was about to take one of the plush seats in the waiting area when he noticed an open door a few yards away. He crossed the lobby and stepped inside. For a moment it appeared that the office was vacant. Then he spotted the woman standing next to a brown leather chair off to the side. Her back was to him, and she was deep in thought as she scribbled on a yellow legal pad.

Steele found himself staring at her, his imagination thoroughly captured by what he could see of the woman. She was raven-haired and petite—no more than five-two, he estimated. Even though she was in high heels, the top of her head would barely reach his chin.

His gaze slowly traveled over her slim figure, noting the gentle curve of her hips and tiny waist. Her appearance was classy and sleek. The cut and fabric of her navy summer knit suit was very chic, but at the same time professional. She wore it with a careless ease that suggested she'd selected it for comfort, not effect. He liked that.

Steele leaned against the doorframe, appreciating the soft way her blue-black hair swayed about her shoulder blades as she bent to retrieve a paper that had fallen to the floor. When she stood, she flipped her hair back over one shoulder. The action made one nicely rounded hip rotate in what he considered a very seductive way. A slow smile curved his lips as his eyes slowly traveled over her figure, noting again the gentle curve of her hips and small waist and shapely legs. One small, navy-leather-shod foot was tapping impatiently.

It was the incongruity of that restless movement that sidetracked Steele's concentration enough for him to register what the faceless beauty had just uttered.

"Damn." The softly spoken epithet contrasted with the elegant setting.

"Tsk. Tsk. Tsk. Didn't your mother ever tell you about swearing?"

The woman turned around, and Steele found himself looking into the most arresting face he'd ever seen. She had big, brown, almond-shaped eyes, an oval face and caramel-colored skin that was as flawless and smooth as a fine figurine. Her raven black hair framed a face that could only be described as breathtaking.

Lord, but she was pretty. Who was she? Maybe Chicago was not going to be so bad after all.

"I'm sorry," he said, smiling warmly. "I didn't mean to startle you. I was just surprised to hear one of the unmentionable words pass the lips of such a lovely woman."

Taylor blinked in surprise. For a moment she thought she'd conjured up the handsome stranger who stood before her. God, but he was good-looking. His features were chiseled perfection; his hair, curly and jet black; his skin, a smooth golden bronze. His mouth was finely molded with full, sensuous lips above a cleft chin. And his eyes . . . They were an incredible shade of hazel and contrasted sharply with his coloring. He was tall, over six feet, and broad shouldered with a lean but sculptured body that radiated male-animal virility. Despite the July heat, he was wearing a smoke gray Italian tailored suit that fit his tall, lean frame to utter perfection.

She sensed that he wasn't just a pretty face, though. There was strength in his bearing. Power seemed to emanate from him. She could also see the self-assured way he moved, and she was sure that besides being handsome and charming, he was tough and daring.

And dangerous, said something inside her.

When he flashed her a brilliant smile, displaying even, white teeth, Taylor felt a tug of attraction that went right down to her toes. Good grief, she had to get hold of herself! Michael Steele would be here at any moment. The last thing she wanted was for him to find her behaving like a blubbering idiot over some man.

She tried to sound casual as she said, "You didn't startle me. And yes, that was one of those words my mother told me not to use. She also told me not to talk to strangers."

"Ah, a very wise woman," he said easily. "In general her advice was sound, but I'm not a stranger."

God, his voice. It was low and husky and impossibly sexy. "Have we met before?" she asked, finding herself responding to his light flirtation.

Hazel eyes held brown ones. "Trust me," he said in that low, husky voice of his, "you'd remember."

Taylor couldn't stop the involuntary shiver that slithered along her spine in response to the sexy drawl. She tried to tell herself that it was due to nervousness about her upcoming meeting with Michael Steele, and not the man who stood before her. "So we are strangers?"

"Strangers are simply people who haven't met."

She tried to suppress the smile that played at the corners of her lips. "That's an interesting way to look at things."

"I think so." He smiled and walked toward her, moving with a casual masculine grace. Her heart flitted as he paused in front of her, standing so close she could feel the heat that radiated from his body and smell the spicy scent of his after-shave. Only sheer willpower kept her from taking a step back. "Allow me to introduce myself," he said, extending his hand. "I'm Michael Steele."

Taylor felt as if she'd been doused with a bucket of cold water. *Michael Steele!* That was who she had been drooling over? Instantly her guard was up. He was much younger than she'd imagined—maybe thirty-five, thirty-six—and far more dangerous. Good manners dictated that she take his hand. "It's nice meeting you, Mr. Steele," she said coolly. "I'm Taylor Quinlan."

His eyes narrowed slightly, but that was the only sign that he'd noticed her change in demeanor. "It's nice to meet you, too," he said, taking her hand.

She tried to ignore the warmth his hand generated and the fact that he held hers a fraction too long. She pulled her hand back and swallowed hard, fighting the awkwardness that swept over her. The man had her at a distinct disadvantage. "Mr. McCall just stepped out," she said, fighting a case of nerves. "As soon as he returns, we'll head down to my office."

"No rush," he said, continuing to study her. "It'll give us time to get acquainted."

That was the last thing she wanted. She had absolutely no interest in getting to know him on any level. If things worked out as she hoped, this would be their one and only meeting. A polite, dismissive smile etched her mouth as she tried to put some distance between them. "I must say I'm a little surprised. I'd have thought that someone of your caliber, an attorney with a near-perfect defense record, reputed to be something of a sorcerer—that you knew everything there is to know about everything and everybody."

He chuckled—a rich, throaty sound that made her pulse quicken despite her resolve. "I've met some prosecutors who thought that. Based on the directions I was given to your office, you must have thought something along those same lines. Didn't anyone ever tell you that men..."

Her eyes narrowed. He was just like a lot of her male colleagues. She finished the sentence for him: "Don't like outspoken women? But they respect aggressive men."

Without missing a beat, he said, "I was going to say, 'Didn't they ever tell you that men don't ask directions?' You should have drawn a map. Your office is damn hard to find."

Taylor flushed, but she was saved from having to respond because at that moment Matt chose to step into the room.

"Were you able to decipher my notes—" Matt's voice trailed off when he noticed the man standing next to Taylor.

"Matthew McCall, this is Michael Steele," Taylor said by way of introduction.

"It's a pleasure meeting you, Mr. Steele," Matt said, moving into the room, his hand outstretched.

Steele stepped forward and shook Matt's hand.

Taylor took a deep breath, then plunged right in. "I wish you'd reconsider about letting Mr. McCall act as your co-counsel instead of me. He's been Craig's attorney for more than twelve years, and he has some criminal defense background. Of the two of us, he's really the better qualified."

Steele gave her a contemplative look. "I'm sure Mr. McCall is a fine attorney, but let's leave things the way they are," he said smoothly. "Now, if you don't mind, is there someplace we can talk in private?" His words were spoken easily, but there was a finality behind them that made it clear this was a closed subject.

After a brief, strained silence, Matt coughed. "Oh, sure, I understand."

"I don't," Taylor said, not willing to give up. "I don't see why—"

Matt held up a hand, halting her words. "It's all right."

No, it wasn't all right, and she wanted to scream in frustration. She looked at Matt sharply. He seemed relieved more than disappointed. That he was already trying to make the best of a bad situation only intensified her anger.

"If you'll excuse Mr. Steele and me," she said through clenched teeth.

"Nice meeting you," Steele said, cupping her elbow. Electricity coursed through her body. She sucked in her breath, then released it slowly, trying to hide the jolt he had given her. Beside her, Steele chuckled. The fact that he was aware of her reaction introduced a vaguely alarming element into the atmosphere. Damn! Why couldn't he be short, fat and bald? That would have certainly made it a lot easier to work with him. It was going to be hard enough dealing with him without this added complication of unwanted sexual attraction.

"This way, please," she said, amazed at how calm she sounded as she turned and walked out of the office, across the carpeted lobby and down a narrow corridor. She quickened her steps, forcing him to relinquish her elbow. Then she realized that having him walk slightly behind her was just as bad. She could feel his eyes on her, studying her, stripping away her secrets. She quickened her steps. She didn't understand her attraction to him. She'd worked with powerful men before. Even a few handsome ones. But none had ever affected her in this manner. The sooner they got this meeting over with, the sooner she could go back to her safe cocoon.

Her secretary, Brenda, a young, pretty blonde, looked up from her computer screen as they approached. Brenda's face broke into a smile at the sight of the extremely handsome man walking next to her boss. Taylor was tempted to tell her to stop gaping, but instead deposited the legal document in Brenda's In box for typing. Brenda's smile slipped slightly at the look on her boss's face. She dropped her eyes to her keyboard and resumed typing the document she'd been working on.

Steele walked ahead of her into a wide, spacious office and took the chair she indicated in front of the big oak desk. She closed the door, then sat down in the leather swivel chair behind the desk.

For a moment neither spoke. His hazel eyes, keen and direct, inspected her face as if he were an examiner and she a candidate—which she supposed she was. The direct and glittering stare, in contrast to his sensuous mouth, was disconcerting.

Seconds ticked by, and still he said nothing. She was on the verge of asking him what was the point of this meeting when he finally broke the silence. But his question was the last thing she'd expected him to say.

"Why don't we begin by your telling me why you believe your cousin is guilty?"

Chapter Two

Taylor felt as if she'd just taken a punch in the solar plexus. She had no idea how to answer the question. She shuffled through some papers on her desk. She knew that Steele would perceive her move as buying time, which was exactly what she was doing. She needed time to think—to decide how much to tell him. His straightforward question revealed that he was an extremely perceptive man. The kind of song and dance she could have given Friedman—or Matt, for that matter, if the question had arisen—wouldn't work with Steele. Nothing but the truth, albeit an abbreviated version, would do. She'd tell him about Craig's temper and his father's suicide—that was common knowledge anyway—but nothing else.

Having decided her course of action, she looked up. Her eyes briefly touched Steele's, then flicked away. "It's not that I believe Craig killed Allison," she said, feeling as if she was navigating a mine field. "It's just that I think he's *capable* of having done so."

If there was any doubt in Taylor's mind that her response sounded lame, that doubt vanished the instant Steele fixed her with his gaze. For a few dramatic moments he said nothing, merely stared at her with eyes that left her feeling that he could see right through to her very soul. Taylor suspected she'd just discovered one of the secrets to his legal success.

"Given the right provocation, I think we're all capable of committing murder," Steele said with more than a hint of cynicism. "But you haven't answered my question. Why do you think Barrett could have killed his wife? Was there violence in the marriage?"

She shook her head. "Not to my knowledge."

"Was she afraid of him?"

An image of Allison's flashing black eyes and saucy brown-skinned face sprang to mind. She couldn't imagine Allison afraid of anyone. "No," she said, shaking her head. "I don't think so."

"Have you ever observed any violence on the part of Mr. Barrett toward anyone?" Then he added dryly, "Disregarding his TV antics, of course."

She was now treading on dangerous ground. "That's not the reason," she said, trying to sidestep the question. "You don't understand." She ran a hand over her face in frustration. How could she explain her reservations about Craig's innocence without exposing too much family history?

"Then why don't you enlighten me?" He leaned back in the chair, folded his arms across his chest and looked her straight in the eyes. It was clear from his body language that he wasn't budging until he got some answers.

She approached it in a different way. "Craig is like his father. Uh—uh, high-strung."

"If you're trying to say his father committed suicide, I know. But that has no bearing on the case."

Taylor cleared her throat. "I guess what I'm trying to say is that Craig is something of a...loose cannon. He always has been." She stood and paced in front of her desk. "Outside of a few close family members, I doubt if anyone knows that side of him even exists. People see his Montel Williams good looks and charismatic ways, and don't look any deeper." She paused and looked at her clasped hands for a moment.

When she lifted her head, the unhappiness in her eyes stirred Steele's protective instincts, and he had a crazy impulse to wrap his arms around her. He cleared his throat. "Just take your time," he coaxed.

Taylor drew a ragged breath. "My parents died when I was ten, and I went to live with the Barretts. Our families were very close, so I was around Craig a lot even though he's eight years older than me. He was the fair-haired child. Everyone loved him...wanted to please him. Consequently he always got what he wanted. Maybe that's why he doesn't deal with rejection very well. He gets...well, irrational when he doesn't get his way."

Steele sat up, immediately alert. "What do you mean by irrational?"

She gave a tiny shrug. "Temper tantrums leading to out-of-control behavior. Throwing things around, smashing objects."

Steele's lips pulled down in a frown. "Can you be more specific?"

That was exactly what she'd been trying not to be, but apparently nothing less would do. She walked around the desk and sat back down as she tried to think of an incident that illustrated what she meant but didn't disclose too much. "One particular event stands out," she said at last. "I had just turned twelve. Craig was home for the summer from college. He'd had his eye on this little red convertible, but before he could get the money, Mark Rodgers bought it. Craig offered to buy the car from him, but Rodgers refused to sell it. Craig was furious. He vowed that he'd make Rodgers sorry."

"Did he?"

She nodded. "He and some of his friends held the guy by his feet upside down off a bridge and threatened to drop him unless he agreed to sell the car to Craig. Mark learned the hard way not to cross Craig, that it was simply easier to give him what he wanted."

Steele thought about that, then shrugged. "It sounds like a dumb college prank. You were only twelve. Isn't it possible you misconstrued the situation and made it more sinister than it really was?"

She shook her head sadly. "I've seen too many rash and reckless acts on his part to have misconstrued the situation. I'm not saying Craig is a cold-blooded killer. He's impulsive and acts out when he doesn't get his way." She issued a weary sigh. "My point is that Allison is the only thing Craig ever wanted that he didn't get. And believe me, he wasn't handling it well. It's true what they said. He did threaten her. I heard him. At the time I didn't think he meant it. None of us did, but now..." Her voice trailed off. She stared at him bleakly. "Now do you understand why I can't work with you on this case?"

Unfortunately Steele did, and a whole lot more. "What I now understand is why you've let Barrett run rough-shod over you."

The statement shocked her. "I've done no such thing!"

"What do you call letting Barrett talk to the police, the media and anyone else he damn well pleases? And let's not forget the matter of today's coroner's inquest."

Her eyes widened. He knew about that?

"Oh, yeah," he said, nodding as if he'd read her mind. "I know that Craig attended the inquest and that you and McCall accompanied him. What the hell were you thinking? I'm surprised you didn't let him testify."

Taylor tilted her chin upward at an angle that was decidedly defiant. "I'm not stupid," she said angrily.

"No, you're not. But you've never handled a criminal case." His voice was deliberately harsh. "It's obvious you know nothing about criminal procedure. No competent attorney would have set foot in that courtroom, let alone allowed his client to do so."

"How dare you!" she snapped.

"You need to hear some hard truths and stop looking at things like some victimized heroine in a romance novel," he went on. "It seems to me that you've done nothing but wallow in self-pity. This case isn't about you. If you thought you couldn't be objective, you shouldn't have agreed to represent Barrett in the first place. But you did, and now he's entitled to your sound legal judgment."

Taylor had to hang on to her temper. "That's what I've given him," she shot back.

"In a pig's eye!" he snarled. "I read that report you and McCall sent me. If you ever decide to give up law, you've got the making for a first-class career as a fiction writer. Because that's what that report was." Steele paused at the stricken look on her face. A part of him felt like a louse for attacking her in this way, but if they were going to work together they needed to clear the air. "Make no mistake about it," he went on, "your cousin is going to be charged with murder. It's just a matter of time. While you've been immobilized and holding Barrett's hand, the police have been busy building a case against him. From what my investigator has been able to determine, the evidence they have against him is strong and getting stronger."

A ripple of apprehension coursed through her. "What do you mean, it's getting stronger?"

"Your cousin's alibi has more holes than a sieve." He gave her a hard look. "Barrett was not with Pamela Olsen at the time his wife was murdered, as he claims."

She looked at him, puzzled. "But Pam gave a sworn statement to the police. *Craig was with her.*"

His eyes didn't waver from hers. "How could Barrett have been with Ms. Olsen when she wasn't even in town at the time the murder occurred?"

Taylor felt as if a rug had been pulled out from under her. Figuratively speaking, it had. "Craig wasn't with Pam?" she asked, gripping the arms of her chair. Bone-chilling cold invaded her body as her mind registered the horrible truth.

Steele shook his head. "Maybe for a part of the evening, but not for all of it and certainly not during the time the murder was committed."

"Are you sure?" She ran her tongue over suddenly dry lips. "Maybe your investigator is mistaken."

He shook his head again. "Hawk Longtree is one of the best P.I.'s in the business. He checked out Olsen's claim. Oh, it required some digging, but he found a gas-station attendant in Springfield who is willing to swear that at eight-fifteen on the night of the murder, he was changing Pamela Olsen's tire. I also have a copy of the credit-card receipt she used to pay for the work. Even if she'd driven eighty miles an hour from Springfield to Chicago, she couldn't have made it back to her Hyde Park apartment by ten-thirty, the time she and Craig are supposed to have been together.''

She closed her eyes. *Craig killed Allison.* ''This is a nightmare.''

''Tell me about it,'' Steele agreed dryly. At her bleak expression, he realized what she was thinking and quickly sought to reassure her. ''Hey, that doesn't mean he's guilty.''

''Why else would he lie?'' Taylor asked in a low, tormented voice.

His heart turned over at her bleak look. Again he had to fight the urge to wrap his arms around her and tell her it was all right. He cleared his throat. ''Scared people do it all the time.'' He gave her a wry smile. ''They see the possibility of doing time. They feel backed into a corner and feel as if they have to account for every minute of their time. In a sense, they're right. That's when the lies start. Unfortunately those lies have a way of coming back to haunt the accused...as they will for Barrett.'' He paused, then added, ''His credibility with the cops and the public has no doubt been shot to hell.''

Taylor gave herself a mental shake as she struggled to take it all in. ''I keep thinking there has to be some mistake. The police would have uncovered his lie if that was the case.''

''Not necessarily,'' Steele said, leaning back in his chair. ''It means the police have done a lousy job of investigating this case so far, but don't count on it remaining that way. Your cousin is news. He's a television personality whose wife has been brutally murdered. Every newspaper and TV station in the country is covering this story. You can bet your bottom dollar they'll be combing through every shred of information that comes out. If the police don't uncover Barrett's lie, some hot-shot reporter will." He made this statement with conviction. "Be that as it may, it doesn't solve our immediate problem—that of working together on this case."

"I don't see how—"

He held up a hand, halting her words. "When I originally agreed to let you act as co-counsel, I did so because of your background in constitutional law and civil rights. I thought you would be able to pick up the slack until my senior attorney could take over in about a month. However, his condition is more complicated than his doctor initially thought, and he's now on indefinite medical leave. If I had known how you felt, I never would have agreed to let you assist me, but if you leave now it would generate too much media speculation." He looked at her, puzzled. "What I don't understand is why you agreed to represent Barrett in the first place, knowing how you felt."

Taylor wrapped her arms around herself and stared at him bleakly. "Craig's mother, my Aunt Ida, asked me to represent him...or to at least work with his defense team. Like many African-Americans, she doesn't fully trust the legal system." Taylor swallowed hard. "At first I refused, citing the fact that we were related. Then she went to work on Craig. He thought it was a great idea that Matt and I represent him. He approached Rich Haraman, the senior partner, with the idea. Craig has brought a lot of money into this firm, and I have no doubt that Haraman could see a hefty legal bill coming out of our participation in the case. Naturally he was agreeable."

Steele shook his head. "You still should have said something."

She turned tortured eyes on him. "What was I going to say? I couldn't tell anyone that I thought Craig might have killed Allison. I feel like a heel as it is. And what if it got back to my aunt? She would have been devastated. I couldn't take the chance. I owe her so much. She practically raised me. Besides, I was able to convince Craig to hire a criminal defense attorney as lead counsel, and you said you'd only need me for a few weeks. I thought I would be able to get off the case before things went too far."

Steele nodded slowly. "Yeah, but that's not the way things have worked out." He looked at her curiously. "I take it neither Barrett nor McCall know how you feel."

Taylor shook her head. "Why don't we save ourselves a lot of grief. Let Matt take my place. That's what should have happened in the first place. He's more qualified and better suited to assist you. This whole thing has been as hard on him as it has been on Craig. I think it would help if he knew he was doing something concrete to help Craig. Besides, he truly believes in Craig's innocence."

Steele frowned. "McCall is too emotionally involved. It's impossible for him to be objective." He shook his head. "I can't let him work on the case. He'll continue treating Barrett with kid gloves, and Barrett will continue taking advantage of the situation. I know I came down hard on you about letting Barrett attend the inquest, but my hunch is that was McCall's doing."

She flushed and looked away. The man was entirely too astute.

He issued a weary sigh. "I can't handle this case alone, so if you really don't think you can be objective, then I'm going to have to drop it."

Taylor's eyes flew to his face. "You can't do that! You can't refuse to represent Craig because we can't work together!"

Unfortunately his greater fear was that he would very much like to work with her. Aloud he said, "This has nothing to do with my wanting or not wanting to work with you, and frankly you've got to stop looking at this case so subjectively. You're not the first lawyer to have reservations about a client's innocence. It's how you handle it that is important. You can't let it cloud your judgment. You think Barrett may be guilty. But *thinking* he's guilty and *knowing* it are two different things." He hesitated, then said, "In the early days of my career, I was involved in a case in which my co-counsel and I had this same kind of disagreement, although I didn't know it at the time.''

Taylor studied him, trying to gauge his sincerity. He didn't strike her as a man who shared his confidences lightly. He met her scrutiny without flinching.

"In that case, my co-counsel was a close friend,'' he added.

Taylor's eyes narrowed. The way he'd looked when he said "close friend" left her with little doubt that the friend had been female and that they'd been a lot more than friends.

He cleared his throat. "I'd just graduated from law school and was working at a law firm in New York City. My friend had practiced for a few years, so I was really flattered when she asked me to work on this criminal case with her.''

Surprised at his openness, Taylor settled back, feeling some tension fade in the wake of genuine interest in what he was saying.

"Our client was a young naval officer and father of three who was accused of killing a furrier in the commission of a robbery of the man's business. Grimes looked guilty as hell, but he maintained that he was innocent. He said he'd been on a camping trip with his wife in another state at the time of the robbery, but he had nobody but his wife to vouch for his whereabouts. That's the same as having nobody at all. On the other hand, the store owner's wife and two customers who were present during the robbery all separately picked Grimes out of a police lineup as the man who robbed the store and killed Mr. Carter.

"We put on what I thought was a good defense, but Grimes was found guilty and sentenced to twenty-five years to life in prison. Naturally I appealed. While I was working on the appeal brief, I discovered that my friend hadn't checked out some leads we had found earlier. When I confronted her, she said she'd thought Grimes was guilty from the very beginning and hadn't seen any point in running down what was no doubt worthless information."

Taylor shifted uncomfortably. She knew where he was headed, but she asked the question anyway. "And was it worthless?"

He shook his head. "Not by a long shot. It was a critical link that led to other evidence. If that evidence had been brought out at trial, it would have totally exonerated Grimes."

Her mouth had suddenly gone dry. "What happened to him?"

"It took me three years to get a rehearing on the case." Steele's voice was suddenly bitter. "Unfortunately Grimes was unable to deal with the degradation of prison life. He committed suicide before a new trial date could be set."

A strained silence followed. It was Steele who finally broke it.

"That experience taught me that in criminal matters things are not always what they seem, and that preconceived notions of guilt are just as powerful as actual evidence against your client. You have to put aside personal bias."

Taylor had to wonder if that experience had also taught him not to trust anyone, especially women. But she simply said, "Do you think that's realistic?"

He shrugged. "Sure. You do it all the time in civil cases. It's no different in criminal matters. When you decide to represent someone, you put aside your personal bias and give your client the best defense possible." Now he was looking at her closely. "Can you do that?"

There was a brief silence as she considered his words. How could she say no? Hadn't he said he'd drop the case if she refused to assist him? She couldn't let that happen. One thing their conversation had shown her was that regardless of Craig's guilt or innocence, Steele was the best person to represent him. And if there was any possibility that Craig was innocent and she'd done nothing to help him, she'd never forgive herself. She drew a deep breath and nodded. "I'll try," she said softly.

For a moment she thought Steele hadn't heard as he continued to study her. She watched as a spark of some undefinable emotion appeared in his hazel eyes, signifying he, too, had reached some decision.

"Good." He nodded. "I think that under the circumstances your role should be that of a researcher-writer. I'll develop the legal strategy and be the sole litigator, if it comes to that."

She gave him a sideways look. "Isn't that what you'd have done anyway?"

He grinned. "Pretty much. I guess I'm used to doing things my way, but in this instance it should keep any conflict over the case to a manageable level."

She nodded, but she had no illusion that working with Steele was going to be easy. They were both strong willed and stubborn, and not likely to compromise. "Where do we go from here?"

He issued a weary sigh and got to his feet. "Let's go see that cousin of yours."

AT FIRST CRAIG REFUSED to admit that he'd lied to the police. When he realized Steele wasn't buying it, he issued a frustrated sigh and began pacing back and forth, clearly agitated.

"Believe me," he said, "I know I shouldn't have lied, but I didn't know what else to do." He went to the wet bar in the corner of the study and poured himself a drink. For a moment he just stared into the cool liquid as if it might hold the answers to his problems. "When the cops heard about my argument with Allison, they started looking at me as if they knew they'd found their killer. I was scared."

Taylor stood and walked to the French doors. The sun was just setting; its reflection off Lake Michigan brought out blues, greens and golds from the wide, artistically landscaped backyard. The McCalls' home could best be described as a mini-mansion. It was an elegant two-story structure nestled on two acres of prime real estate in Winnetka, a suburb about twenty miles outside of Chicago. From this angle Taylor could see manicured lawns, a tennis court and the three-car garage. The walls of the study, like the living room, sported several original paintings and expensive antiques.

All in all, it was a very impressive home. Normally, no matter how troubled or upset she was, her burden was lifted in this tranquil setting. Not today, though. She took a deep breath and turned her attention back to the discussion.

"Didn't you think the police would find out?" Steele was saying. "I did, and they certainly will, too. It was a serious mistake not telling them the truth...a mistake that's going to have to be rectified."

Craig froze in midstep and whirled around, shaking his head vehemently. "If you're suggesting that I go to the police and tell all, you can forget it. I won't do it!" He punctuated the statement with a swig of Scotch.

Steele threw him a hard look. "What makes you think you have a choice? You can either come clean with the police or start looking for another lawyer. There's no way I'm going to represent a liar. And what about Ms. Olsen?"

Craig frowned. "What about her?"

"Your lie opens her up to an accessory-to-a-murder charge. Are you willing to drag her name through the mud, maybe even see her do jail time because of your lie?"

That prospect sobered Craig as nothing else had done. "All right," he said, dropping heavily into the nearest sofa chair. "You win."

That earned a disgusted look from Steele. "This isn't a contest."

"I really made a mess of things," Craig said, shaking his head. "Not just for myself, but for Pam, as well. I thought the worst that could happen was that my relationship with Pam might come to light and give the prosecution a reason to call her to testify. I never figured they would drag her into this."

A moment of uncomfortable silence followed this. Taylor broke it. "What's done is done. What we need to do now is clarify your statement and move on."

Steele's eyes softened as he looked at the woman who sat on the sofa across from him. "Yeah, I guess we'd better do it as soon as possible." He glanced at his watch. "After we leave here, we'll stop by the station. We can also get a copy of the police report while we're there."

"Okay," Taylor said, placing a small tape recorder on the cocktail table next to Craig. "I think we should record our interviews so we'll know for sure that we're getting everything. I'll have Brenda transcribe the tapes."

Steele glanced at her and nodded approvingly. "Good idea."

"Ah, before you turn that thing on," Craig said, his eyes sliding from the tape recorder across to Steele, "there's something else you ought to know."

Steele gave him a let's-hear-it look.

Craig drew a ragged breath. "I was at Allison's house the night she was murdered."

Steele swore. Frustrated, he ran a hand over his curly hair. "Lie to me one more time about anything—what you had for breakfast, what day of the week it is—I mean anything, and I'm history." He pinned Craig with a hard look before adding, "And so are you. Got that?"

"Yeah," Craig nodded.

"What were you doing at Allison's that night?" Steele's voice was as hard as nails.

"We'd had words the day before. I—I had to talk to her."

"And did you?"

"Yeah, but not for long. Our discussion quickly deteriorated, and she asked me to leave. She was upset."

"About what?" Steele fired the questions at him in rapid succession.

Craig licked his lips, then stared bleakly into his drink. "About something I did," he mumbled.

"Which was?" Before Craig could answer, realization dawned. "Please tell me you didn't choose that night, of all nights, to strike her."

"Damn it, Steele, I didn't mean to hit her!" Craig blurted. "It just happened!"

"This is great!" Steele muttered. "Just great!" He passed a weary hand over his face. "All right, start at the beginning and tell us what happened." He looked at Taylor and some of his anger faded. "Start the tape."

Taylor's breath caught in her throat at the look he gave her. Flustered, she was all thumbs as she flipped on the tape recorder.

Steele cleared his throat, then turned back to Craig. "You said you went over to see Allison to clear the air because of an argument the two of you had the day before?"

"That's correct."

"What time did you get there?"

"I'm guessing, but I'd say somewhere a little after ten."

"I need more than a guess, but we'll go on for now. What happened then?"

Craig took a long swallow of his drink, as though fortifying himself. "I tried to apologize, but she didn't want to hear it. She said I needed to accept the fact that we were finished, that if things worked out the way she wanted she was going to walk away with a hefty amount of my money, as well as become the next Mrs. Gordon Ridgeway."

"Ridgeway? The publishing mogul?" Steele whistled. "Interesting. What happened next?"

Craig issued a bitter laugh. "At that point I lost it. I started yelling at her. Before I knew it, the argument had escalated. She started screaming and throwing things at me. She was hysterical, so I grabbed her and shook her. When that didn't stop her hysterics, I—I slapped her. It wasn't very hard, but I needed to make her stop yelling. I was afraid someone would hear and call the police. I'm not proud of my behavior, but I didn't know what else to do."

"Did she calm down?"

"Somewhat. She told me to get out, that I was no better than that creep Ted Larson."

"Larson?" Taylor's head shot up. "I thought he'd left town. Was he still harassing Allison?"

Craig nodded. "Apparently he'd returned. He had been calling and following her."

At Steele's blank stare, Taylor explained. "Larson is a personal trainer that Allison got involved with right after she and Craig separated. When she dumped him, he persisted in calling and following her around. All that was supposed to stop when she got a restraining order against him."

"Naturally," Steele said dryly, "you didn't tell the police about Larson because you didn't want them to know you'd been at Allison's." He released a heavy sigh. "We'll check him out. What did you do next?"

"I drove around for a while, thinking. I realized that I really was a fool, that I'd jeopardized a perfectly good relationship with a good woman because of my obsession with Allison."

Too bad he hadn't come to that realization earlier, Taylor thought. It could have saved them all a lot of grief.

Craig swallowed the last of his drink. "I drove over to Pam's. She wasn't home, but I let myself in with the key she'd given me."

"What time did you get there?" Steele asked.

Craig paused to think. "Around eleven, maybe eleven-thirty."

"What time did Ms. Olsen arrive?"

"Around midnight."

"How did she react when you asked her to tell the police you'd been with her the night Allison was murdered?"

He smiled bleakly. "She just wanted to help me."

Steele nodded as if the answer didn't surprise him. "One more question, then we'll call it quits for now.

Even though Taylor and McCall advised against it, you went to the police and gave them a statement that we now know was less than candid. You knew that you couldn't tell the truth, so why did you feel a need to give them a statement?''

Craig threw Taylor an uneasy look. "I'm a television personality, and that means I need public support. I was trying to do damage control."

"In other words," Taylor said, "you were trying to save your skin?" She made no attempt to hide her anger.

"What's wrong with that?" he asked defensively. "I've worked hard to get where I am. I'm not about to let it all slip away. I know that sounds bad, but..."

"All right," Taylor said, feeling suddenly tired. She looked at her watch. "Mr. Steele and I have to head down to police headquarters and get a copy of your statement." Her eyes moved to Steele. "I'm assuming you want to review his statement and the police report tonight."

"Yeah, I do," Steele said, standing. "By the way, I caught Vanessa Norris's show this morning. I don't want any more off-the-cuff comments about your relationship with Allison to anyone. Not just reporters, but friends, relatives, neighbors... I mean *anyone.*"

"My staff, crew and audience members are bound to have questions," Craig spluttered. "My reputation as a talk-show host is build on my being open and honest. I can't go around saying 'no comment.' How long do you think I'll have a talk show if I alienate the viewers?"

Steele gave Craig a hard look. "You won't have to worry about putting on a show if you're in a jail cell. I have no problem with your talking to your staff and audience participants. All I ask is that you keep your mouth shut about matters relating to this case. I don't want a repeat of what happened this morning. Anyone who wants a statement about this case talks to me or Taylor. Is that clear?"

"Yeah." Craig issued a weary sigh. "What if—"

He was interrupted by a soft knock at the door, then Heather McCall stepped into the room. Her face was slightly flushed, and her brown eyes seemed overbright with excitement. "Pardon me, but Detective Donaldson is here. He wants to talk to Craig."

All eyes turned to Steele, who was frowning.

Detective Donaldson? Could it be *Frank* Donaldson? Steele turned the name over in his mind. No…it couldn't be. Donaldson was a fairly common name. But Steele had a sinking feeling in the pit of his stomach.

He nodded at Heather, then waited as she went to collect their visitor. A moment later she escorted the detective into the room. At first Steele didn't recognize the slender red-haired man standing in the doorway. The years had not been kind to Detective Donaldson. Although he looked to be in his early fifties, Steele knew he was actually just a few years older than his own thirty-six. He was a little underweight by police standards, and his skin and eyes had a pouchy, jaundiced look that made Steele wonder whether he'd developed a drinking problem. But the long, thin face was basically the same, and so was the dark, loose-fitting cop suit.

"Barrett, I'm glad I found you," Donaldson said, moving into the room. "I'd—" Then he did a double take when he saw Steele. "What the hell—"

"Donaldson," Steele said by way of greeting.

The police officer continued to stare at him for a moment before coming to some decision within himself. "I heard that Barrett had retained a high-priced, out-of-state attorney, but I didn't know it was you." His voice was icy cold, his stance aggressive.

"Won't you have a seat?" Taylor said, trying to defuse what she sensed was a potentially dangerous situation. "Can I get you anything? Coffee?"

Donaldson grunted what she thought was a no and dropped into a chair across from Craig.

Taylor's eyes narrowed as she poured herself a cup of coffee. In her two previous run-ins with Donaldson, she'd found him cold and inflexible. Today he was doubly so. Michael Steele was clearly not one of his favorite people.

"Is there something we can do for you, Detective Donaldson?" Steele asked smoothly.

"I just came by to let Mr. Barrett know that I would like to take him up on his offer to take a lie-detector test."

Taylor gulped, almost spilling her coffee at this latest revelation. Craig seemed to be having quite a lapse in memory, she thought, shooting him an angry look. Her cousin was deeply involved in studying the pattern in the carpet.

Steele didn't blink an eye. "I'm sorry, Detective Donaldson, but I can't agree to let my client do that."

It was perhaps a very good thing that the McCall residence was a modern structure with strong sealed windows. As things went, Taylor was sure that the drapes swayed and the windows rattled in response to Detective Donaldson's howling. "What the hell do you mean you can't agree!" He pointed an accusing finger at Craig. "Barrett already said he'd take it! Damn it, he can't change his mind. Everything is all set up!"

Steele gave Donaldson a moment to calm himself. Then he said, "When my client made that offer, he was upset and distraught over his wife's death. He didn't know what he was saying. I'm sure you wouldn't want to hold Mr. Barrett to any statements he might have made when he wasn't himself and wasn't represented by counsel."

"Come on, Steele, what are you trying to pull?" Donaldson growled. "You're not some young pup still wet behind the ears. You know how we do things. Barrett agreed to come down to the precinct and be questioned. We had every right to take his statement. Everything was completely aboveboard."

"If that's so, why did my client feel he didn't have a choice in the matter?"

Donaldson shrugged. "Hell, I can't read minds. But if he's innocent, he should want to cooperate with the police."

Steele gave him a humorless smile. "Ah, but that's just it. He got the impression that you guys don't believe him."

"Should we?"

"He didn't kill his wife."

Donaldson shrugged. "You say so, but I'm not so sure."

Steele's hand tightened on the arm of the sofa. Now they were getting to the part he wanted to know about. "Why not?"

Donaldson hesitated, but when he spoke there was a hard edge to his voice. "I'm sure you'll understand if I don't answer that question, Counsel."

Steele considered that briefly. Without expression he said, "The state's attorney race is coming up in a few months."

Donaldson's voice hardened even further. "I don't like what you're suggesting."

"Neither do I. I'd hate to see you make a major-league mistake."

"I'll worry about that," Donaldson snapped. "You worry about your client. Maybe he didn't kill his wife, and maybe he did. Until that gets settled, make sure he doesn't disappear."

"I got your message," Steele said coldly. "Now you get mine. Your office has been leaking information about my client to the press. I want it stopped, and I want it stopped now. I'm holding you personally responsible."

Donaldson's face darkened with anger. Without answering, he pushed himself out of his chair and stomped from the room. A moment later the front door slammed.

Taylor turned and stared at Steele, puzzled. "Call me crazy, but why do I have the feeling that you know Donaldson?"

He looked at her for a moment, then sighed. "I'm afraid we do know each other. I defended the man who killed his wife and children."

Chapter Three

What had started out as a bad day had gotten decidedly worse. Taylor and Steele talked to Craig for a few minutes more, then headed down to the police station, where they met with Captain Evans. Steele clarified Craig's statement regarding his alibi and registered an official complaint about the leaks coming out of the department.

Captain Evans was cordial and polite, but he was as unresponsive as Donaldson had been. He claimed that he had no idea where Norris was getting her information, but insisted it wasn't from the department. He was equally unresponsive to their questions relating to other suspects, and he refused to comment at all on Ted Larson.

The air crackled with tension as Steele continued to press. Captain Evans's patience came to an end when Steele asked for a copy of the police report. The captain stalked to the door and bellowed for Donaldson to bring him a copy. A few minutes later Donaldson stepped into the room, tossed a folder onto the desk in front of Steele and stalked out. If Taylor had thought Donaldson was difficult to deal with before, the man was now like Attila the Hun. His dislike of Steele was almost a palpable force.

For his part, Steele was cool. He pressed hard for more

information, but it was clear to Taylor that they could expect no cooperation from the police department.

ON THE WAY BACK to Taylor's office, they stopped at Mama Rose's, one of Chicago's best soul-food restaurants, where they bought take-out barbecue ribs, potato salad and coleslaw. Taylor told herself that she and Steele needed to talk about the case; that was the only reason they were having dinner together.

After they had eaten, they reviewed the police report and Craig's statement. Then Taylor settled down into the sofa and stared at him over the rim of her wineglass. Steele was sitting at her desk. He'd removed his jacket and loosened his tie and looked utterly devastating. She wondered fleetingly what it would be like to be loved by him. Would he be patient and gentle or wild and adventuresome? She gave herself a mental shake. Her imagination was running away from her. Yet understanding that didn't change anything. She swallowed hastily and fought to repress the thoughts running through her mind.

"I think I've exercised a great deal of restraint. Don't you think it's time to tell me what's going on between you and Donaldson... especially since it appears to be affecting this case?"

Steele ran a hand along the back of his neck. When he finally spoke, his voice was weary. "It was a couple of years ago... Donaldson was a D.C. cop then. I guess he pulled up stakes and moved here to Chicago after the trial."

Taylor pulled her legs under her and leaned back against the sofa cushion, waiting for him to continue.

"My client was an executive for a Fortune 500 company," Steele said. "He had been having some back problems, and the medication he'd been taking no longer worked. He had a few hours of free time so he dropped by his doctor's office. His doctor checked him over and gave him some samples of a new product for back pain. We learned later that there were no side effects in the vast majority of patients, but in a relatively small number of people the medication could produce extreme drowsiness. At the time neither my client nor his doctor was aware of that.

"Anyway, Jack took one of the pills while he was still at the doctor's office. The doctor's office was in a mall, so he decided to run a few errands. By the time he climbed into his car and headed home, it had been about thirty minutes since he'd taken the medication."

"Let me guess," she said. "By that time the medication had kicked in."

"Like a ton of bricks. Jack nodded off—just for a moment—but in that moment his car drifted across the center line into Mrs. Donaldson's car, hitting her head-on. She and the two kids were killed instantly."

"How awful," Taylor said. For a moment she didn't think he'd heard her. He looked so sad and alone. She wanted to reach out and take his hand, but the demons from the past were there holding her back.

Steele slowly nodded. "Yeah, it was a tragedy all around. Donaldson took it real hard. He made a lot of noise and got the media involved. The next thing Jack knew he was on trial, charged with second-degree murder."

"But it was an accident," Taylor insisted.

Steele nodded glumly. "I know, and that's what the jury ruled, but Donaldson didn't view it that way. He made all kinds of wild allegations from Jack having bought off the judge to collusion between myself and the prosecutor."

Taylor gave him a thoughtful look. "From his reaction to you today, I'd say he hasn't been able to put the past behind him. No doubt your involvement in the case only reinforces his belief that another rich man is trying to buy his way out of a murder charge."

Steele nodded. "I'd say that's a sure bet."

Her eyes narrowed as a more disturbing thought occurred to her. "You hear stories all the time about cops setting people up. Do you think Donaldson would do something like that?"

Steele shook his head. "Donaldson is meaner than a junkyard dog, but he's a good cop. I don't think he'd resort to tampering with evidence. I just think he lacks objectivity, and it'll be hard to get him to see our side of things."

"So I guess counting on the police for any help is out of the question."

Suddenly Steele's face changed as he smiled. It was a dazzling smile that took her breath away. "Hey, no pain, no gain." When he smiled, those incredible hazel eyes of his sparkled.

"Yeah, but it's a complication I could live without," Taylor said, trying to ignore the way her heart had begun to pound. His masculinity drew her, pulled at her, like a moth to a flame. She coughed nervously. "Now that you've read the police report, you see what we're up against."

Steele didn't mince words. "It's pretty damaging." He propped his feet on the corner of her desk and leaned back in the chair, his lazy attitude suggesting that what he was about to say didn't amount to much. Taylor knew better. "The neighbor, Lee Trebeck, claims he heard Allison arguing with someone, presumably Craig, the night she was murdered. He also claims that he saw a man roughly matching Craig's description running from the direction of the condo just before the police arrived. Then there's the unalterable fact that Craig threatened to kill Allison, presumably because he was jealous and alternatively because she was demanding a hefty share of his assets in the divorce settlement. Furthermore, Craig has no alibi for his whereabouts during the time the murder occurred."

"There is a lot of evidence," Taylor countered, "but it's all circumstantial."

"Sure it is," Steele agreed. "Anything less than an eyewitness who saw Craig bludgeon Allison to death is circumstantial, but the prisons are full of people who have been convicted on less circumstantial evidence than the police have against Craig."

Taylor thought for a moment. "Okay, let's say Craig is indicted. The prosecution still has a long way to go to get a conviction. They've got no murder weapon, no one who actually places him at the crime scene and no real motive. All this talk about jealousy or crime of passion is pure conjecture."

He smiled that killer smile at her. "That's true." Steele rose and walked to a sideboard, where he poured himself a cup of coffee. He looked at Taylor, asking with a gesture of his hand if she would like a cup. She shook her head. "We've got a little time on our side," he said, returning to the chair, "I suggest we make the most of it."

She nodded in agreement. "The case was referred to the State's Attorney's Office for investigation, but it's a sure bet they are going to charge Craig with Allison's murder."

Steele took a sip of coffee. "Normally I would say it could go either way, but this is an election year. The State's Attorney is running for re-election. I don't think he wants the opposition to accuse him of being soft on crime or giving preferential treatment to Craig because he's a celebrity. They have a good circumstantial case, and I think they'll run with it. But their case isn't airtight by any means."

Taylor nodded. "There's bound to be holes in it like in any case. Finding those holes and persuading a jury of their relevance is another matter."

He took another sip of coffee, then set the cup on the desk and picked up a legal pad and pen. "Then we'd better start looking for them. We'll take it from the top and identify the holes as we go along." He lowered himself into the cushions of the sofa next to her. "Tell me about Barrett and his wife."

She gave him a sideways glance. "Aren't we going over previously covered territory?"

A faint smile flickered briefly at the edge of his sensual mouth. "Humor me."

"Very well," she said, trying to ignore the fact that he was sitting so close to her. She could feel the heat radiating from his body and could smell the faint, spicy scent of his after-shave. Damn, he even smelled good. She cleared her throat, then began, "Craig and Allison met about a year ago. After a brief courtship, they were married. No one with the possible exception of Craig gave the marriage much of a chance, so it came as no surprise when they separated six months ago. I didn't see much of Craig while they were married." She gave a wry little smile. "Craig and I aren't close, and Allison and I never really hit it off."

He looked surprised at that. "Did she have any close friends—female or otherwise?"

Taylor shrugged. "Not to my knowledge. She and Heather were friendly, but I wouldn't characterize even that relationship as close. Their husbands were close, so they were thrown together. As for friends from the past, she never mentioned any and we didn't meet any."

Steele was having a hard time concentrating on what Taylor was saying. She had the softest lips he'd ever seen. He wondered fleetingly how that luscious mouth would feel pressed against his. To feel her tongue...

"It's funny," she continued, "but I never thought about that before. Don't you think it's odd that we never met any of her friends?"

"Uh-huh," he said vaguely. "We'll check her out."

Taylor shifted slightly, looking uncomfortable. "The separation wasn't unpleasant, at least from Allison's perspective. Craig was paying her fifteen thousand dollars a month, and as you know, she was demanding a hefty share of his assets in the divorce settlement. Not bad for a girl who didn't have two nickels to rub together when she married him, do you think?"

Steele's thoughts were totally focused on Taylor. He loved the way she pursed her lips when she was thinking. At the precise moment that thought was going through his head, she ran the tip of her tongue over her lower lip. It was purely a nervous gesture on her part, but to him it was totally sensual and erotic.

Steele gave himself a mental shake and tried to concentrate on what she was saying.

"It only took Craig a few months to get Allison out of his system. He started seeing Pam Olsen about three months ago. Things were getting pretty serious between them when Allison stepped back into the picture, claiming that she'd made a mistake and wanted him back. Fool that he was, he was not only willing to take her back but rescinded their prenuptial agreement. She had a powerful effect on men."

She wasn't the only woman with a powerful effect, Steele thought.

"He was in a fool's paradise until Heather McCall inadvertently let slip that Allison was seeing Gordon Ridgeway. Craig confronted her and they argued. She not only admitted that she was seeing him, but also said that she planned to marry him as soon as the divorce was final."

Steele's eyes narrowed. "So Barrett thought she'd been stringing him along to get as much as she could from him before moving on to a bigger fish."

"Exactly," Taylor agreed. "They had several arguments, culminating with the infamous one where Craig threatened to kill her."

"How did the cops hear about it?"

Taylor shrugged. "It was common knowledge among our friends that they had a tumultuous relationship. An anonymous caller tipped off the police about the threat."

Steele pursed his lips. "We need to see if we can listen to a recording of that call."

"Why?" Taylor asked. "It probably wouldn't be admissible in court, and there are any number of people that can testify to what the caller said."

"I know," he said thoughtfully. "It's just that anonymous callers bother me. Especially when they're trying to feed a motive for the crime to the police." Steele sighed. "Donaldson will no doubt blow up the anger and jealousy aspects of their relationship. He'll probably try to get copies of Barrett's shows in which an altercation occurred to show his propensity for violence. I'm glad that incident you told me about was almost two decades ago, so too far in the past to be relevant—otherwise I'd be a little concerned."

Taylor shifted uncomfortably. "So what if he's a little hot tempered," she argued. "This is a murder trial. He's not vying for Mr. Congeniality in the Mr. America pageant."

Steele gave her a hard look. "Yeah, but testimony like that in a murder trial can get a person convicted real fast. It's too easy for a jury to make the leap from a man with a history of violent behavior to a man who could commit murder." He pulled on his lower lip in a gesture that Taylor found decidedly seductive.

"But the prosecution has to be able to link them up," she said, pulling her thoughts back to the matter at hand. "It's our job to point out to the jury that the connection doesn't exist."

Steele picked up his coffee cup and took a sip. "You're right, and we're going to be able to do that because we have two definite advantages."

Taylor gave him a speculative look. "And they are?"

Steele used his fingers to count off his points. "First and foremost Barrett is innocent. That means all the circumstantial evidence gathered against Barrett has been given the wrong interpretation. What we have to do is analyze that same evidence and give it the correct interpretation.

"Second we've got a little time on our side. The State's Attorney will have to assign this case to one of the attorneys in his office. My guess is it'll go to one of the senior attorneys. That's good, because that person probably already has a substantial caseload and is going to have to spend a couple of weeks clearing his calendar before he can really jump into this one. While time is with us, we're going to conduct our own investigation. I want to focus primarily on Allison. Maybe we'll find something in her background that will tell us who hated her enough to want to kill her."

Taylor nodded. "We should also check out the men in her life—Ridgeway and Larson. Now is probably the best time to interview them, while their guards are down." She smiled. "Though I doubt that either man will say anything that will implicate himself."

He returned her smile. "They wouldn't intentionally. But this would be the most likely time for them to slip up, while the police investigation is focusing on Craig."

Taylor yawned. "Okay, I'll track down their addresses and pick you up at your hotel around ten in the morning." She stood, and he followed suit. "We have a lot of questions, but I'm not sure how many answers we're going to get."

Steele shrugged. "Actually we only need the answer to one—if Craig didn't kill Allison, who did?"

IT WAS an intriguing question, but it was not the one that haunted Steele and kept him wide-awake late into the night staring at his bedroom ceiling. No, that was a question of a more personal nature. An image of soft brown eyes and raven black hair flashed before him. He still couldn't get over his reaction to Taylor Quinlan. After his disastrous experience with Daphne, he'd sworn he'd never work with a co-counsel, never with someone whom he wasn't in perfect accord with over the manner in which the case should be litigated and never with someone he was attracted to. Yet today he'd broken all three rules.

He sighed heavily. He needed his head examined, he thought wryly. Once Taylor had confirmed what he'd suspected—that she questioned Barrett's innocence—he should have sent her packing. No ifs, ands or buts about it—that's what he should have done. It was the only logical thing to do. The case was complicated enough without the added distraction of a co-counsel who questioned his every decision or vice versa. It was a recipe for disaster.

He knew that, but instead of doing what logic dictated, he'd found himself trying to determine if she could put aside her reservations about Craig's innocence and help develop the best defense possible. She'd said she could. And although he only had his instinct and her word to go on, he'd believed her. Actually he'd been surprised that she even had such concerns. She didn't strike him as a rash or impulsive person who made snap decisions. It didn't make sense, but neither did his behavior. For years he'd gone out of his way in order to work alone and now he was almost relishing the idea of working with Taylor.

He rolled over onto his side. Why was he jumping through so many hoops to keep her on the case? It would have been a hell of a lot easier to let her off the case the way she'd requested and try to find a replacement. The press be damned! It wouldn't have been easy, but it might have been the safer course of action.

His lips curved into a slight smile as he thought of the way she tilted her chin. She was a stubborn little thing. It certainly wasn't going to be easy working with her. The woman clearly had a mind of her own and was likely to voice it. Loudly. But instead of being put off by that fact, adrenaline coursed through him at the prospect of going head-to-head with her over the case and other things....

He plopped on his back, frowning at the ceiling. He needed to get out more if he was salivating over a woman he'd just met. He didn't understand his attraction to her. She wasn't the first beautiful woman he'd worked with. Images of a half-dozen women came to mind, but Taylor was certainly the most intriguing, the most compelling woman. He'd felt it the moment he laid eyes on her. It wasn't just her physical beauty. There was something about her that left a lasting impression. She was captivating, intelligent, vibrant, alive, sexy. And yet there was a sadness deep in the back of those big brown eyes of hers. A sadness that he sensed went far beyond any concerns about her cousin's innocence or the case itself. He doubted if most people noticed, but he had and he'd wanted to wrap his arms around her and make the pain go away. He couldn't remember a time he'd felt so strongly attracted to a woman or so protective. And he had a hunch she was just as attracted to him as he was to her.

His body hardened just thinking of her. Lord, he wanted her. But that was not in the cards, and he might as well accept it. He was not going to get involved with Taylor. He'd let desire cloud his judgment once before, and the results had been disastrous. No, he was going to put Taylor Quinlan out of his mind and focus strictly on clearing Barrett's name. He sighed heavily. Unfortunately, he had a feeling both were easier said than done.

TAYLOR HADN'T BEEN ABLE to get Steele out of her mind. She'd alternated most of the night between wondering if she was doing the right thing in not telling Steele the whole story and fantasizing about him. She'd close her eyes, and his image would appear and along with it, thoughts and feelings she'd thought long since buried.

"How much farther?" Steele asked, breaking into her thoughts.

"Just a few blocks," she said. She could feel his hazel eyes on her but she kept hers trained dead ahead, not daring to look at the man who sat in the passenger seat next to her. She didn't want to be aware of him as a man because that awareness forced her to acknowledge her attraction to him. In the close confines of her Toyota, she couldn't avoid acknowledging that she found him fascinating. Something about him pulled her, drew her toward him. But it scared her senseless. Chronologically she might be twenty-eight, but she was ill equipped to deal with a man like Steele. Not that she even wanted to, she told herself sternly. She wasn't interested in an affair, and that's all she could ever have with him.

"How did you talk Donaldson into letting us into Allison's condo?" she asked, pulling her thoughts back to the matter at hand. "As Allison's next of kin, it's Craig's property now and we're his legal representatives, but I'd thought Donaldson would try to keep us out as long as possible."

Steele shrugged. "He really didn't have much choice. The evidence team finished up with the condo last night, so technically it isn't a crime scene anymore, which is why I want to take a look at it this morning. I want to see the place the way the police saw it."

"Do you know if they found anything?" she asked.

"If they did, Donaldson isn't talking. But from his sour mood, I don't think so. Let's hope we have better luck."

She turned off Michigan Avenue, then hooked south onto Lake Shore Drive, entering one of the city's most exclusive areas. At the intersection she turned onto a street lined with two-story condominiums. About midway down she pulled up to the curb in front of an elegant two-story structure, surrounded by a neatly manicured lawn and huge oak trees. As they climbed out of the car, they were met by the security guard Craig had hired to patrol the premises and keep nosy reporters and curiosity seekers out. They followed him up the walkway.

Taylor watched as he fished a key from his pocket, opened the front door and stepped aside so they could enter.

"Thanks," Steele said. "We'll lock up when we're done here."

The guard nodded, then hurried away. They stepped into a wide entryway. To the left of the entry was the living room, and to the right was the dining room. Taylor followed Steele into the living room and glanced around.

"What are we looking for?" she asked, watching Steele as he prowled the room.

He paused, pushed his navy suit jacket back, his hands on his hips, surveying the spacious living room. "Something the police might have overlooked." He shrugged. "I don't know. Anything that doesn't fit."

She threw him a sideways glance. "Donaldson and his men have probably been through this place with a fine-tooth comb. Don't you think if there was anything to find, they'd have found it?"

"Maybe. But you'd be surprised how often cops overlook evidence, especially when they're convinced they already know who did it."

"That's a frightening thought."

"I know," Steele agreed, "but it's human nature. If that's what happened here, then the police only looked for evidence that would corroborate their belief that Craig was the killer, which means they could have overlooked something or misinterpreted a clue."

Taylor grinned. "And we're going to find this clue and give it the correct interpretation? I think you're dreaming."

He returned her grin. "I've had a number of dreams since taking on this case. Some of them quite X rated." The words were out before he could stop himself.

Suddenly what had started as lighthearted banter had turned to something else. Something dangerous to her well-being. She cleared her throat, trying to break the sexual tension that swirled around them.

"Ah, I'll take this side of the room. Why don't you check out that side," she said, pointing to the far side of the room. She needed to put some distance between them. The farther away he was, the better she'd like it.

He smiled, signifying he'd recognized her ploy, but thankfully he didn't say anything. Gradually her errant heart began to resume a steady beat as she got into the search.

Taylor lifted a nearby lamp, peeked inside the shade then checked underneath. She moved on to the sofa table near the entryway, checking the contents on top and inside. Other than some mail that was neatly stacked on the tabletop, she found nothing of remote interest. She turned and looked at Steele. He was kneeling on the floor, peering underneath a large floor sculpture.

She sighed and picked up the bundle of mail. According to the postmark, all of the letters had been posted after Allison's death. Nothing of any interest, she thought, leafing through the bundle. Circulars, a woman's magazine, a couple of bills, a letter... She paused

when she saw the name on the envelope: Illinois State
Senator Barry Denning. Taylor recognized the name immediately. He was a power broker in Illinois politics.
Denning, an arch-conservative whose views on family
values and welfare reform had made him a household
name, was also the front-runner in the gubernatorial
race. She turned the letter over. The stationery was expensive looking—too nice for its content to be the standard computer-generated political fare. Curious, she tore
the envelope open. Inside was a personal note thanking
Allison for a recent contribution to the senator's gubernatorial campaign. She frowned. That didn't sound like
Allison.

"Steele," she said over her shoulder, "take a look at
this."

"Did you find something?" he asked, coming to stand
next to her.

"I'm not sure." She handed the letter to him for inspection. "I just can't see Allison interested in politics,
let alone making a contribution to anyone's campaign."

He quickly skimmed the letter, then shrugged. "It's
probably just a tax write-off, but we'll check it out."

They spent several more minutes checking out the living room, but didn't find anything out of the ordinary.
They moved on to the family room, where the body had
been found. Taylor tried not to look at the bloodstains on
the carpet or the plants and books that littered the floor.

While Steele inspected the French door and the area
directly outside, Taylor prowled around the room. Even
in its present disarray, it was still a lovely room, she
thought. The predominant colors were black and white
with splashes of red. Very dramatic, as its owner had
been.

Along one wall was an armoire that was closed, but she
knew it housed a TV, VCR and stereo. The opposite wall
held a couple of paintings and a complete wall of books,
hundreds of them, covering every imaginable subject. A
book lover herself, she thought of her own apartment,
where books were everywhere. But with Allison it had

been a different story. She remembered the first time she had seen Allison's collection, she'd complimented her on her selections. Allison had laughingly explained that they were her decorator's idea. As far as Allison was concerned, the books were simply a fashion statement—a way of impressing her friends.

Taylor crossed to the shelves of books and ran a finger along the spines of the books, reading the titles as she went. Out of the corner of her eye, she caught a flash of something yellow protruding out of a book on the third row from the ceiling. Upon closer inspection she saw that it was a bookmark. Probably inserted, she thought cynically, to give the impression that the book was being read.

But to an avid reader such as herself, the bookmark was like a magnet, and before she knew it, she was standing on tiptoe and pulling out the book and inspecting the title. It was Herman Melville's *Moby Dick*. She smiled—not a book likely to be read by Allison, she thought, sliding the book back on the shelf. Farther down on the shelf a popular bestseller had been placed on its side, as though someone had been reading it and set it down for the moment.

She chuckled and moved down to the next row, continuing to run her finger along the book spines. About midway down was another book containing a bookmark. She lifted it out and read the title: *Killers without a Conscience.* The inside-cover page proclaimed it to be a psychological study of twenty of the country's most cold-blooded killers. She shuddered. A little too morbid for her taste.

She was about to slide the book back on the shelf when the title *How to Drive a Man Wild* caught her eye. She smiled. Now that seemed more Allison's speed. And if she was honest, since meeting Steele, hers, too. Curiosity made her itch to take a peek inside. She glanced over her shoulder to make sure Steele was nowhere near. She pulled the book from the shelf, opened it and read. Her eyes widened as she came across one particularly interesting section. Did people really do things like that? she wondered.

"Did you find something?"

She whirled around, almost bumping into Steele. Where had he come from? And why was he standing so close? She was acutely aware of his clean masculine scent and his presence. Only sheer willpower kept her from taking a step back. "No, I didn't find anything." She wished she didn't sound so breathless.

He cocked his head to the side, looking at the books she was holding. "What have you got there?"

Damn! Why hadn't she left the book on the shelf. Reluctantly she handed him the books. "I noticed a couple of them contained bookmarks and thought I should check them out. Allison could have planted something in one of them." Her answer sounded lame even to her own ears. She could tell by his grin that he didn't believe a word of what she said.

"How to Drive a Man Wild," he read aloud, then looked down at her and chuckled. Her face flamed with embarrassment, and she was sure her discomfort showed on her face. "You don't learn this from reading, you learn it from doing." His voice lowered an octave. "If you need a practice partner..."

"I was looking at that one," she said, pointing to the other book he held. "Since I don't have a background in criminal law, I thought it might be a good resource. Give me an understanding of the kind of criminal mind we're dealing with." Anything but the truth.

His grin broadened as he read the title on the other book. He shook his head. "Not likely."

"You never know, I may even learn enough to teach you a thing or two," she said, taking refuge in haughtiness.

"I'm sure you could," he said. At the husky note in his voice, she looked up at him and wished she hadn't. The way he was looking at her made her feel as if she just stepped in front of a raging fire. She swallowed hard, her mouth suddenly dry.

"You think Donaldson would mind if I took it home?" she said, trying to pretend she was unaffected by his words.

"I doubt it," he said, handing her the true-crime book. She had no choice but to take it, but she refused to look at him as she placed it in her tote.

"Don't you want this one, too?" he teased, dangling the book in front of her. His hazel eyes sparkled with pure devilment.

Her face flamed as she snatched the book from him, but in doing so, their fingers touched. A jolt of electricity shot through her, curling her toes. She swallowed and took a step back. "I've checked this side of the room," she said, trying to lessen the sexual tension that swirled around them, "but I didn't find anything. What about you?"

Her comment pulled him back to the matter at hand. "No," he sighed. "But I think this is one instance where it's not what we're finding that's important. It's what we're not finding."

She frowned. "What do you mean?"

"The police's theory is Allison knew the killer. In fact, let him in, as evidenced by the lack of any sign of a struggle or break-in. That would also explain how he knew the security code. But that's the very part of the equation that makes the least sense to me. If he wanted to make it look like a burglary, why rearm the system and why not take something?"

Taylor nodded. "Yeah, but those are the kind of mistakes that Donaldson thinks that someone like Craig would have made."

He shook his head again. "All the same, it doesn't make sense to trash the place unless the killer was really looking for something."

"But, Steele, this is the only room that was searched, and nothing was taken. Not that there's really much in here worth taking," she said, glancing around the room, "unless you're a book lover."

Steele sighed. "I know. Let's check out the rest of the house."

They checked out the remaining downstairs rooms, then moved upstairs, where a check of the guest bedrooms also turned up nothing. The guest bathrooms were an equal washout. Nothing was secreted in the back of the commode or hidden among the color-coordinated towels or concealed in the toilet paper. Nor did they find anything in Allison's exercise room. They moved on to the master bedroom.

Steele went to work on the canopy bed, looking underneath the mattress and box spring while Taylor checked the dressing table. The top was littered with the standard cosmetics and toiletries. She moved on to the bureau, sliding open the top drawer. There was nothing out of the ordinary inside. Just some flimsy lingerie, a silk lounging creation and three packs of cigarettes.

Along with the cigarettes were two matchbooks. The first had an expensive, gold-embossed cover and bore the name Bayberry. She recognized the name immediately. It was a popular night spot among young black professionals in the Chicago Loop known for blues and its classy clientele. The other matchbook, a plain white cover, bore the name Martin's Bar and Grill. She wasn't familiar with the place but surmised from the address it was in a seedy part of the city. Taylor frowned. Definitely not Allison's turf. She placed the matchbook on top of the bureau to show to Steele.

She moved on to the second drawer. Inside were a number of cashmere sweaters and designer silk scarfs, but nothing to explain why someone would want to kill Allison.

Behind her she heard Steele whistle. "Take a look at this."

He was standing in the doorway of a huge walk-in closet that housed more clothes than most department stores. Rows of designer gowns and dresses, racks of shoes, purses, sweaters and several leather coats and furs.

"She must have spent a small fortune on clothes," Steele said.

Taylor nodded. "Allison always looked nice, but I had no idea she had so many clothes." Taylor fingered several beaded gowns. "And so many incredibly expensive ones at that," she added, reading the labels of a few: "Valentino, Chanel, DKNY, Mackie."

Steele shook his head, frowning. "It doesn't add up," he said absently.

She looked at him, curious. "What doesn't?"

He waved his hand in a manner that was meant to encompass the entire house and all its contents. "The clothes, the house. Not to mention the Porsche and Jeep in the garage." His frown deepened. "This is no fifteen-thousand-dollars-a-month life-style, which is what she was getting from Craig. She had to have some other source of income to maintain all of this."

Taylor shook her head. "She couldn't have. She didn't bring any money to the marriage and she certainly didn't acquire any while she was married to Craig." She shrugged. "Ridgeway is a very rich man. Maybe he was bankrolling her."

Steele nodded absently. "You're probably right, but all the same, I'd like to see her financial records. See exactly how she was financing this life-style."

"I'll talk to Craig. They were still legally man and wife when she died, so he should have access to her accounts. I'll also get a copy of the separation agreement from him, which should tell us what, if any, additional income or assets she had."

"Sounds good," Steele said approvingly.

"Oh, let me show you what I found." She spent a few minutes telling him about the matchbook she'd found in Allison's bureau. When she finished, Steele said, "I'll have Hawk check it out."

"Hawk?"

Steele smiled. "Hawk Longtree. My private investigator. He's flying in today from Washington to help with the investigation." He glanced at his watch. "This is taking longer than I'd planned. Why don't I finish up in here and the master bathroom while you check out the office?''

''Okay, I'll also look for Allison's checkbook and any other financial records that may exist. We haven't come across anything like that in our search, so I guess they're in her office.''

Taylor turned on her heel and headed out of the room. She walked down the hall and into the office. Like the other rooms, the office was tastefully decorated. As she surveyed the room, she thought she detected a faint wisp of the expensive cologne that Craig always wore. But that couldn't be. Craig hadn't been in the condo since the night of the murder. She was just about to cross the room and inspect the papers that littered the desk when a figure dressed in a black nylon jacket and wearing a black ski mask streaked from behind the door, knocking her to the floor. For a moment she was too stunned to react, then she was on her feet.

''Hey, you! Stop! Steele!'' she shouted as she tore out after the intruder. She dodged a hallway lamp that the intruder pulled to the floor as he sprinted down the corridor. Out of the corner of her eye, she saw Steele tear out of the master bedroom after her. She turned back in time to dodge an overturned chair, only to round the corner and run smack into an overturned table. She went down with a heavy thud.

''Ouch!'' she moaned, rubbing the leg she'd bumped against the corner of the table.

Steele was kneeling next to her immediately. ''You okay?''

''I'm fine,'' she said, waving him on. Steele gave her shoulder a squeeze and took up the chase. Taylor scrambled to her feet and hurried after him. When she reached the front door and stepped outside, Steele was looking up and down the street. The intruder was nowhere in sight.

''Let's check around back,'' Steele said over his shoulder. She raced after him, but when they reached the backyard, it was also empty. It was as if the intruder had disappeared into thin air.

She surveyed the empty yard. "Where could he have—"

The sound of a car engine had them racing into the alley behind the condo. They got there in time to see a late model dark-colored sedan speed away.

"I didn't get the license number," Taylor said, panting. Her breath was coming in short, harsh gasps. "What about you?"

Steele shook his head. "Me, neither. Did you get a look at him?"

Taylor immediately thought of the cologne she smelled when she'd entered the room. Any number of men besides Craig probably used that particular brand. In light of that she decided to keep her suspicion to herself. She shook her head. "It all happened so fast. My sense is the intruder was a man, but all I saw was a black streak." She hesitated, then asked, "You think it was the killer?"

"Dressed all in black with a ski mask over his face. Who else could it have been?"

At that moment the security guard appeared. Steele questioned him, but he said he hadn't seen anyone enter or leave the house. But his face turned beet-red as he admitted he'd been next door the whole time and only came out when he'd seen them in the backyard.

"Damn!" Steele ran a hand over his hair. He took her arm, and they walked slowly around front and back into the house. "If it was the killer, he took an awful big risk coming back here," he said. "I just wonder what the hell he was looking for."

Taylor paused and looked at Steele. "I think the better question is, did he find it?"

Chapter Four

There was one thing to be said in Lee Trebeck's favor, Steele thought as he and Taylor sat across from him in the brightly lit sitting room—he had good taste in women. Well, he amended, as least as far as Taylor was concerned.

After they'd finished up at the condo, they had walked across the street to question him about his 911 call to the police the night of the murder. At first the thin, nervous-looking man had been reluctant to speak with them, then Taylor had smiled at him and Trebeck had melted. Steele couldn't blame him. She had that same effect on him.

Like now—sitting this close to her on the love seat, it was damn hard to concentrate on what Trebeck was saying. Her sweet floral scent was driving him crazy. It had been the same in the car and at Allison's condo. He'd lost count of the number of times he'd just wanted to take her in his arms and kiss her senseless. He was so lost in thought, it took him a moment to realize they'd stopped talking and were staring at him.

"Uh, sorry," Steele said. He began by asking Trebeck to tell them what he had seen and heard the night of the murder. At first Trebeck spoke in short, clipped sentences, but at Taylor's smiles and nods of encouragement he began to open up.

Steele studied him as he talked. Trebeck looked to be in his late thirties. He had a way of leaning forward with his head that gave his long, gaunt face a wide-eyed, frightened look. He reminded Steele of Barney Fife, the deputy chief on the old "Andy Griffith Show."

"I gather you think the man you saw was Craig Barrett?" Steele asked when Trebeck had completed his narrative.

"Who else could it have been?" Trebeck replied.

Steele pinned him with a hard look. "I don't know and frankly I don't see how you could know, either. It was dark out and the man was almost half a block away."

A shadow of annoyance crossed Trebeck's face. "I know what I saw."

"But you didn't get a good look at him," Steele persisted. "Are you willing to put a man's life at risk because of what you think you saw?"

Trebeck recoiled as if he'd been struck. "My eyesight is just fine. And I have to say, I won't shed a tear if Barrett is arrested," he said bluntly. "He deserves everything he gets."

Steele's eyes narrowed at the venom in his voice. Trebeck clearly disliked Craig. Steele couldn't help but wonder to what extent his dislike of Craig colored his perception of the events of the night of the murder.

"So you believe Barrett killed his wife?" Steele asked calmly.

"Of course I do," he snorted. "Every time he went over there, it would end in a big fight." He shook his finger at Steele. "I always had a bad feeling about him."

"Did you ever witness any of these so-called fights?"

Trebeck hesitated. "Well, no, but I heard them."

"You heard loud voices," Steele corrected. "You can't say categorically the voices you heard were Allison's and Craig's or Allison's and some other man's. Ms. Barrett did have other male visitors, didn't she?"

"Well, yes," Trebeck admitted grudgingly, then added, "but he was the only one she argued with all the time." Then with more force he said, "Barrett didn't deserve such a fine woman. I told Allison so myself, but she just laughed. She saw his handsome face and that million-dollar smile, and like everyone else she thought he was some kind of god. It's a damn shame that it took this tragedy for the world to see him for the monster he is.''

Before he could challenge Trebeck's assertion, he felt Taylor's hand on his arm, telling him she'd ask this one. "Perhaps I misunderstood," she said in that sweet voice of hers, "but according to your testimony at the coroner's inquest, I was under the impression you didn't know either Mr. or Mrs. Barrett especially well. Am I mistaken?''

Trebeck gave his head a vigorous shake, then glanced down at his hands like a nervous rabbit. "No, we weren't friends or anything." He looked up, his Adam's apple working. "It was an observation. I'd see Allison...ah, Mrs. Barrett out jogging and we'd speak. Sometimes when she had a problem with an appliance, I'd run over and fix it for her. She was a very lovely lady." His voice softened and his eyes took on a sad, wistful look before he caught himself.

Steele's eyes widened as realization dawned. Trebeck had had a crush on Allison! He looked at Taylor and knew she'd picked up on it, too. But it had been like that all morning. It was as if they could read each other's mind. He'd never been so aware, so in tune to anyone in his life, and he wasn't sure if he liked it.

"When did you last see Allison Barrett?" Steele asked, breaking the connection.

"The afternoon of the murder. I was out walking my dog, and she was out jogging.''

"Did you speak to her that day?''

Trebeck nodded.

"How did she seem? Was she nervous, upset or angry about anything?''

Trebeck shook his head. "Oh, no. She was in a real good mood. She was all smiles. She said she'd finally hooked a big one.''

"She'd hooked a big one?" Taylor repeated. "Did you ask her what she meant?"

"No, but I wish I had." He looked sadly at Taylor. "That was the last time I saw her alive."

"You said you first heard the argument around ten-thirty," Steele said, breaking the strained silence that had sprang up. "How can you be so sure of the time?"

Trebeck's thin lips curved into a small lopsided grin. "That's easy," he said. "My wife and I watch cable television every night. We start with the 'Dick Van Dyke Show,' which comes on at nine, and go straight through to 'I Love Lucy' at eleven o'clock. Then at eleven-thirty we watch 'The Tonight Show.' The fight started while we were watching 'Mary Tyler Moore' which comes on at ten-thirty."

Trebeck's testimony was going to be hard to refute, Steele thought grimly.

He changed tack. "If you were so concerned about Mrs. Barrett, why didn't you go over when you first heard the argument?"

"Ah, my wife didn't think . . . ah, want me to." Trebeck seemed to find something on the floor quite interesting.

A jealous wife? Steele wondered. Maybe they ought to speak to Mrs. Trebeck. He wondered if her slant on the situation was the same as her husband's. "Is Mrs. Trebeck here?" he asked. "We'd like to talk with her."

Trebeck's head shot up, and his blue eyes grew as round as a saucer. "What for? I told you everything I know. My wife can't tell you anything more."

"Maybe Mrs. Trebeck saw something you missed," he pressed. "It'll only take a minute."

"My wife isn't feeling well. I'd rather you not bother her. All this has been very trying for her."

"We could come back at another time and talk to her," Taylor suggested.

"I'll think about it." Trebeck was noncommittal.

Steele decided to let the matter drop. He'd have Hawk follow up. However, before he could ask another question, Trebeck rose. "If you don't mind, I have to get back to work."

Steele stood and Taylor followed suit. "Thanks for your help," he said. "If you think of anything else, please call either Ms. Quinlan or me." He pulled out his wallet and took one of the business cards that Taylor had given him the night before and handed it to Trebeck.

But from the vague way Trebeck nodded, Steele wasn't going to hold his breath waiting for him to call.

AFTER THEY LEFT the Trebecks', Taylor and Steele canvassed the neighborhood. They rang doorbells, asked questions, interviewed reluctant neighbors up and down the street, hoping someone would remember seeing a suspicious individual or car the night of the murder. No one did, or would admit it if they had. But Taylor wasn't entirely surprised. Most people were reluctant to get involved with the police, especially when it came to a murder investigation.

Their last stop was at the condo directly to the left of Allison's. Steele rang the doorbell, and a moment later Taylor heard a rustling sound on the other side of the door. A tall, slightly overweight brunette opened the door. Taylor guessed her to be in her late forties, though her dyed shoulder-length black hair made her look older. She wore baggy blue jeans and a blue denim work shirt.

"I'm Taylor Quinlan," she said. "And this is my associate, Michael Steele. We represent Craig Barrett. We'd like to ask you a few questions about Allison Barrett."

"Sure, come on in," the woman said.

Steele placed his hand at the base of her back, and she stepped across the threshold. It was just a courteous gesture, but his palm seemed to burn right through her suit jacket and camisole, straight through to her bare skin. She drew a sigh of relief when he relinquished his hold on her to take the wing-back chair flanking the living room sofa. She took a seat next to their hostess on the sofa.

Sitting on a bar stool on the other side of the room was a gray-haired man nursing a beer. Like the woman, he wore faded blue jeans and a denim work shirt.

Taylor looked at Steele and signaled that he should take the lead.

"We just have a few questions, Mrs..."

"It's Marti Kramer, hon," she said, batting her lashes prettily at Steele, "but you can call me Marti. That's Ned," she added, jerking her head in the direction of the man sitting at the bar stool. "Say hello, Ned."

Ned refilled his beer glass and ignored them.

"Shame about that Barrett woman, isn't it? The papers are hinting the husband did it," Marti said.

"That's why we wanted to talk to you," Steele replied. "We were hoping you could shed some light on the circumstances surrounding her death."

Marti frowned. "I wish I could, but like I told the police, I really didn't know her. She kept pretty much to herself. She was kind of stuck-up...real hoity-toity. You know the type." She stuck her nose in the air and bent her right hand downward to emphasize the point.

"What can you tell us about her?"

She shrugged offhandedly. "Not much. She was here when we got here. Ned and I moved here about three months ago from Los Angeles. I'd see her out jogging. I was always telling Ned that someone as skinny as she was had no business out running like that." She shrugged again. "Like my mother always told me, no one wants a bone but a dog."

Taylor's mouth twitched. Marti certainly had an interesting way of phrasing things. Out of the corner of her eye, she could tell from the twinkle in Steele's eyes that he'd had the same thought.

"To your knowledge, did she have many visitors?" he asked.

Marti laughed. "Hey, I have better things to do with my time than spy on my neighbors. You should talk to Mr. Trebeck. He's in the condo across from Mrs. Barrett's. He was always trying to talk to her."

"I'm sorry, I didn't mean to offend you," Steele said smoothly. "I just thought since you were next-door neighbors you might have occasionally observed people coming or going." He punctuated his words with a dazzling smile.

Taylor threw him a sideways look as if to say: *She's not going to fall for it.* But with Marti's next words, Taylor knew she had.

"I'm not one to gossip, but I might have noticed some of her guests . . . occasionally."

"Can you tell us what you saw?" Steele pressed. "Did she have a lot of visitors?"

"I guess she had a normal amount, although most of them were men." Marti frowned, thinking. "I only saw her in the afternoon. I think she slept until late in the day, hon. Ned and me here—early to bed, early to rise—that's our motto. We never saw or heard Mrs. Barrett until late afternoon. One of those night people, I s'pose. Five, six o'clock she'd be out running. Sometimes I'd see her in the evening, dressed to kill when she was going out— which she did quite a bit. Right, Ned?"

Ned still hadn't acknowledged that anyone else was in the room, let alone responded to any of Marti's prompts. Taylor doubted if the woman even noticed; she talked enough for both of them. Steele nodded encouragement and Marti went on.

"Course now if her husband didn't kill her and it was some lowlife, I bet he got in here when the security cameras were off."

Steele looked up, surprised. "They're not always on?"

"They are now," she stressed, "but it took Mrs. Barrett to get herself killed to get the condo association to provide the security we've been paying for. You see, Ned, I told you we're wasting our money living here. What's the point in having high-tech security if it's not working half the time."

Ned took a swig of beer and kept looking out the window.

"Think you can do something about that, hon? Tell the judge about our lax security or something? We're supposed to be safe in here at night, though Lord knows if someone wants to get you nowadays they'd do it in broad daylight if they had mind to, wouldn't they, Ned?"

Marti was beginning to ramble. Taylor gave Steele a look, signaling they ought to wrap things up.

"Well, if you think of anything, please give us a call." Steele handed her his business card.

She gave Steele a coquettish smile as she slipped the card inside the breast pocket of her shirt. "I certainly will. You know no place is safe nowadays. People kill you just as soon as look at you."

"Coulda been that slender redheaded fellow she was arguing with," Ned said in a slightly slurred voice that startled the other occupants in the room.

Taylor and Steele exchanged quick looks. This might be that clue that the police overlooked. She tried to stem her mounting excitement.

Marti looked at Ned and frowned. "What are you talking about? Arguing? Mrs. Barrett?"

"Was it the night of the murder?" Steele asked, ignoring Marti's words.

"I didn't hear any arguing, Ned," Marti said. She looked at Steele. "He doesn't know what he's talking about. That was the night of my girlfriend Genoa's pool party. We were over there—until he got as drunk as a skunk anyway." She threw Ned a pointed look, then turned back to Steele. "He got sick and Genoa's husband helped me bring him back and put him to bed."

"What time was that?"

Marti frowned. "It was a little before eleven, but he couldn't have heard or seen anything. He was out cold."

"Ned," Steele said, "did you hear an argument that night?"

Ned ran his fingers through his sparse white hair. "I came down to the kitchen to get a drink of water. I glanced out the window, and they were out on her deck...." His voice trailed off. "I don't know. Sorry. I mighta dreamed it." He stared into his glass for a moment, downed the remaining contents and refilled it.

"When do you think you might have heard or dreamed it?" Steele pressed.

Ned shook his head. "I don't know." His belch signaled the end of the conversation.

"Don't listen to him," Marti insisted. "He didn't hear any argument."

Taylor looked at Steele. He gave her an imperceptible nod that seemed to say he agreed they weren't going to get anything further out of the couple and should wrap things up.

Thanking the couple, Taylor and Steele rose and walked to the door. Outside the condo, standing next to the car, Taylor said, "The man Ned saw doesn't sound at all like the person Trebeck claims to have seen."

Steele nodded. "It would also mean the murder may have occurred closer to eleven-thirty, which would make it more difficult for the prosecution to argue that Craig had the opportunity to kill Allison." He sighed and climbed in next to her. "But Ned would make a lousy witness."

"You're right about that," Taylor agreed. She put the key in the ignition and pulled away from the curb. "Where to next? Ridgeway or Larson?"

He glanced at his watch. "It's getting late. I need to check in with my Washington office. I also want to talk to Hawk. Why don't we head back to the office and interview Ridgeway and Larson tomorrow?"

"Okay, that will give me time to check on phone messages and schedule an appointment with Denning."

"Sounds good," Steele said.

They spent the remainder of the trip discussing the discrepancies between Ned Kramer's and Trebeck's recollections of the night Allison was murdered, as well as speculating on what the intruder had been looking for. Before he knew it, they were stepping off the elevator on the twenty-seventh floor of the law firm. He paused outside Taylor's office. For a moment neither he nor Taylor said anything. Then he coughed, clearing his throat. "If you don't have any plans for the evening, maybe we could get together." Damn! He was acting like some schoolboy asking a girl out on a first date.

Taylor looked at him, surprised. He couldn't blame her. After the admonishment he'd given himself about maintaining a professional distance, he'd surprised himself. He'd decided to ask her out on the spur of the moment, provoked by instinct and urges he didn't understand. Every reason he'd laid out the night before for keeping her at arm's length still remained, except that he suddenly wanted to prolong his time with her.

Before she could protest, he said, "We need to talk about the case. I'd like to get your impression on today's events. We don't have a lot of time and we need to stay on top of things. Besides, getting to know each other will help if this case goes to trial."

Taylor was torn. One part of her wanted to accept his invitation because she was so strongly attracted to him. But the cautious part of her questioned the wisdom of spending time with him in anything other than a professional capacity. In a social setting it was too easy to let down her guard, let something slip. God, there was too much at stake to take that kind of risk.

Then she gave herself a mental shake. For heaven's sake, she was a mature woman! So she was attracted to him. What was the big deal about that? He was only asking her to have dinner with him. Why not accept?

"I don't have any plans," she heard herself say. "Dinner would be fine. There's a great Italian restaurant, Saavedra, not far from your hotel. I'll meet you there," she added. Somehow that made it seem less like a date. "Say around seven?"

"Good," he smiled. "I'll see you then."

As she watched him walk away, she wondered, *What have I gotten myself into?*

TAYLOR WAS still wondering as she rummaged through the bedroom closet, looking for the black pumps she planned to wear on her date that evening. No, she told herself firmly, it was a dinner meeting. She frowned; that still sounded too much like a date. Business meeting? She didn't know what to call it, but it certainly wasn't a date. She might have even believed it if she hadn't left work early to run by one of the exclusive shops that lined that part of Michigan Avenue known as the Magnificent Mile and purchased a "snazzy little black number." It had cost a small fortune but it was worth it. It had a halter top and fit her slender frame to perfection. Not that she was trying to impress Steele, she told herself. She simply wanted to look nice for her business meeting.

With plenty of time yet to dress, she walked into the living room, curled up on the sofa, and picked up the book, *How to Drive a Man Wild.* She'd only read a few pages when she put it down. Who was she kidding? There was no way she could have a relationship with Steele. Even if they didn't have this issue of Craig's mental condition between them, there was still the issue of her own medical history. And she'd better remember that and stop fantasizing about Steele and things that were never going to be.

As if to reinforce her resolve not to think about him, she leaned over and picked up the true-crime book and opened it to the bookmarked page. She settled back into the cushions as she became engrossed in reading a fascinating account of a young, charismatic black male, who could only be described as a "lady-killer"—in more ways than one. His unsuspecting victim, Margaret Willis, only discovered his true personality when she refused to continue supporting him. By the time the police connected him to her murder, he was long gone. With only a composite sketch to go on, the killer had been able to evade the authorities for the past four years. Not very good police work, Taylor thought, turning the page to the next story.

It was the tale of a three-decade-old crime. As far as friends and neighbors knew, Robert Vance was exactly what he seemed, a quiet, unassuming, twenty-seven-year-old farm-equipment salesman. There was no air of intrigue or criminality about Vance, no hint of violence in his manner or life-style. In short, nothing to explain the gruesome murder of Vance's wife or his sudden disappearance. To this day, the police couldn't say what happened to him. Taylor shook her head. "Probably dead by now," she muttered, then glanced briefly at the clock. She'd read a little longer, then get dressed.

The next account was that of a young girl who had been charged with killing her foster parents by setting the house on fire while they slept. What was unusual about the crime was the age of the killer—thirteen—and the fact that the girl had shown absolutely no remorse for the crime. She'd been charged with two counts of first-degree murder, but because of her young age, had been tried as a juvenile and sentenced to a mental-health facility for the criminally insane. She'd been released from the facility at the age of twenty-one and promptly disappeared. But one day, the writer speculated, she would resurface and so would tales of other crimes.

Taylor shuddered and dropped the book on the sofa. What could have happened, she wondered, to turn a child into a monster? Had she been the unfortunate offspring of a mentally ill parent? The story hit entirely too close to home. She shuddered again and wrapped her arms around herself. She wouldn't think about it. She glanced at the clock. It was still too early to dress. Restlessly she clicked on the television. The early edition of the evening news was just starting. Predictably Allison's murder was the top story.

"Sources close to the investigation tell KBN news that police have narrowed their investigation and are now focusing their attention on popular daytime television talk-show host Craig Barrett."

A picture of Craig was flashed in the upper right-hand corner of the screen.

"As you know," the anchor continued, "Barrett has maintained a squeaky-clean imagine, but close friends of his estranged wife say it was a facade—that there is a very dark side to the man we have all come to love."

Then came an interview with several of Craig's former groupies, who recounted instances where Craig had supposedly stalked and terrorized Allison. "Whatever the case," the anchor continued, "Barrett is reputed to have been angry and bitter over Allison's claim to half his assets, as well as losing her to publishing mogul Gordon Ridgeway. Barrett is reported to have threatened Ms. Barrett's life only days before she was found brutally murdered in her Lake Shore Drive condo."

Taylor clicked off the TV and stared at the blank screen. The anchor had played up Craig's celebrity status, as well as the troubled aspects of his ill-fated marriage. The reporter's characterization of Craig and Allison's marriage made it sound much more volatile than it had in fact been. It was clearly an attempt to show Craig in the worst possible light, but more than that, the words cast him in a light that could only be damaging in the court of public opinion. The innuendos and mudslinging had started. How long before some sharp reporter started digging into Craig's background? Dredging up his father's suicide. Would they stop there or keep digging until...

She closed her eyes, halting the direction her mind was taking her. She drew a deep breath, struggling to compose herself. She didn't want to look like a basket case when she met Steele. Shakily she pushed herself off the sofa and headed into the bathroom to dress.

Forty-five minutes later she entered the foyer of the restaurant. Steele was prowling around near the entrance to the dining area, tall and lean in an impeccably tailored double-breasted light brown suit. As she walked toward him, she couldn't help noticing the number of people, mostly women, who glanced his way.

Steele, on the other hand, looked only at her. Suddenly she felt incredibly shy and awkward. She straightened her shoulders and dug up a smile all the while her insides were doing jumping jacks. "Hi," she said.

For a moment he didn't say anything. He just stood there staring at her. "You look beautiful," he said finally. His voice was low and husky.

Her heart did a flip-flop at the way he was looking at her. "Thank you," she managed to say. "Ah, why don't we go on in?"

She felt a warm glow when he took her elbow and escorted her down the short corridor into the dining area.

"Have you been here before?" Steele murmured as he lowered himself into the chair opposite Taylor.

Taylor nodded. "Once or twice. The food's great."

"The last time I was in Chicago, I came here for dinner," Steele said, glancing about the room. "It's a nice place."

"Nice" was an understatement, since the kitchen regularly drew five stars in every restaurant guide in the city. Clearly Steele wasn't the type to be swayed by others' opinions or he was just hard to impress. She smiled as she admitted to herself that she had been trying to impress him.

"What's so funny?" Steele asked. He had caught the small smile flitting across her lovely face, a real one this time, and was curious as to its cause.

"Nothing," Taylor said hastily.

"No, come on, tell me."

Lamely she said, "Just that it's nice to be here, that's all." Quickly, lest he think she meant with him, she added, "I really like this place and I've hardly ever gotten here for dinner, that's all."

He sat back in his chair and looked at her. "Okay. Now, what were you really thinking?"

"Just like a lawyer. You don't believe anything anyone says."

He grinned. "I do when they're telling the truth. Just now your eyes slipped out of focus slightly. It's the first time I've seen that happen. I guess that's because it's the first time you told me something that wasn't true."

Taylor stared down at the silverware. She felt like a heel. If only she could tell him the entire story.

"All right," she said, looking up at him. "I was really thinking that you have a reputation for being hard to impress and that I'm glad I'm here with you in a purely professional capacity, that I am not interested in you as a man. Satisfied?"

Steele clutched his hand to his heart. "Well, that will teach me to ask." He grinned. "Next time...lie. I'm not sure my ego can deal with your straightforward honesty."

He thought she would laugh at his little joke. Instead, she quickly turned her head to the side, but not before he glimpsed her sad expression.

"Is something wrong?" he asked, concerned that he might have offended her in some way.

She plastered a smile on her face. "I guess I'm just a little tired."

His eyes narrowed, but he didn't press. "Maybe we should order," he suggested. By the time their orders were taken, her mood had lifted and she was giving him a rundown on her afternoon activities.

"I called Senator Denning's office and made an appointment for us for tomorrow at two," she concluded. "What about you? Did you get in touch with Mr. Longtree?"

Steele smiled. "Yeah. His plane got in a few hours ago. He'll check out the bar identified on the matchbook we found at Allison's, as well as interview Mrs. Trebeck. See if she has a different slant on things." Steele paused and took a sip of wine. "I also arranged for security to be tightened at the condo."

"Frankly," Taylor sighed, "we didn't uncover anything today that points to anyone other than Craig as having killed Allison. Trebeck firmly believes he did it."

"I know," he said. "He's going to make a great witness for the prosecution. They're going to use him to establish the time of the murder, as well as to place Craig at the crime scene." He sighed. "If Ned was a more credible witness, we could use him to counter Trebeck's claim."

Taylor nodded in agreement. "And Donaldson would be forced to consider that someone other than Craig could have killed Allison. If only we'd gotten to the condo earlier, maybe we'd have found what the intruder was looking for."

"And maybe not," Steele argued. "Our intruder had a distinct advantage over us. He knew what he was looking for." He issued a frustrated sigh. "Look, why don't we talk about something else for a while?"

"Like what?"

"You, for instance," he said, giving her a dazzling smile. "I meant what I said about wanting to get to know you better. So why don't you tell me about yourself?"

"There's really very little to tell," Taylor hedged. It was hard enough pretending she was unaffected by her handsome co-counsel, while trying to focus on the conversation with Steele looking at her like that. There was no way she could also effectively sidestep questions about her family. He was entirely too astute and would pick up on a song and dance. It would be best to steer clear of the topic entirely. "I'm sure the life you lead is far more exciting than mine," she said lightly. "You strike me as sort of an Indiana Jones."

"I wouldn't go that far," he laughed. "The life of a criminal defense attorney is not at all glamorous like television and the movies would have you believe. The hours are long, and many of your clients aren't exactly choirboys. So you get to visit them in a lot of seedy places like federal prison."

"When you put it like that," she teased, "maybe 'exciting' isn't really the right word."

"That's an understatement," he said, returning her smile. "Now come on, tell me about yourself."

The man had a one-track mind. "I graduated from the University of Chicago Law School four years ago and went directly to work for Haraman and Giusto." She smiled. "Not that there was any question of my going anywhere else. Matt would have had my head."

"You and Matt go back a long way, don't you?"

She nodded. "He and Craig have been best friends since high school. Sometimes I forget he isn't really part of the family."

"Is that why you weren't able to tell him you had reservations about Craig's innocence?"

"That's part of the reason," she hedged. Again she felt on shaky ground, but decided to stick as close to the truth as possible. "It was hard enough thinking Craig might be involved in Allison's murder, but to give voice to that thought was untenable. I didn't know what else to do but ask to be removed from the case."

Steele took a sip of his drink. "Your leaving would have led to too much media speculation," he said. "In a situation like this, you have to be conscious of public opinion. The last thing we need is to have the press claiming you left the case because you believe Craig is guilty. And that's exactly the slant they would have placed on it. From what I've seen of the reporting so far, it's going to be a first-class media circus."

She thought back to the news broadcast she had seen earlier in the evening. "You're right," she said grimly. "I've already had a dose of that."

"What do you mean?"

"I caught the early edition of the news. The lead story was Allison's murder." Her mouth tightened. "They're already laying the groundwork to portray Craig as a modern-day Dr. Jekyll and Mr. Hyde."

Steele sighed. "Before this is over, you're going to hear a lot worse than that. I hope Craig and your family isn't harboring any deep, dark secrets. A lot of dirty laundry is going to be aired before this is over."

Taylor shuddered, causing her wineglass to tip over. She quickly began to mop up the mess.

Steele covered her hand with his, halting her action. "I'm sorry. I didn't mean to upset you."

The warmth from his hand penetrated the cold that had seeped into her, and for a moment she let his hand cover hers. "You didn't upset me," she replied hurriedly, then reinforced her words with a faint smile.

His eyes softened at her attempt to put on a brave front. "How is Craig's mother holding up?" he asked gently.

Taylor picked up her fork and drew imaginary circles on the table. "Naturally she's worried, but she's a very strong woman."

"You love her very much, don't you?" he said quietly.

She nodded, not trusting herself to speak.

Curious, Steele looked at her. "I guess that's why I'm surprised you and Craig aren't closer. You were only ten when your parents died. The perfect age for a girl to want an older brother."

She hesitated, not sure how to answer his unspoken question. She couldn't tell him the real reason: that Craig's mother had been a source of conflict between them. Craig saw her as smothering and obsessive, but because she knew what fueled Aunt Ida's concerns, she saw her as loving and protective. But she couldn't tell him that. "Craig was in his last semester of high school when I went to live with the Barretts," she said finally. "Then he was off to college. I guess the eight-year age difference and him being away at school made our becoming close impossible. Most of the time it was just me and Aunt Ida."

Her answer must have satisfied Steele because he nodded, then asked how she liked living in Chicago.

This was definitely safer ground. "It's kind of a love-hate thing. Summers are great but the winters are grueling." She grimaced. "I don't think I'll ever get used to this blistering cold." She looked at him and smiled. "How about a little equal time here? I'd like to know more about Michael Steele. How did you get to be such a hotshot criminal lawyer, for instance?"

He grinned. "Is that what I'm supposed to be?"

She nodded. "The terror of the courtroom. Prosecutors tremble at the mere sight of you. You're the avenging angel of the innocent, the man judges respect and juries adore. And you've never lost a case since going out on your own. That's pretty impressive stuff.''

He shrugged, diminishing the significance. "I'm good at my job for the same reason you're good at yours. I work hard and I pick my battles carefully.''

Her eyes widened in mock surprise. "Is this the same man that represented the college freshman accused of killing his drug dealer in cold-blooded murder? The case that everyone said was a sure loser?''

His teeth flashed white against his brown skin as he laughed loud enough to make people at several tables turn their heads to look. Unabashed, Steele said, "Okay, you got me. I like a good fight. Representing the underdog makes me feel like I'm doing something worthwhile. When I was a kid, the one thing I wanted to be was a cowboy. I was always the guy in black—the hired gun— getting off the train in some dusty Western town—ready to take on the bad guys.''

She laughed. "Some would say you got your wish by becoming a trial lawyer." She sipped her drink and studied him. He really had gotten his wish. He spent his life defending individuals against the system. Many of his clients were rich and powerful and paid huge sums for his services. But others were poor and downtrodden and needed a champion.

"You must be offered more cases than you could possibly handle," she said. "How do you decide which ones you'll take?''

"Instinct and interest. And I have to believe that the person, if he in fact committed the crime, isn't going to be a menace to society if I get him off.''

"How can you represent someone you know committed a crime?'' she asked. As a case in point, she told him about the criminal cases she read about earlier.

Steele nodded. "I'm not familiar with the first two, but I remember that last one. It was out of Philly. It got a lot of local attention at the time." He shook his head. "I wouldn't have taken that kid's case. I don't represent psychos or anyone I flat out believe did whatever they're being accused of or at the very least didn't have a good reason for doing what they did.''

"That's reassuring to hear," Taylor said softly. "Is that why you took Craig's case? You're that sure of his innocence?''

He nodded. "Yes, but like I said, it's just a feeling. It's the same feeling that told me to keep you on the case.'' He smiled. "I have to admit I did have some reservations, but from all accounts, it was the right decision. You handled yourself like a real pro today. You located the Senator Denning letter, the matchbook and found our friendly intruder. Besides, I admire your honesty. You didn't have to tell me how you felt. You could have just as easily kept your reservations to yourself, but you didn't. That took guts.''

Taylor's quickly lowered her lashes, but not before he'd seen the flash of pain in her eyes.

Steele looked at her sharply. What had caused that bleak look? he wondered. It was the second time tonight he'd seen it. He had also noticed it earlier in the day. They would be talking, and suddenly she would look as if she'd lost her best friend. What demons chased her? he wondered. He was just about to question her when she launched into a discussion of the case.

He hesitated. There was still so much he wanted to know about her, about those glimpses of sadness that he'd observed but she was as skittish as a colt. If he pushed too hard, she'd bolt. Reluctantly he let her pull him back to the case. "Okay," he said, "here's what I want you to do.... "

Chapter Five

Taylor stepped off the elevator and headed in the direction of her office. It had been a grueling morning. It had started with an eight-thirty trip to the McCalls to talk to Craig and get his signature on a power of attorney. Armed with that authorization, she'd proceeded to the First National Bank, where she'd been granted access to Allison's financial records and safe-deposit box. From there she'd gone on to Phoenix Development Corporation, ending with a trip to the Secretary of State's Office. Her neck ached and her eyes burned, but she was pleased with what she'd found. She hoped Steele would be, too.

Just thinking of her handsome co-counsel caused a smile to spring to her lips. While there had been a few tense moments during dinner last night, she'd really enjoyed herself. Afterward she'd been too keyed up to sleep, and when she finally drifted off, her dreams had been full of Steele. Heat rushed to her face when she thought of the X-rated content of at least one of those dreams. The man was certainly wreaking havoc with her senses.

When she reached the office, she decided to check in with Brenda before going to see Steele.

"Any messages?" she asked, plopping in the chair next to the secretary's desk.

"Tons." Brenda grinned, handing her a stack of phone messages and the correspondence that had come in that morning. "Judge Greenspan's clerk called. She said to tell you the status in the Burns case will be in two weeks. I noted it on your calendar."

"Thanks," Taylor said, absently going through her messages. Nothing too pressing. Several clients had called. Vanessa Norris. Her aunt. Most could wait. She instructed Brenda to call her aunt and tell her she'd get back to her. The one from Vanessa Norris she dumped in the trash can and headed to Steele's office.

As she drew nearer, her heart began to pound in anticipation. *Stop it!* she told herself sternly. She had absolutely no interest in Michael Steele. He was a colleague, nothing more. At the door she paused, drew a deep breath, knocked, then entered.

Steele was sitting behind his desk, poring over a large computer printout. Her eyes roamed over him. God, no man had a right to look that good, she thought. He'd removed his jacket and rolled up his shirtsleeves. His white linen shirt was stretched taut over his lean, muscular chest. She caught a glimpse of dark hair on his arms and wondered if there was a thick pelt of dark hair on his chest and stomach, as well.

It was as if she'd voiced her thoughts aloud, because he looked up and she saw the fire burning in the depths of his hazel eyes.

"I got the information you wanted," she said, trying to pretend she was unaffected by his heated gaze. "Want to hear it?"

"Sure," he said. He put the printout aside, then leaned back in his chair, regarding her steadily.

She moved self-consciously into the room and took the chair across from his desk. She cleared her throat and began. "You were right to be suspicious about Allison's finances. Her condominium is owned by Phoenix Development Corporation. Supposedly she was just renting. However, I couldn't find any rent receipts. So I dropped by the company and got the royal runaround, which really piqued my curiosity."

"So what did you find?" he asked, smiling.

"According to the Secretary of State's Office, Phoenix Development Corporation is owned by Senator Barry Denning."

Steele sat up, immediately alert. "Denning and Allison were involved? That's incredible."

"I know," she said, "but I can't imagine any other reason for her living rent free in one of his ten-thousand-dollar-a-month condos."

He gave her a thoughtful look. "I can't wait to hear Denning's explanation."

"You and me both," she agreed. "I also talked to Craig. He confirmed that Allison was virtually penniless when they got married. As far as he knows, the fifteen thousand a month he was giving her was her only source of income."

Steele nodded absently. "That's what I thought."

"I also ran a credit check on her," she said. "There was no indication that she had any stocks, bonds, mutual funds or other investments, and I didn't find anything of that nature in her safe-deposit box."

"Was there anything inside?"

Taylor consulted her notes. "A life-insurance policy, a few pieces of jewelry and her will. Her parents are dead. She left everything to a younger brother, Edward Garrison."

Steele nodded again. "I'll have Hawk see if he can locate him. But back to the question of assets, just because you didn't find any doesn't mean none exist. It could just be that she didn't have any in her name."

"I know," Taylor agreed. "But I haven't been able to locate any secret accounts, past or otherwise."

Something in her voice made Steele look at her sharply. "Are you telling me you think she has additional assets?"

Taylor's eyes sparkled with excitement. "I'm sure of it. Look." She handed him a copy of Craig and Allison's separation agreement. "That document was drawn up five months ago. If you turn to page four, you'll note the only assets attributed to Allison are a Porsche, some jewelry and the personal effects that are now inside her condominium. But look at the footnote at the bottom of the page."

She waited until he'd read the paragraph and looked up again.

"At first blush," she continued, "that footnote could be read to mean that Craig has assets that weren't considered in this agreement, but Matt is sure all of Craig's assets are accounted for on pages two and three. So that footnote has to refer to assets that Allison acquired between separating from Craig and the drafting of that document."

Steele pulled on his lower lip as he studied the footnote. "Why didn't the drafter just come right out and say what they were?" He looked at Taylor and frowned. "And why haven't we found any record of these supposed assets?"

"In answer to your first question, I think the footnote was written in that manner because he also had some questions about them."

Steele contemplated her words for a moment before saying, "Then I guess the only way we're going to get any answers is by looking at the actual documents used to prepare this agreement. But there weren't any documents listed in the police report of items removed from the condo, and we certainly didn't find anything like that in our search and they weren't in her safe-deposit box." Suddenly his hazel eyes widened, and Taylor knew the same thought had occurred to him that had occurred to her. "Do you think that's what our intruder was looking for?" he asked.

Taylor leaned forward. "I'd stake my life on it. He didn't find them and we didn't, either, because they weren't there. Craig remembers Allison grumbling about not being able to locate the insurance policy for her diamond bracelet. He thought it was because she'd left the policy, as well as her other documents, with her lawyer. However, I checked with him this morning, and he didn't have them, which means they'd have to be with Jasper and Kline, the accounting firm that drew up the separation agreement.''

Steele gave her a thoughtful look. ''Let's hope she didn't get around to collecting them. I'd like to know what assets she had.'' He glanced his watch. ''I hope they can see us today.''

Taylor smiled. ''I already called and made an appointment. They're expecting us right after lunch. I thought we could stop by and talk to Mr. Jasper before our meeting with the senator.''

''Very good,'' Steele said approvingly. ''I just hope this isn't a wild-goose chase.''

''I don't think it will be,'' Taylor answered in a rush of words. ''In fact, I think it will support our theory that someone other than Craig could have killed Allison.'' She leaned forward slightly. ''I checked out Allison's bank accounts. There wasn't much in checking, just a few thousand dollars, but she had over three hundred thousand in savings.''

Steele gave a low whistle.

''You're telling me.'' Taylor nodded. ''Even if we assume Allison saved every dime Craig gave her since they separated, she'd still only have ninety thousand dollars.''

''The money could be from Ridgeway,'' he said, then added, ''but that's a hell of a lot of money coming from some sugar daddy.''

''I'll say,'' Taylor agreed. ''But I don't think that's where the money's from. And Craig swears he didn't give it to her.''

Steele looked at her sharply. ''You've got something?''

''I looked at her deposits into her saving's account since she separated from Craig,'' Taylor said, barely able to contain her excitement. ''The three hundred thousand was the result of two deposits—both made in the last five months and both from bearer bonds that were liquidated into cash.''

''What are you saying?''

Hazel eyes met brown ones. "I think Allison had gone into business—the blackmail business. The question is, after five months of being bled dry by Allison, did her victim decide to cut his losses and just kill her?"

IT WAS an intriguing question and one that Taylor hoped they'd find the answer to in the documents Allison had left with the accounting firm. If the documents identified additional assets as they hoped, those assets could quite possibly lead them to Allison's blackmail victim. That was probably why the intruder had been willing to take such a big risk coming to the condo. He'd probably been looking for the documents—the one thing that could connect him to Allison's murder. It might not be enough to prove the victim was her killer or that Craig was innocent, but it would be enough to establish reasonable doubt in the minds of the jury if Craig was ever charged with Allison's murder. And that was all the defense needed to do to prevent a conviction.

Taylor tried to stem her mounting excitement as she followed Steele into the office of David Jasper, president of the prestigious accounting firm of Jasper, Kline & Iocca.

"Mr. Steele, what a pleasure it is to meet you." David Jasper's wrinkled face beamed as he pumped Steele's hand. "I've read so much about you. And I must say, I've followed your work closely. I'm something of a criminology buff."

"You're very kind," Steele said smoothly. "This is my associate, Taylor Quinlan."

"Ah, yes," Mr. Jasper said smiling at Taylor. "We spoke on the phone. Won't you be seated?" He pointed to two comfortable-looking chairs flanking his desk.

"I hope you don't mind our barging in on you on such short notice," Steele said after they were seated.

"Not at all," the accountant said with a dismissive wave of his hand. "I assume you would not be calling upon me unless it was a matter of utmost importance."

Steele nodded. "That's correct. Ms. Quinlan and I are hoping you can shed some light on a situation for us."

"I'll do what I can. What is it you seek clarified?"

Steele looked at Taylor, signaling that she should take the lead.

Taylor handed the accountant a copy of the separation agreement. "I believe your firm drafted the property-assessment portion of this document for our client and his wife."

Mr. Jasper peered nearsightedly at the document. "Ah, yes." He nodded. "The Barrett separation agreement. We prepared that section." He placed the document on his desk and looked from Steele to Taylor. "Is there a problem?"

Taylor shook her head. "Not at all. Everything appears to be in order."

Mr. Jasper gave her a smug little smile. "We at Jasper and Kline pride ourselves on our work. Your client's document was prepared by Harold Lamden, one of the finest accountants this firm has ever had."

"Following up on that same line of thought," Taylor said, "are your clients always required to document their financial worth?"

The accountant blinked, clearly surprised by her question. "Oh, heavens, yes," he said. "Human nature being what it is, we require documentation of financial worth, as well as a signed consent for release of information so that in the event we need to verify the accuracy of any information provided or dig a little deeper into a client's finances, we may do so."

Taylor leaned forward and handed him a legal document. "Mr. Barrett has authorized Mr. Steele and me to review any documents Mrs. Barrett may have left with your firm."

At Mr. Jasper's look of confusion, she tactfully added, "Apparently there was some kind of mix-up resulting in neither Mrs. Barrett nor her attorney getting back the documents she provided to Mr. Lamden."

Mr. Jasper looked at her, surprised. "We still have them?"

Taylor nodded. "That's my understanding."

"I see," he said slowly. His wrinkled face puckered into a frown. "Perhaps if you could tell me what it is you're looking for, I could clarify it for you."

Taylor shook her head. "We have reason to believe that Mrs. Barrett's documents identify assets that are not accounted for in this agreement. The footnote on page four seems to suggest that. Under the circumstances, a review of the actual documents would be called for."

"Ah, yes. I quite agree," the accountant said after a brief study of the agreement. "I must say I'm a little surprised. Mr. Lamden was usually most clear in his writing." He removed his bifocals and began polishing the lens with a white linen handkerchief. "Er, well, I'm afraid you've caught me in a . . ." He coughed delicately. "This is very embarrassing."

Taylor looked at Steele. This was not the reaction she was expecting. "What do you mean?" she asked cautiously.

Mr. Jasper shifted uncomfortably in his chair. "We're very selective about who we employ professionally, as well as in regard to our support staff, but sometimes a bad apple slips through. Betsy Boyd was our bad apple—or should I say Mr. Lamden's." He gave them a pained look. "I'm sure if Harold had been himself, he would have rectified the situation, but the poor man was quite distraught over his mother's untimely death."

Mr. Jasper issued a tiny sigh, then continued speaking as if to himself. "Harold was devoted to his mother. Absolutely devoted, and when she died suddenly of a heart attack . . . well, it knocked him for a loop. He was devastated and for a time had to be hospitalized. When he came back to work, I gave him the Barrett file. I knew he'd jump right into it. Do a good job. I . . ." He gave a nervous little laugh. "Forgive me. I'm rambling. Well, what I hadn't counted on was Ms. Boyd's gross incompetence and Harold's inability to deal with it. We tolerated the situation as long as we could. But after Ms. Boyd misplaced all those files, we—"

Steele, who'd been content to let Taylor do the questioning, now spoke up. "Whoa, back up. What do you mean, she misplaced what files?"

The accountant cleared his throat and shifted in his chair. "This is a very delicate situation, and we've been handling our little problem discreetly."

"Are you saying you don't have the Barrett file?" Steele asked incredulously.

"We have it," the accountant said quickly. "We just don't know where it is. We think that file and several dozen others were sent to one of our two warehouses in the city. However, Ms. Boyd didn't retain a copy of the tracking sheet. So we don't know how they were labeled or which warehouse they were sent to. Nothing like this has ever happened before at Jasper and Kline."

"How did it happen this time?" Taylor asked.

"Incompetence. Sheer incompetence. Naturally we terminated Ms. Boyd's employment."

"Naturally," Steele said dryly. "Did you question the secretary before you fired her?"

Mr. Jasper flushed under Steele's scrutiny. "We didn't realize the extent of the problem until she'd left. By then it was too late. The woman had disappeared."

"Disappeared?" An image of a woman on the run flashed in Taylor's mind. "Did you notify the police?"

"Oh, heavens, no," Mr. Jasper said, realizing the direction her mind was going. "There was nothing nefarious or suspicious about her disappearance. After leaving the firm, she got married and moved downstate. We've tried to locate her but haven't had much luck. I'm afraid we didn't get her married name or the city she moved to before she left."

Taylor looked at Steele. It was a setback, but it was not insurmountable. "Perhaps if Mr. Lamden looked at the agreement," she suggested, "something might jog his memory."

Mr. Jasper shook his head. "I afraid that's not possible."

"I know you're concerned about his mental state, but we'll be discreet," Taylor said, seeking to reassure him.

"But you don't understand. Mr. Lamden is no longer with us."

"Do you have his address?"

"Oh, dear," Mr. Jasper said, clearly flustered. "I'm not explaining myself very well." He drew a deep breath. "Like I said, Mr. Lamden was very distraught over his mother's death and sank into a deep depression. We should have seen it coming but we didn't. He seemed to be doing so well."

Taylor was instantly on guard, preparing herself psychologically like a prizefighter about to take a body blow. As if from a distance, she heard Mr. Jasper say, "Mr. Lamden is dead. He committed suicide."

HAROLD LAMDEN WAS DEAD! It was the last thing Taylor had expected. Any question of foul play had been ruled out. Lamden had simply gone home one evening, washed down a sleeping pill with a glass of red wine, gone out to the garage, climbed into his car and turned on the ignition. He'd died of carbon-monoxide poisoning.

Mr. Jasper was all apologies. He assured them he'd do whatever he could to help locate Betsy Boyd. He even offered to let them conduct their own search of the warehouses to look for Lamden's files, but it did little to rectify the situation.

The trail that had seemed so hot only hours before had suddenly turned stone cold. No matter how she looked at it, without those documents, Taylor saw little hope of identifying Allison's blackmail victim.

Taylor's spirits were at an all-time low by the time they entered Senator Barry Denning's campaign office.

"Cheer up," Steele whispered as they waited for the young blond receptionist to announce their arrival. "Our luck is bound to change."

She gave him a wry smile. "It can't get any worse. Things—"

They looked up as the door of the inner sanctum opened, and a man walked out. It wasn't the senator. Steele and Taylor stood up.

"Mr. Steele. Ms. Quinlan. I'm Kane O'Rourke, Senator Denning's administrative assistant." O'Rourke was just shy of six feet tall. He wore a practiced smile along with oval wire-rimmed glasses, a dark navy suit, a pristine white shirt and power red tie.

"The senator's tied up on a call to D.C., but if you'll come with me, I'll see what I can do for you until he's free."

Steele and Taylor followed the administrative assistant down a carpeted hall into a plush office. It was large, and the entire back wall was of glass and offered a magnificent view of Lake Michigan. The other walls were covered with photographs showing the rich and powerful preening with the senator. Movie stars, two presidents, a general and a couple of astronauts. On a large mahogany desk was a picture of the senator and his family.

Steele and Taylor took the seats O'Rourke offered and waited for him to speak. After pushing some papers to the side, O'Rourke sat down on the edge of the desk and crossed his arms over his chest. "So, what can I do for you folks?"

"Mr. Steele and I represent Craig Barrett," Taylor began. "We'd like to talk to the senator about Allison Barrett."

"Oh, yeah—" O'Rourke nodded "—the woman that was murdered. I'm sure the senator will help in any way he can, but I'm not sure just what it is you want."

"It's my understanding Allison Barrett was a contributor to the senator's gubernatorial campaign," Steele said, picking up the conversation.

O'Rourke shrugged offhandedly. "She may have been, but I can't say for sure. We have a lot of contributors. You'd be amazed at the number of people in this state

that agree with the senator on family values and man-
datory sentencing for violent felons.''

"Forget the campaign rhetoric," Steele said. "Just
answer the question. Was she a contributor to the senator's campaign?"

"You can't expect me—or the senator, for that matter—to remember all of his supporters. Senator Denning
is very well respected in this state, and a lot of affluent
people support him." His words were spoken calmly, but
the slightly amused look in his face had been replaced by
a thoughtful expression, and a small worry line puckered his forehead.

Steele leaned back, placed his right foot on top of his
left knee and regarded O'Rourke steadily. "Frankly I'm
surprised you don't remember. It can't be that often that
the senator would take time out of his busy schedule to
write a personal thank-you note to a contributor. And it
certainly isn't every day that someone purchases a ten-
thousand-dollar ticket to a private fund-raiser." He
cocked his head to the side and looked at O'Rourke curiously. "Yet when we checked, we couldn't find any
record of such a check having ever been written. I'm sure
you know that cash donations of that amount must be
reported to the Internal Revenue Service. You wouldn't
want anyone to get the wrong impression, would you?"

The color drained from O'Rourke's face. All the
cocky, practiced élan seemed to drain out of him like
water out of a bathtub. If he was acting, he was good,
Taylor thought. O'Rourke stood up. "I think you'd better talk to the senator."

"That's why we're here," Steele said smoothly. "You
think that phone call to D.C. is about over?"

O'Rourke blinked at him twice, then nodded.

The moment he was out of the room, Taylor turned to
Steele. "The letter we found at the condo didn't men-
tion any dollar amount, and I forgot to look for a check.
How did you know it was a cash donation?"

"Shh," he whispered, giving her a mischievous grin.
"I thought that was a nice touch, didn't you?"

Taylor grinned back. "You're terrible—"

The door opened. O'Rourke stepped aside for a distinguished-looking man in his early fifties. The first thing Steele noticed was that his pictures didn't do him justice. Denning looked like the American ideal of Who We Want Running Things.

Tall and ramrod straight, the man looked like Harrison Ford. His tawny brown hair was even graying at the temples, but instead of making him look old, it gave him an air of aristocratic bearing.

"Mr. Steele. Ms. Quinlan." Senator Denning walked toward them, confident, self-assured, his hand outstretched. "I understand you have some questions about Allison Barrett. Lovely woman." He shook his head, and his voice had just the right degree of concern when he said, "It was a tragedy."

Steele nodded. "Why don't you begin by telling us how you met Ms. Barrett?"

"I met her through my wife about eight months ago at a political fund-raiser," he said easily. "She seemed like a charming woman, but I really didn't know her all that well."

Steele gave him a hard look. "Senator, let's not beat around the bush. We both know you were more than casual acquaintances." He let the implication hang in the air.

Denning turned to his administrative assistant, who was standing off to the side with his arms crossed over his chest like a sentinel. "Kane, that will be all." The door had just barely closed behind him before Denning whirled around. "I resent what you're implying. If this is some attempt to smear—"

"Not only was Allison one of your *supposed* contributors," Steele continued as if he'd not spoken, "she lived in one of your ten-thousand-dollar-a-month Lake Shore condos rent free."

The only indication that Senator Denning had been affected by his words was a slight tremor of his hand. He'd make a hell of a poker player, Steele thought.

"That's correct," the senator said, "but it's not what you're thinking."

Steele's gaze never left Denning's face. "Senator, I'm not your judge or jury. My client is being accused of murder. I'm simply trying to get to the truth. Why don't we begin by your telling Ms. Quinlan and me exactly what *was* the nature of your relationship with Allison."

"There was no relationship."

"Senator, there's no point—"

"I'm telling you the truth!" he said angrily. He drew a deep breath, then said in a calmer voice, "There was nothing between Allison and me. However, before I say anything more, I must have your word this conversation won't go any further." Senator Denning's head swiveled from Steele to Taylor. "The press and my opponent would have a field day if any of this got out. I—I'd be ruined."

Steele gave him a hard look. "Senator, a woman has been murdered. All things considered, that could be the least of your problems."

"Do I have your word?"

Steele shook his head. "We can't make any promises. Why don't you tell us about you and Allison?"

For a long moment Denning didn't say anything, then he nodded as if he'd reached a decision. He plopped down on the sofa across from them and stretched out his long legs. "It's not what you're thinking," he said finally. "There was nothing between Allison and me. She and my wife, Myra, were friends."

Taylor slanted Steele a sideways glance that seemed to say that she found Denning's assertion hard to believe.

"Myra is very active with women's issues," the senator explained. "You know—child care, health care and domestic violence. So when Allison confided in her that she was married to this brute and wished to leave but couldn't because she lacked the financial means, Myra prevailed upon me to help, which I did." He cleared his throat. "I was concerned about people misconstruing a loan, so I agreed to let her stay at the Lake Shore condo.

She needed to get away from her husband. The condo was vacant. It was all aboveboard.''

"You let her live there rent free for almost six months?" Taylor couldn't keep the skepticism out of her voice.

The senator shrugged. "Well, I guess we should have been more diligent, not let her take advantage of our good nature, but being a poor businessman is not a crime."

If that was all there was to it, Taylor thought.

"Why didn't you come forward and give this information to the police?" Steele asked.

The senator stood. "Surely you can appreciate my position." His voice pleaded for understanding. "I'm in the middle of a very tight gubernatorial race. I can't get involved in a murder investigation. The press and my opponent would have a field day."

"Don't you think your constituents are smart enough to see through any media hype?" Steele asked.

Senator Denning shook his head. "It's not a question of being smart but rather being constantly bombarded with negative information. After a while people believe it. And that's why I didn't come forward. Put yourself in my place. Why should I jeopardize everything I've worked for for the past twenty-five years for a woman I barely knew?"

Taylor's eyes narrowed. And this coming from the man who thought the way to solve the state's rising crime problem was through people getting involved!

"Besides," the senator continued, "I really don't know anything that would aid the police or you in your investigation. The only thing I know is what Allison told me." He looked at them shrewdly. "Anything I'd have to say would only further implicate Barrett in his wife's murder."

Steele chose to ignore the senator's veiled threat. "Did you ever visit Mrs. Barrett at her condo?"

"Of course not!"

The senator's show of righteous indignation didn't faze Steele one bit. "When was the last time you saw her?"

Denning frowned as he thought back. "It was months ago."

"Alone?" Steele pressed.

The senator gestured toward the door. "Good day, Mr. Steele, Ms. Quinlan," he said coldly.

"Is there anyone who can corroborate your story?"

Denning nodded. "My wife, Myra. If you'd like to speak to her, she'll confirm my story."

"Thank you," Steele said, standing. Taylor followed suit. "I think we'll do that."

Senator Denning nodded. "I'll have Kane call her and let her know you're on your way over."

At the door Steele turned and asked, "By the way, where were you the night Ms. Barrett was killed?"

The senator threw him a stormy look. "I was right here, working on a speech. I'm sure Willie, the night watchman, can vouch for me. Now if you don't mind..."

MYRA DENNING WAS WAITING for them when they ar-rived. She confirmed her husband's story, but that was to be expected, Steele thought. It had taken them at least thirty minutes to reach the senator's Evanston home, which was certainly enough time for the couple to have rehearsed their story. And Myra Denning was the con-summate politician's wife: polished, sophisticated and adept in sidestepping difficult questions. She also struck Steele as a woman who wasn't about to let her hus-band's indiscretion destroy his political career or the years she'd invested in him. No doubt, she wanted to be First Lady as much as her husband wanted to be gover-nor.

"Well, what do you think?" Taylor asked when they were once again seated in the car.

Steele shrugged. "Their story is certainly plausible, and they'll stick to it come hell or high water. Maybe I'm too cynical, but I don't believe a word of it."

THEIR NEXT STOP WAS to see Gordon Ridgeway. Ridgeway lived in Highland Park, an affluent north-shore suburb about thirty miles outside of Chicago. As Steele rapped the brass knocker on an elaborately carved door, Taylor looked out on the lush green lawn. Ridgeway had certainly done well for himself, she thought. He'd been born dirt poor, in the Mississippi Delta, one of ten children of sharecroppers. Working sixteen hours a day, seven days a week, he'd turned a fledgling newsletter into one of the country's leading monthly magazines for black women, as well as amassed a vast fortune by the time he was forty.

Her musing was interrupted as the door swung open. A man somewhere in his early fifties, dressed like a penguin, stared coolly at them. "May I help you?"

"I'm Michael Steele. This is Taylor Quinlan. We're attorneys representing Craig Barrett. We'd like to see Mr. Ridgeway." Steele took a business card out of his wallet and handed it to him. Taylor did likewise.

The butler took the cards, looked at them briefly, then said, "Please come with me."

Steele and Taylor walked into a foyer that was larger than Taylor's entire living room. The floor was black-and-white marble, and the three-story white staircase was covered in black plush carpeting. A spectacular crystal chandelier hung in the center of the foyer. Then she noticed a well-dressed, short, dark-brown-skinned man standing on the second floor of the balcony watching them.

"Ms. Quinlan?" the butler said, pulling her attention back. "This way, please."

She followed the butler and Steele into a sunlit lounge off the foyer. "Please wait here. I'll see if Mr. Ridgeway can see you." The butler gave them a hint of a bow, turned on his heel and left the room.

Taylor walked over to a desk and picked up a silver-framed photo. "Look at this." The picture was of Allison and a much older man whom she recognized from Allison's funeral as Gordon Ridgeway. Taylor couldn't

help but wonder what had attracted a man like Ridgeway to Allison. She knew exactly what had attracted Allison to him—his vast fortune.

"Looks like a match made in hell," Taylor observed.

"Yeah," Steele agreed. "There's no fool like an old
fool."

There was a whisper of noise behind them, and they
whirled around. The man she'd seen on the staircase
stood in the doorway watching them, tense and alert.
Close up he looked to be in his early forties. He might
have been attractive if his face hadn't been scrunched into
a scowl. "I heard you tell Phillips that you represent
Craig Barrett."

Taylor looked quickly at Steele and signaled that he
should begin the questioning.

"That's correct," Steele said cautiously. "You have us
at a disadvantage. You know who we are, but we don't
know who you are."

"I'm Daniel Ridgeway," he said, moving into the
room. "Why do you want to see my father?"

"We'd like to talk to him about Allison Barrett,"
Steele said smoothly.

Ridgeway frowned. "I don't see how he can help you.
He was in the hospital the night Allison was murdered.
Besides, from what I read in the papers, it sounds to me
as if the police have a pretty good idea of who killed her."

Steele chose to ignore Ridgeway's dig. "Your father
and Mrs. Barrett were engaged. Perhaps he might remember something she said that will aid our investigation. I'm sure he's just as anxious as Mr. Barrett to
apprehend Allison's killer."

Ridgeway snorted. "My father and Allison talked
about marriage but . . ." His voice trailed off.

Steele frowned. "You make it sound as if things were
up in the air, but I was under the impression the marriage was to take place as soon as her divorce was final."

Ridgeway shrugged offhandedly. "Oh, I know Dad
was quite taken with her. She was pretty in a cheap kind
of way, and I know she flattered his ego, but he would

have come to his senses before he walked down any aisle.''

Steele's eyes narrowed. "You didn't like Ms. Barrett, did you?''

"I couldn't stand the sight of her," Ridgeway growled. "And I'm not going to pretend otherwise. My father was forty-two years older than Allison. He'd only known her four months. Dad thought he'd gotten himself some kind of queen, but what he had was a snake—a no-good, conniving snake!''

"I take it you know the type?" Taylor asked, picking up the questioning.

"Of course I do. She's not the first gold digger I've dealt with.''

Taylor's eyebrows rose a fraction. "Dealt with? That's an interesting choice of words. Just how did you deal with her?''

For a moment Daniel Ridgeway looked taken aback, but he recovered quickly. "I didn't kill her," he said. "I did something better. I convinced Dad that for the good of the company, she should sign a prenuptial agreement. And then I told her what I'd done. I wanted her to know that she was not going to get her hands on Dad's money.''

"Perhaps she really did care for your father," Taylor suggested.

Ridgeway rolled his eyes. "Oh, please! She had no more interest in Dad than the man on the moon. It was his money, plain and simple, that she was after.''

"That's enough!" a voice boomed from the doorway. Three pair of eyes swiveled in the direction of the sound.

The man who stood in the doorway was short, no more than five-eight, with close-cropped white hair, sharp brown eyes and leathery black skin. He was dressed simply in a navy blue single-breasted suit and crisp white shirt and tie.

Daniel Ridgeway stood wringing his hands. "Dad, let me explain—''

"I think you've said enough," he said, spearing his son with a cold look. "Get out! I'll deal with you later!''

"Dad, I didn't mean—"

"I said get out!" There was steel in the old man's voice. Taylor watched as Daniel Ridgeway slunk out of the room.

"I must apologize for my son's behavior," he said, taking a nearby chair. "He meant well, but he had no right to say those things about Allison."

He probably had thought far worse, Taylor mused, but aloud she said, "I gathered he wasn't too pleased about your coming marriage to Allison."

Ridgeway nodded. "He's my only child. Naturally he's very protective—"

"Of you or his inheritance?" she challenged.

Ridgeway's mouth curved into a slight smile. "Probably both. As far as the company is concerned, he's been running it the last few years. Naturally he would be concerned about my coming marriage's impact on the company and our shareholders. But my son loves me and he's only interested in my happiness. He'd have come around."

Taylor doubted it, but schooled her features so not to betray her thoughts. "So you *were* planning to marry Allison?" she asked.

Ridgeway lit a cigar and leaned back in his chair. "Allison was a beautiful, sexy and exciting woman. What man wouldn't have loved to have been married to a woman like that?"

"Would you?" she asked.

"Of course," Ridgeway answered smoothly.

Taylor couldn't help but wonder if he was being entirely candid. "It didn't bother you that Allison was involved with her personal trainer, Ted Larson, at the same time she was engaged to you?"

He shook his head. "Ms. Quinlan, I'm afraid you've been listening to gossip. That relationship was over."

"So it didn't bother you that she probably didn't love you?" Taylor did nothing to hide her skepticism.

Ridgeway leaned back and took a drag on his cigar. "I'm seventy-two years old," he said finally, "and even when I was younger, I wasn't a particularly attractive man. I didn't care what people thought about my pending marriage to Allison before her death and I certainly don't care now. She may not have loved me, but she gave me something more. She made me feel young, alive, happy. You can't put a price tag on those things."

Taylor looked at Steele sharply. Could she have been wrong about Allison blackmailing someone? Maybe the money in her account had come from Ridgeway. There was no delicate way to ask, so she just came right out with it. "Were you supporting her?"

He smiled. "I gave her a few expensive trinkets, but on some things I'm very old-fashioned. I think a man ought to be married to a woman before he begins supporting her."

"Then how do you explain her lavish life-style?" she asked.

Ridgeway shrugged. "I never really gave it much thought. I assumed Barrett was still supporting her."

"Do you know anyone who had any reason for wanting to harm her?"

"You're suggesting, I presume, that somebody other than Barrett killed Allison and fixed it so it looked as if he did it? Perhaps Ted Larson?"

"You think that unlikely?"

"I'm afraid I do," Ridgeway said slowly. "Allison wasn't afraid of Larson, but I can't say the same for your client. She told me her life with him had been pure hell...."

Taylor frowned as Ridgeway continued speaking. She couldn't put her finger on it, but something wasn't right. He said all the right things but... Then it hit her. He had been at Allison's funeral, but hadn't shed a tear. Not at the funeral home or at the cemetery. It seemed strange for a man whose fiancée had just been brutally murdered to exhibit so little emotion. He was either supremely good at concealing his grief, or Allison's death just hadn't affected him that much.

She wondered which it was.

AS STEELE WATCHED Ted Larson put the moves on an older female patron at the Lake Shore Country Club, he wondered if Larson's good looks weren't responsible for much of his success as a personal trainer. Larson's skin was a golden brown, and he appeared to be somewhere in his late twenties. While he lacked the money and sophistication of Denning and Ridgeway, he more than made up for it in good looks. He was just under six feet, with large, deep-set dark brown eyes and close-cropped reddish brown hair. Steele looked at his hair again: reddish brown. Could it have been Larson that Ned Kramer had seen the night of the murder?

Looking at him flirt outrageously with the blonde, Larson didn't look like a cold-blooded killer, but Steele had been involved in the criminal-justice system long enough to know that looks can be deceiving.

Steele watched Larson lean over and whisper something in the blonde's ear. She giggled and turned beet-red. Larson chuckled, then sauntered over to where he and Taylor stood. He gave Steele a cursory glance before turning his attention to Taylor.

Steele disliked him on sight.

"Well hel-lo, pretty lady," Larson said, flashing Taylor a brilliant smile. "If I had known Barrett had such a lovely cousin, I'd have been out here sooner."

He was all but panting, Steele thought.

"Let's go into the lounge," Larson suggested. He moved close, like a bloodhound scenting his prey, but Steele moved faster and took Taylor's arm, fastening her to his side. He felt her turn and look at him, but he refused to look at her as they followed Larson into the club's waiting room. Steele made sure he took the seat next to Taylor on the lumpy couch.

Larson picked up a towel and plopped into the love seat across from them. "You're barking up the wrong tree if you think I'd lift a finger to help Barrett," he said, mopping his brow.

"Why do you think Craig killed Allison?" Steele asked, not liking the way Larson's eyes continued to roam over Taylor.

"Because he said he would. He was obsessed with her. Her engagement to Ridgeway was the last straw."

Steele gave him a cool look. "I'd say you had a stronger reason for killing Allison than my client. She dumped you, and you didn't like it, not one little bit."

"That's no doubt Barrett's slant on things," Larson said dryly.

"Then why don't you tell us yours?" suggested Steele.

"Allison and I were friends, although I'm sure Barrett never believed that."

Steele didn't, either. "I would imagine you've got a lot of *friends,*" he said sarcastically.

Larson grinned and shrugged offhandedly. "What can I say? I know how to treat a woman, that's all." His eyes slid flirtatiously toward Taylor. "And if my friends want to help me out with little tokens of their appreciation, what's wrong with that?" He lowered his voice an octave. "When you're good to your friends, then your friends are good to you."

A muscle ticked in Steele's jaw. "Then why did you follow Allison around, hassling her after she dumped you?" he asked tersely. He felt Taylor's hand on his arm signaling him to take it easy.

Larson rolled his eyes. "I don't run after women. But I also know a woman sometimes says no when she really mean yes. We got our signals crossed, that's all, but everything was cool. A woman doesn't have to drop a building on my head."

His "God's gift to women" attitude grated on Steele's nerves. "No, she just had to get a restraining order against you," he said.

"Too bad she didn't get one against your client, isn't it?" Larson replied. "Maybe she'd be alive today."

"So you deny that you were stalking her?" Steele answered, trying to hang on to his temper.

"I never stalked her!" Larson said, annoyed at Steele's persistence. "I may have bumped into her a time or two. It was unavoidable. We ran in the same social circles. But I wasn't bothering her."

"That's funny, the night she was murdered Allison told Craig you were still stalking her."

"Barrett's lying!" Larson snarled. "If I was such a threat to her, don't you think she'd have said something to someone other than Barrett?" He gave Steele a hard look. "Give me a break. He was the last person she'd tell anything to."

Score one for him, Steele thought. The fact that they had no one to corroborate Craig's allegation was the reason Donaldson hadn't followed up on it.

"Where were you the night Allison was murdered?" Steele asked.

Larson rolled his eyes. "I've already gone through all this with the cops. Why don't you just read the police report?"

"Just answer the question," Steele said coldly.

Larson gave an exaggerated sigh. "I was at the opening of that new club on Canal Street." He looked at Taylor and smiled. No doubt that was supposed to be his famous lady-killer smile, Steele thought. "You have heard of the Green Onion, haven't you?"

"What time did you get there?" Steele asked, ignoring the fact the question had been posed to Taylor.

"I met a friend there around nine-thirty, and we hung out until about midnight. I even got my picture taken a time or two. You know the kind where the date and time is listed at the bottom of the photograph. I'll make sure you get copies."

"And you didn't see Allison that evening?" Steele asked.

"How could I? I was at the club." Larson ran his left hand lazily up and down his chest. "Look, man, I liked Allison. We were close. I wouldn't have harmed a hair on her head."

Steele's eyes narrowed. It was an interesting choice of words when you considered Allison's head had been bashed in, but aloud he asked, "Did she ever say anything to you about a problem she was having with anyone?"

"Besides Barrett?" At Steele's stormy look, Larson sighed. "A lot of chicks didn't like her—Pam Olsen, Heather McCall, to name a few—but I don't know anyone who would have wanted to see her dead."

"What about Daniel Ridgeway?"

"He didn't have the balls." Larson stretched his long legs out in front of him. "Actually I didn't think Barrett had it in him, either. I always thought of him as being a little worm. But I guess you never know about people...." His voice trailed off as something apparently occurred to him.

"What?" Steele prompted. "Did you remember something?"

Larson nodded. "Yeah, it was something that happened at Allison's. I'd put it out of my mind. I guess it's because Allison didn't take what he said seriously." He shook his head. "Nah. It's too bizarre."

"Why don't you let us be the judge of that," Steele suggested.

"You know the guy that's running for governor?"

Steele tried to stem his mounting excitement. He could feel the same energy coming from Taylor. "Senator Denning?"

"Yeah, that's him. Well, anyway, Allison said he threatened her. Well, not him exactly," Larson corrected, "some blond-haired guy that works for him."

Kane O'Rourke, Steele thought. "When was this?"

"About a week before she died. He came by the condo making a lot of noise about how she'd better keep her mouth shut. It's a good thing I just happened to stop by. I threw him out."

"Did she say why Denning had sent him?"

"No." He chuckled. "But I can think of only one thing that would get a man like that all riled up."

Steele gave him a thoughtful look. "And what's that?"

Larson shrugged. "An affair. Denning must have thought she was going to blow the whistle on him." He cocked his head to the side and gave them both a quizzical look. "What else could it have been?"

Chapter Six

"You think Larson's telling the truth about hearing Kane O'Rourke threatening Allison?" Taylor asked. She and Steele were sitting on the sofa in his office, sipping coffee and digesting what they had learned from their interviews.

Steele ran a weary hand over his face. "Frankly I don't know if I believe any of them—the Ridgeways, Larson or Denning. They all have a reason to lie."

"Yeah," Taylor agreed, "but if Allison was blackmailing anyone, it was most likely one of these men. And that man could be the killer." Even as she spoke the words, she knew a part of her still had doubts about Craig's innocence. She coughed and looked at Steele. "Why don't we put our heads together and review what we know about each man?"

Steele nodded approvingly. "That sounds like a good idea." He watched the gentle sway of her hips as she walked to his desk on the other side of the room. When she leaned over and the soft fabric of her dress faintly outlined her gentle curves, he found himself lost in an erotic fantasy of naked bodies on cool, crisp sheets.

"Let's start with our strongest suspect," she said, coming back and taking a seat next to him on the sofa.

It took Steele a moment to dislodge the fantasy that had gripped him. "Okay," he said, loosening his tie and rolling up his sleeves. He pulled a small black notebook out of the breast pocket of his shirt and flipped it open. "I think Senator Denning tops the list. He claims his relationship with Allison was strictly aboveboard, but all signs point to an affair. Politically he couldn't have withstood a sex scandal. All the polls show him to be the front-runner in the gubernatorial race. He's on the verge of becoming the next governor of Illinois. There are even some political analysts who suggest he's planning a presidential run in eight years."

Taylor nodded, picking up the story. "Then along comes Allison, a woman he had an affair with several years back—threatening to derail his train. He tries to buy her off—she gets greedy. He sends O'Rourke to scare her, but it doesn't work."

"Or maybe," Steele interrupted, "he just realized that as long as she was alive, she was a threat." He shook his head. "He wasn't about to let it all slip away—that's a strong motive for murder."

Taylor leaned back and gave him a thoughtful look. "I agree disclosure of an affair would have damaged his political career," she said slowly, "but I don't think that it would have destroyed it. A sharp politician like Denning may have been able to turn a negative situation like that into a positive by breaking the story himself and asking the voters' forgiveness."

"Too risky," Steele said. "Besides, Denning is a very proud and arrogant man. He doesn't strike me as the type who could have gone public with that kind of story." He shook his head. "He was facing political ruin no matter how you look at it."

"How does O'Rourke fit in the picture?" she asked.

"He's just an errand boy. But he may be a way to Denning. Maybe if he thinks he's been implicated in her murder, he'll turn on the senator."

Taylor nodded in agreement. "Okay, we'll place Denning at the top of the list and eliminate O'Rourke." She took a moment to write, then looked up at him. "Let's move on to Gordon Ridgeway," she said. "He was working awfully hard to portray himself as a man who was looking forward to his coming marriage, but frankly I thought he was relieved that he didn't have to go through with it."

"You think he was being pressured into marrying her?"

She shrugged. "It's possible, but I don't think he killed her."

Steele took a sip of coffee. "Neither do I. He doesn't fit either Ned's or Trebeck's description of the man they saw the night of the murder. Now, Daniel Ridgeway is another matter."

Taylor pulled her legs under her and leaned back against the sofa. "He definitely had reason for wanting Allison out of the way. The poor guy worked hard helping to build a publishing empire, and was about to get the boot."

Steele gave her a sideways glance. "Aren't you forgetting the prenuptial agreement?"

"I don't think he was all that sure that his father would have insisted that she sign it." She shook her head. "He had a lot to lose if he didn't—not just the company, maybe even his inheritance. That's a pretty good motive for killing someone."

Steele stretched his arm across the back of the sofa. "So what's wrong with this picture?"

She sighed. "It doesn't square with our blackmail theory. I can't imagine what Allison could have had on him."

"Neither can I," Steele said. "He seemed pretty straitlaced. But let's not eliminate him as a suspect just yet or, for that matter, foreclose other reasons besides blackmail for Allison's murder. Which now brings us to Ted Larson." He rubbed the back of his neck. "As much as I dislike the guy, I can't see him caring enough about Allison to have killed her, nor any basis for her to blackmail him."

"You're right," Taylor said slowly, "but this whole thing with Allison and Larson is screwy. He's suppose to be a gigolo, a boy-toy, right?"

Steele nodded.

"Which means he romances women, not out of any kind of love, but strictly for money. The women he's involved with know that. So when Allison dumped him, why was he still hanging around?"

Steele gave her a thoughtful look. "What do you think was going on between them?"

Taylor drew a deep sigh. "I don't know. It's just that Allison and Larson's *supposed* relationship doesn't make sense. Allison wouldn't have given a poor man the time of day, as a lover or friend. While Larson isn't poor, he's definitely not in the same league that she was used to playing in. Then there's Larson himself. He wouldn't continue hanging around a woman who wasn't paying for his charm."

"You're looking at this too logically," he said. "What we're talking is the illogical—unbridled passion, lust. Things that defy logic." Hazel eyes gazed deeply into brown ones. "Chemistry is a strange thing."

She shifted uncomfortably under his scrutiny. "Uh, that's true," she said, "but I don't know...." Her voice trailed off.

His eyes continued to hold hers as he said, "Sometimes we're attracted to people who are all wrong for us. Our minds tell us not to get involved, but our emotions take over and we can't help ourselves. We act totally out of character."

She sensed he was no longer talking about Allison and Larson. "That sounds like Heather and Matt McCall," she said, searching for some way to defuse the situation. "They're certainly an odd couple."

"What about you?" he asked. His voice was low and incredibly sexy. "Haven't you ever felt that way?"

Of course she had. She felt that way right now, but she wasn't going to tell him that. She moistened her lips with the tip of her tongue, and his eyes instantly dropped to her mouth. All of the searing heat and the undercurrents they'd been trying to avoid seemed to swirl around them, bursting to life.

"What do they say?" Steele continued in that same low, husky voice, his gaze still locked with hers. "Truth is stranger than fiction."

The intensity of his gaze made her pulse leap, and she knew that he wanted to kiss her. She was never so sure of anything in her life. And God help her, she wanted him to kiss her, too.

Kiss me, she wanted to say, but the words stuck in her throat. However, she thought, if she leaned forward slightly... As if her body had a mind of its own, she felt it move toward his. His mouth was just a whisper away. His head began to lower. His mouth drew nearer. Her eyelids closed—

"I'm glad you're still—"

Taylor felt as if she'd been doused with a bucket of cold water as their heads simultaneously swiveled in the direction of the sound. Through passion-filled eyes, an image of a tall black man dressed in blue jeans and a navy blazer registered in her mind.

Steele's voice was husky as she heard him say, "It's Hawk." She looked into hazel eyes that were as dazed as her own.

"Come on in," Steele said, waving him in. "I want you to meet Taylor Quinlan. Taylor, this is Hawk Long-tree."

"Ms. Quinlan," he said in a deep baritone voice.

Taylor's face flamed with embarrassment as she took his outstretched hand. *That's Hawk?* she thought, staring up at the incredibly handsome man who stood before her. Hawk was in his late thirties. He was at least six-one, with piercing black eyes, wavy black hair and chiseled, high cheekbones that reflected Native American ancestry somewhere in his African-American heritage. Jeans and a burgundy turtleneck accentuated his lean, athletic build. He looked more like a model than a private investigator.

"You're busy," Hawk said. "I'll come back later." He turned to leave.

"Why don't you stick around?" Steele insisted. "We've been going through our list of suspects trying to make sense of what we've learned thus far."

Hawk took a seat in the chair across from the sofa. Steele then spent a few minutes outlining what they'd found. When he was done, Hawk nodded. "I agree the killer is most likely one of these men. From what I've been able to determine, other than Craig, they were the only ones Allison was involved with in the last year or so. But you can eliminate Gordon Ridgeway. His alibi checks out. He was in the hospital, being treated for a light case of food poisoning, the night she was murdered."

Steele ran a weary hand over his face. "Did you find anything else?"

Hawk consulted his notes. "I checked out that bar on the matchbook you found at Allison's—Martin's Bar and Grill. It's a dive in a real seedy part of the city. Not the kind of place you'd think Allison Barrett would frequent. But, according to the bartender, she was something of a regular."

Taylor nodded. "Sounds like the kind of place you go to when you don't want to be seen."

Hawk looked at her approvingly. "My sentiments exactly. I suppose it was because she didn't want anyone to know she was seeing Larson. According to the bartender, they've been meeting there about once a month for the last year or so."

Taylor sucked in her breath. "That's before she married Craig. They've been involved that long?"

"Apparently." Hawk put his notes away. "But it's not all that strange. The woman was married, as well as engaged. Having a lover on the side might not be something she'd want to broadcast."

Steele nodded. "As much as I'd like the killer to be Larson, he's probably our weakest suspect. Denning and Daniel Ridgeway both had stronger motives for wanting Allison dead."

"And in Denning's case," Hawk said, "I don't know how he met Allison, but it certainly wasn't at any fundraiser like he claimed. I talked to Craig. He confirmed what Taylor suspected—that Allison had absolutely no interest in politics. He also said that while they were married neither of them attended a fund-raiser for the senator, and that's when the meeting supposedly occurred."

Steele's dark eyebrows slanted in a frown. "The good senator is bucking for the number-one spot on our suspect list. Hawk, why don't you lean on his assistant? He's the weak link in the chain. What about Lamden's files?"

Hawk shook his head. "I checked out both warehouses, but there's no way in hell you can walk in either of them and find Lamden's files or any file, for that matter—unless you know the exact row and bin number. Even though they're filed in alphabetical order, there are thousands of document for every letter in the alphabet."

Steele gave him a hard look. "Then you'd better find Betsy Boyd."

"There's not much to go on," Hawk replied, "but I'll do what I can."

Steele nodded. "See if you can locate Allison's brother. Talk to Craig. Maybe he can give you some background information."

"Hawk, would you also check out Larson?" Taylor asked. "Unlike Steele, I'm not ready to discount him as a suspect."

Hawk grinned at the sour look his friend threw his lovely co-counsel. "Will do."

Taylor sighed. "If only we knew what it was that Allison had on her victim."

Steele gave her a pointed look. "Whatever it is, it may be worth killing for."

"HAND ME the other printout." Hawk dropped the computer printout on the floor, then leaned back in his chair and looked at the man seated across from him. It was close to midnight. Steele had taken Taylor home, then came by Hawk's hotel, where they'd spent the past few hours poring over Allison's phone records. "Steele?" Getting no response, Hawk leaned forward and waved his hand in front of his friend's face. "Earth to Steele!"

Steele slowly raised his head and stared at him. "Did you say something?"

Hawk smiled at Steele's blank expression. "Do you want to talk about it?"

"No." His face was closed, as if guarding a secret.

Hawk ignored the curt response. "Do you want to know what I think?"

"No," he repeated.

Undaunted, Hawk continued, "You haven't been yourself since you took this case on. Or should I say, since you met Taylor Quinlan." A knowing smile crept across his bronzed, high-cheekboned face before he added, "She really knocked you for a loop, didn't she?"

Steele remained unmoving for a long moment, then his posture relaxed and he nodded reluctantly. "She's not like any woman I've ever known. She's beautiful, intelligent, sexy. And we're so in tune with each other, it's almost scary."

"Call me crazy, but isn't that good?" asked Hawk.

"Yes and no." Steele spoke slowly, as if each word was being pulled from deep within him. "I guess I'm afraid I like her a little too much."

Hawk looked confused. "So what's wrong with that? You said you'd resolved your concern about working with her. She said she could be objective."

Steele didn't say anything.

"Don't you believe her?" Hawk pressed.

That was the big question. Steele rubbed his hand along the back of his neck. "I believe her," he said slowly, "but something is troubling her. I can see it in her eyes."

"And you're afraid it might have something to do with this case," Hawk said. He leaned back in his chair and regarded his friend for a moment. "Steele, we all have secrets. And Taylor may have one that bothers her, but that doesn't mean it has anything to do with Barrett or you."

"You're probably right," he said vaguely.

"Frankly I think you're making a mountain out of a molehill. You're looking for reasons not to get involved, but what are you always telling me? You've got to trust someone."

"I know, but..." he replied bleakly. He was torn. One part of him wanted to accept Taylor at face value because he was so strongly attracted to her. But that other part, the cautious part, warned that lowering his guard would only lead to disappointment and heartache. *Remember,* an inner voice whispered, *you've been fooled before.* If that betrayal had taught him anything, it was that you couldn't trust your feelings. Especially those feelings called love, trust or desire for commitment.

He raked a hand over his hair, then let out a deep sigh. "I know I'm not making a lot of sense, but Taylor's driving me nuts. I don't know what to make of her. All I know is that I don't want her under my skin... or constantly in my thoughts."

Hawk looked closely at his employer and friend. In the five years he'd known Steele, no woman had ever come close to penetrating the shell he had wrapped around his emotions... until now.

"I hate to tell you this, but she's *already* under your skin." He smiled, cocking his head to the side to study Steele. "You're falling for her."

"That's crazy!" Steele denied vehemently. "You know my views about getting involved with someone I'm working with."

"Then what was that cozy little scene I walked in on?" Hawk grinned. "Looks to me like you've changed your mind."

Steele shook his head. "I don't know what you think you saw, but I haven't changed my mind," he said, his tone defensive. "I still think it's unwise to get romantically involved with people you work with. All kinds of problems can result."

"C'mon, Steele. Trust your instincts. Give yourself a chance. You can't go through life judging every woman by what Daphne did."

Steele gave him a wry smile. "Isn't this the pot calling the kettle black? Maybe you ought to take a little of your own advice."

"Maybe," Hawk said, his earlier amusement gone. "But we're not talking about me. From everything you've told me about Taylor and from what I've observed, she's perfect for you." He threw Steele a hard look. "I think if you let her slip through your fingers, you'll regret it."

He sighed. Maybe Hawk was right. Maybe it was time to put the past behind him. Take a chance. What did he have to lose?

Chapter Seven

Steele slammed the evening edition of the newspaper on the cocktail table with a loud thud that sent pages fluttering and inserts sliding out.

"What the hell were you thinking?" he demanded, glaring across the cocktail table at Craig.

Craig's reply was to look off to the side. Matt McCall kicked out a chair, inviting him to sit. The *Chicago Banner*'s front page proclaimed in bold headlines—Barrett Assaults Newspaper Reporter.

The story was short, only a few paragraphs. It basically recounted Allison's brutal murder, then proceeded to describe Craig and Allison's tumultuous marriage and subsequent separation. While the story was not very flattering, it was the picture of Craig that was the most damaging. It had been snapped just as he'd made a grab for the camera. The image captured was that of a wild-eyed, disheveled Craig, totally out of control, lunging at the reporter.

Taylor's face was grim as she stared at the newspaper headline. The media was having a field day with Allison's murder. Every rumor, every innuendo ever reported about Craig, no matter how outlandish, suddenly was being given credence and reported as the gospel truth. And if that wasn't bad enough, every news program and talk show was giving the story daily play.

Taylor might have been able to slough off the media hype if they'd made some progress in their investigation. But they were no closer to exonerating Craig now than they'd been three weeks ago. Hawk had canvassed Allison's Lake Shore neighborhood, even talked to Mrs. Trebeck, but had come up with nothing. Nor had he had any luck in locating Betsy Boyd or Allison's missing brother. Worse yet, he'd found nothing to support their blackmail theory, and they'd not come up with any others. No matter how she looked at it, all signs still pointed to Craig as being Allison's killer.

"Before you string him up, Steele, you ought to know what happened right before that incident," Matt said, coming to his friend's defense. "The network had just informed him that his show was being canceled. After working his butt off to make it one of the top-rated talk shows in the country for three years straight, this is how they reward him."

This had to be devastating news, Taylor thought. She sat on the sofa next to her cousin and put her hand on his arm. "Oh, Craig, I'm so sorry."

Steele raked his hand over his hair in frustration. "So am I, but you can't lose control like that. If this case goes to trial, I don't want images like that plastered all over the papers and network television prejudicing the jury pool."

"C'mon, Steele," Matt growled. "Cut the man a little slack. He was upset."

"I understand that, but he's doing a damn good job of digging himself into a hole so deep he'll never be able to crawl out." Steele's voice was deliberately harsh, but he needed to impress upon Craig and Matt the seriousness of the situation.

For a moment no one said anything. The silence was finally broken by Heather's cheery voice as she breezed into the room.

"Michael," she scolded. "Stop badgering Craig. I invited you and Taylor here for dinner, not to talk shop. I don't want to hear another word about the murder investigation."

Taylor looked at Heather's open face. She viewed the world in such simplistic terms, and because of that, her faith in Craig's innocence or their ability to clear him never wavered.

She gave Heather a wan smile. "You're right. We won't say another word about the investigation." She drew a deep breath. It would be good to not have to think about the issue of Craig's innocence and family secrets for a few hours.

"Good." Heather beamed. "Now, Craig, I think you should call Ida right away. Before that story hits the stands. It's bound to upset her." She turned to her husband. "Why don't you go down to the cellar and select a nice bottle of red wine while I check on dinner?"

Matt nodded and followed her and Craig out of the room.

Taylor stared at Heather's retreating back. When Mrs. Kent, Matt's long-time housekeeper, had died suddenly of a heart attack shortly after the couple had married, Taylor hadn't believed Heather would be able to manage the McCall household or the four-person staff. She'd always seemed like such a scatterbrain. At least, that's how she'd been during the brief period she'd worked at the law firm. But from all accounts, the household was running smoothly. Taylor turned, prepared to make some comment along those lines to Steele. But the words stuck in her throat.

Steele was watching her. Their eyes met, and for a moment the way he looked at her made her head spin and she was glad she'd dressed with special care for the evening. Not just because Heather expected her guests to dress for dinner but because she had wanted to feel beautiful and desirable and, yes, an inner voice whispered, to impress Steele. Meeting Steele had awakened feelings in her that she'd never felt before and didn't understand. She just knew he made her heart skip a beat. What she was going to do about it she had no idea. Both had tried to put that little scene a few weeks before out of their minds, but it was as if a veil had been lifted. The air seemed to crackle with tension when they were together, and it was getting increasingly hard to tell herself that she shouldn't get involved with him.

She looked away, feigning interest in a recent painting that Heather had acquired. "This painting really makes the room," she said.

Steele quickly turned, forcing his attention toward the painting. He put his hands in his pockets in a gesture that reminded her of a little boy told not to touch anything. "This house is really beautiful," he said, his voice slightly strained.

She followed his gaze to the vaulted ceilings, the tapestries, the baby grand piano and the room's expensive furnishings.

"Yes, it is," she said, following his lead.

Steele looked at her curiously. "It has to be worth at least two million," he said. "Being an entertainment lawyer must be a lot more lucrative than I would have imagined."

Taylor nodded in agreement. "It is when you also manage someone as successful as Craig and you're getting fifteen percent of his earnings. Of course, Craig isn't Matt's only client. Just his most successful."

Just then the McCalls stepped back into the room. "Dinner will be ready shortly," Heather announced. "Matt, darling, why don't you get everyone something to drink?"

While Matt played bartender, it gave Taylor a moment to study her cousin's best friend. She hadn't noticed before, but he looked as if he'd lost weight. He was worrying himself sick, and it was beginning to affect his work. Just the other day, he'd had to give her his computer password so she could finish a brief that he'd forgotten was due that day. And this morning she'd gotten a call from George Avery of Avery & Associates, the brokerage house that handled the bulk of Craig's investments.

"Matt, could you give George Avery a call?" At his look of confusion, she added, "He called me. I guess because I have Craig's power of attorney. Brenda said he has some questions about a financial transaction.''

"I'll take care of it," Matt mumbled. He ran a weary hand over his face. "I'm sorry you were bothered."

"How are things going for you?" Taylor asked gently.

Matt gave a humorless laugh. "We can't breathe for falling over a reporter, but Heather and I can deal with it. It's Craig that I'm worried about. The press has been doing a real hatchet job on him. People we thought were friends have either dropped him or are selling their stories to the tabloids. I'm not sure how much more of this he can take."

Taylor felt a tug of sympathy. Not many friends would subject themselves to the kind of nightmare Matt was enduring for the sake of his best friend. "Craig is lucky to have a friend like you."

Matt dropped his head and stared into his drink, embarrassed by her words.

"Uh, Craig tells me you're trying to locate Allison's brother," Heather said, breaking the silence that had settled on the room.

Taylor threw her a grateful look. She'd been searching for something to say that would ease Matt's embarrassment. "Hawk hasn't had much luck in locating him. We've been able to trace his whereabouts up until about four years ago, and then the trail abruptly ends."

"I'm surprised he hasn't come forward," Heather said. "If not out of brotherly love, at least to claim his inheritance."

"We haven't made the contents of her will public," Steele explained. "So he doesn't know he's her beneficiary. From what we've been able to determine, they may not have been that close. They had the same father but different mothers. Allison was the out-of-wedlock child and carried her mother's maiden name."

Heather nodded. "Maybe that's why she spent so much time trying to pretend she was something she wasn't. Like having all those books around. We knew she didn't read them.''

Out of the corner of her eye, Taylor saw Steele smile and threw him a warning look.

"What?" Heather said, obviously noticing the exchange.

"When Taylor and I were at the condo, she borrowed two of the books. Ask her to tell you the titles," he teased.

She threw him another warning look, but Steele just laughed. Then he proceeded to tell Matt and Heather in great detail the names and content of each book. She wanted to strangle him.

Matt covered his mouth, trying not to laugh. Heather, however, didn't see what the men found so amusing and said so.

Steele's eyes danced with merriment and, for a moment, Taylor thought he was going to say something embarrassing but, thankfully, he simply said, "Taylor thinks the true-crime book will aid in the investigation."

At the mention of the investigation, Matt sobered. He shook his head. "The killer couldn't have just disappeared into thin air," he said, forgetting Heather's admonishment not to talk about the murder. "Someone must have seen something."

Taylor sipped her drink. "If they did, they're not talking."

"Can you really blame them?" Craig asked. He had come up behind them. "I feel as if I'm in a nightmare that I can't wake up from. I've lost my show, my girlfriend and my good name. They're even hounding my mother."

At the mention of her aunt, Taylor felt a twinge of guilt. She'd generally spent Sundays with her, but since Allison's murder and the subsequent investigation, she'd not been able to make the forty-five minute drive to her southside apartment. "How is Aunt Ida?"

He looked at her, his expression bleak. "You know what a worrywart she is, but she's hanging in there. But it's not easy. She's being hounded by Norris and several other reporters. They've even resorted to rummaging through her trash. But what really has her upset are the interviews they're now conducting with the neighbors about things that happened over the years. Mom thinks they're going to dredge up Dad's suicide. I told her not to worry, but you know Mom."

Taylor's heart jumped in her throat; the last thing they needed was some reporter snooping into Uncle Bob's suicide. What if they kept digging? There was no telling what they might find. She shivered.

Steele touched her arm. "You okay?" She could hear the concern in his voice. She plastered a smile on her face and nodded. She could tell from the way he kept staring at her he was not convinced.

"I hope you told her that Taylor and Steele are going to get to the bottom of this," Heather said. Her voice rang with conviction.

"I know you're doing all you can," Craig said, "but it's hard to be optimistic when everyone is treating you like a criminal." He paused and looked at them with tortured eyes.

"I don't see why the police are just focusing on Craig," Matt said heatedly. "Why aren't they checking out Gordon Ridgeway and Larson?"

Steele nodded. "I'm sure they have, but at this point there's nothing to connect either man to Allison's murder, whereas there are any number of people who heard Craig threaten Allison."

Craig's head shot up. "I was angry! I didn't mean it!"

"We all know that," Matt said, clapping his friend on the back. He speared Steele with a hard look. "Don't you find it odd that Gordon Ridgeway has never issued a statement to the press expressing his condolences over Allison's death?"

Steele shrugged. "It's a little strange, but I don't think you can draw any inference other than it wasn't a love match."

"All the same," Matt pressed, "his lack of emotion isn't normal. Even if he wasn't in love with Allison, you would expect some sorrow or expression of sympathy on his part."

"Not if he's the killer," Craig snarled.

Steele shook his head. "What reason did he have for killing her? He wanted a trophy wife and he didn't make any bones about it. Make no mistake, he held the upper hand in that relationship. If anyone was walking the straight and narrow, it was Allison, not Gordon Ridgeway."

Craig stared gloomily into his drink. "The only thing I know is that I didn't kill her, but someone sure as hell did." He looked at them, his expression bleak. "And whoever that person is knew her well enough to be able to slip in and out of the condo without being detected. As far as I know, only two men fit the bill—Gordon Ridgeway and Ted Larson. If Ridgeway didn't kill her, then it had to be Larson."

"My money is on Larson," Matt agreed. "Heather thinks he was stalking Allison. He was always lurking somewhere in the shadows."

"What did Allison say?" Steele asked.

"She shrugged it off," Heather said. "She wasn't afraid of him. She only got the restraining order because she was mad at him about something."

Craig frowned. "I thought it was because he was bothering her."

Heather shook her head. "That's not what she told me. She said it was to teach him a lesson."

This was the first time she'd heard that. Taylor pounced on her words immediately. "What kind of lesson?"

Heather shrugged. "I asked, but she didn't say." She threw Craig an apologetic look. "I'm sorry, but as far as men go, I think she might actually have cared about him."

Taylor's eyes narrowed. Maybe there really was something to their relationship. If that was the case, would she have confided in him?

IT WAS SEVERAL HOURS later before Taylor was able to pose the question to Steele. Under the guise of showing him the grounds, they'd finally been able to slip away from the others. They were standing in the garden talking.

"I think we should question Larson again," she said. "If he was following Allison around, he may have seen something. Or for that matter, if they were close like Heather thinks, maybe she confided in him, told him something that will help to clear Craig."

Steele threw her a pointed look. "If you recall, Larson thinks Craig is her killer."

"Nevertheless, I think we should question him. If he and Allison were really friends, I think he'd want to help catch her killer."

Steele looked at the woman who stood next to him. Talking about the case was the last thing he wanted to do. Moonlight glistened through her hair; a light breeze picked up a few dark strands to play with. She was, without a doubt, lovely and alluring.

Steele deliberately looked away. He tried not to think about how attracted to her he was. He tried not to think about the fact that she was his colleague, but it was no use. She was the most compelling woman he'd ever met, and he really wanted to get to know her better.

"I don't know," he said finally. "He certainly hasn't shown himself to be willing to help so far. Frankly I think questioning him would be a waste of time. I think we'd be better served keeping the heat on Denning. He had a lot to lose if the press got wind of an affair."

Taylor dropped her eyelashes to hide her disappointment.

But not quick enough. Steele's heart flip-flopped at her crestfallen look. "I guess it wouldn't hurt to have a go at him again."

Taylor beamed up at him. "Great," she said. "Let's do it tomorrow. Maybe we'll get some fresh leads." She sighed. "This case is so frustrating, I just want to scream."

He gave her a wry smile. "Criminal cases are tough. The defense always has an uphill battle. People don't come forward with information because they don't want to get involved. And then there are those people like Trebeck who remember things that may have never happened. It's frustrating, but it always seems to work out in the end."

She sighed. "I'm glad you can be so optimistic."

"There's really little point being otherwise." He looked toward the house and smiled. "Speaking of optimism, Heather seems to abound in it."

She laughed. "She was a secretary at the firm before she married Matt. In fact, that's where they met. We used to call her Mary Sunshine."

Steele chuckled. "They're certainly an interesting couple. She isn't the type of woman I'd have thought he'd have married."

"Is that a tactful way of saying she's not too bright?" she teased.

Steele shook his head. "She's brighter than you think. Matt is just such a serious guy." He shrugged. "I'd have thought he'd marry someone he had more in common with, but they seem to have a very solid marriage."

"That's true," Taylor said slowly. "But I have to admit that when Matt announced they were getting married, Craig and I were a little concerned. He'd only known her a short time and, like you said, she didn't seem his type. Apparently, love conquers all."

The way Steele was looking at her made her shiver, and she rubbed her arms. "Why don't we go inside?"

She'd just taken a step forward when her heel caught on a piece of broken tile. She would have taken quite a fall if Steele hadn't caught her.

"You're all right," Steele whispered, his arms wrapped tightly about her.

Taylor could only nod as she tried to ignore the feel of his hand on her back, the well-honed, muscular body beneath his jacket, his manly scent, his heat. But it was no use. Energy pulsated from him with such force that goose bumps rippled over every surface of her skin, and a warm glow began to grow and unfurl deep inside her. It took all her willpower to resist the urge to close her eyes and rest her head on his shoulder and give in to a complexity of emotions too difficult to confine.

This was sheer madness, an inner voice warned. She had to fight her attraction. With supreme effort, she pulled out of his arms. "I'm sorry to be so clumsy," she said, avoiding his probing gaze. No way would she let Steele know how he affected her or how she hungered to be in his arms. "I guess I'm tired. I think I'd like to call it an evening."

"Sure," he said, his voice slightly strained.

Inside, Steele wished the others a pleasant evening, then escorted her out of the house to the waiting car. Within minutes the Corvette was purring smoothly along the city streets. She sank back against the opulent leather seat, letting her head rest comfortably as she idly scanned the passing shops and deserted sidewalks and tried not to think about her attraction to the man who sat next to her.

"You sure you want to go straight home?" he asked, breaking into her thoughts.

No, she wasn't, but it was definitely the safer course of action. She looked at him questioningly. "I'm sure. Why?"

"I thought we could drive around for a while. You could show me a little of the city, then later we could stop in at one of the blues clubs that Chicago is famous for."

She was tempted, but she was confused enough about her feelings for Steele. "Some other time, okay?"

"Taylor, you know I'm attracted to you, and I think you're just as attracted to me," he said, his voice low and incredibly sexy.

She shivered. "I can't deny that I'm attracted to you," she said, "but I don't think it would be wise for us to follow through on that attraction."

"Why not?" He gave her a quick glance before turning back to the road.

"Well, we work together," she said in what she hoped was a convincing voice. "Things could get a little awkward."

"I think they already are."

"Steele, don't." She swallowed and turned her head toward the passenger window.

For a moment she thought he was going to argue. Out of the corner of her left eye she saw him shift in the seat and stare dead ahead. As the minutes ticked by and he didn't say anything, the silence became tense, strained. The leisurely pace they'd been traveling at also seemed to pick up.

She stared blindly out the window, not daring to look at him. The Corvette roared along, passing one car then the next. Horns blared and tires squealed as space opened as he zipped in and out of traffic. Several irate drivers who Steele had tailgated threw them angry looks as he passed.

Steele ignored them. He ignored everything. His focus was on one thing and one thing only, Taylor thought: getting the evening over with as quickly as possible now that she had rebuffed him. And that hurt terribly.

As the speedometer edged close to sixty, Taylor began to get a little concerned. "Steele, could you slow down a little?"

"I don't think that would be such a good idea," he said, continuing to look straight ahead.

His voice was calm, but it had an underlying quality to it that demanded a glance in his direction. He was looking in the rearview mirror at something.

A twinge of alarm registered at the back of her neck. "What is it?"

"We're being followed," Steele said, his eyes glued to the rearview mirror.

"Are you sure?" she asked, twisting in her seat, looking out the back window.

"Yeah, I'm sure. There's a dark-colored sedan about two cars back. The headlights are out. It's been following us since we left the McCalls'. It also looks suspiciously like the car that joker we encountered at Allison's was driving."

Taylor's eyes widened in alarm. "If that's Allison's blackmail victim back there, why is he following us?"

Steele shrugged. "We must have rattled his cage, made him nervous. Hell, I just wish we knew whatever it is he thinks we know."

"Yeah, so do I," she agreed grimly.

Steele threw her a grin, then said, "Hang on, I'm going to see if we can catch this guy."

She felt herself thrown back against the seat as Steele suddenly gunned the engine, made a sharp left turn and joined the freeway traffic pouring past the lakefront area, but his pace was fast. She glanced out the back window. The dark-colored sedan was right behind them.

"He's still there," she yelled. Steele's only reply was to press on the accelerator. The car leapt forward, hungrily devouring the roadway. They passed one car, then the next.

She checked the back window again. The sedan was still there.

A wild screech of hot, disintegrating rubber bellowed in her ears as Steele yanked the wheel into a ninety-degree turn at what felt like a hundred miles per hour and took the off ramp. Her shoulder slammed into the passenger door as the car exited the highway at a high rate of speed. Steele rolled through the stop sign at the end of the off ramp and roared down the street. Cars swerved and stopped, giving them a wide berth. They sailed through an intersection to the sound of beeping horns and squealing tires, and flew around a corner and down a quiet residential street. Luckily there were few pedestrians out this time of night, but those who were jumped back on the curb at the sight of the speeding car.

They raced down one street then another, and at the end of a fairly deserted street, Steele yanked the wheel and executed a U-turn.

"I'm going to try and get closer!" Steele yelled. "See if you can get a look at the driver or his license plates."

Taylor's head was reeling as the Corvette headed in the direction of the dark-colored sedan. The car that had been following them came to a screeching halt and began to back up fast. Then, like Steele, its driver executed a U-turn and drove at breakneck speed in the opposite direction. The Corvette was hot on its tail. The hunter had now become the hunted.

"Steele, we didn't see any license plates because there are none on the car."

"Yeah, I see," Steele said, not taking his eyes from the road. She was thrown against the passenger door as they swerved, narrowly missing a tractor trailer that had jackknifed in front of them. The sedan was still ahead, but they were quickly gaining on it.

She leaned forward, straining to see the driver. She could almost make out the faint outline of a person, when the sedan suddenly swerved to the left, cutting across two lanes of traffic. It took them a moment to change lanes. The sedan sailed through a busy intersection. They did the same. They dodged head-on collisions right and left at top speed. Ahead, Taylor could see the flashing red lights of a railroad crossing, and the gates slowly beginning to descend. But instead of slowing down and stopping, the sedan sailed through the gates, narrowly missing being hit by the freight train. She was thrown violently forward as Steele slammed on the brakes, bringing the car to a screeching halt just inches from the crossing. Through the boxcar opening they saw the sedan barreling away.

"Damn!" Steele punctuated his words by pounding on the steering wheel. "We lost him!"

"Yeah," she replied, her teeth still rattling. "But I don't think I could have survived catching him."-

AFTER THEIR high-speed chase, the remainder of the ride to Taylor's apartment was uneventful. Before she knew it, Steele was bringing the car to a halt in front of her building. He insisted on seeing her inside. He did it with such charm that Taylor couldn't resist. Truth be told, she didn't want to. All those strange, unexpected feelings were catching up with her.

They got off the elevator and walked down the carpeted hall to her apartment. She fished in her evening bag for the key. Steele took it from her and turned the lock. He handed it back to her gravely.

"Where did you learn to drive like that?" she asked, stalling. She didn't want the evening to end.

Steele chuckled. "A client taught me. He was reputed to have at one time been a driver for the mob."

"Well, I guess you never know when defensive driving will come in handy." She smiled.

"That's for sure," he said, returning her smile. "Get a good night's sleep." His voice was low and husky, and he looked as though what he was saying had nothing whatsoever to do with what he was thinking.

"Steele..." she murmured. Her eyes were wide and filled with questions as he slid his arms around her and pulled her against him.

He bent his head, blocking out the light from the crystal fixtures along the wall. Shadows fell across them both. Taylor stiffened slightly but made no effort to pull away. The door was open behind her. She had a clear line of retreat. She just didn't choose to use it. She swayed and raised her hands instinctively. They landed against the hard wall of his chest.

The contact sent tremors through them both. He murmured something, her name? She couldn't really be sure because speech was beyond them both. He lowered his head to hers, and she closed her eyes as his lips brushed hers, lightly, sweetly, so tempting that she could not help but respond.

He deepened the kiss. His mouth moved slowly, sensually over hers, more deeply and hungrily by the second until the erotic pleasure of it brought her arms up around his neck. In response, his mouth became more demanding, intoxicating. She felt her breasts swell, and their sensitive peaks tightened as she burned with desire. She could feel the hard muscles of his thighs through the thin material of her dress as he backed her against the wall, pressing her into it.

Steele pulled her closer. She was lost, engulfed in a world of pleasurable sensations. Minutes passed, but nothing existed but his kiss.

Scrape.

Suddenly Steele went still. He still held her, but he was no longer kissing her. Something had invaded his subconscious, thrusting him back to reality. A sound. What had it been? The elevator door opening? An apartment dweller's television set? He listened. Waiting. Straining to hear. Then he heard it again. And this time he recognized it. Footsteps on carpeting. Someone was slowly creeping down the hallway in their direction!

Chapter Eight

Taylor sensed the change in Steele immediately. One minute he was kissing her senseless, then in the next he whispered, "Someone's coming."

Before she could digest his words, he whipped her behind him and drew a revolver from the back waistband of his trousers.

Her eyes widened at the sight of the gun. From the way he held it in both hands and his aggressive stance, she had no doubt that he knew how to use it.

"You there!" Steele snarled. "Put your hands up and step out where we can see you."

"Don't shoot!" a voice cried. The words were followed by the sound of footsteps moving slowly down the apartment corridor toward them. Taylor could feel the tension in Steele. It was the same tension she was feeling. She held her breath as a long, dark shadow appeared on the floor and slid up the wall. From the shadows Taylor could see he was tall and wore what looked like trousers and a close-fitting top. Her heart beat faster as the figure moved slowly into the light. Taylor's hand flew to her mouth as fear gave way to surprise.

Vanessa Norris!

"What the hell are you doing here?" Steele growled. He lowered the gun and tucked it back into the waistband of his trousers; his stance was still aggressive.

The reporter lowered her arms and let out a long, shaky breath. "I was waiting for you and Ms. Quinlan," she said. "I've been calling your office for weeks, but neither of you saw fit to return my calls."

Norris's words followed so closely on the heels of their high-speed car chase was too much for Taylor. "You're the last person to lecture anyone on courtesy," she said, moving out to stand alongside Steele. Fear and anger made her voice harsher than she'd intended. "You sneak into my apartment building, scare us half to death and now you stand here like you're the injured party! I've got a mind to register a complaint with your station manager."

Norris looked at Taylor, clearly bewildered. "I don't know why you're so upset."

"What do you call—"

Taylor felt Steele grab her right arm, signaling her not to say anything further. The look he gave her spoke louder than words. He thought Norris might have been the person in the car that they'd chased. "How long have you been here?" Taylor heard him ask.

"About an hour or so," the reporter replied. "You were out when I got here, so I parked my car across from the apartment building and waited. When I saw you drive up and go inside a few minutes ago, I slipped in through a side door and took the stairs up."

Well, that answered the question, Taylor thought.

"Look, we need to talk," Norris said, taking a step forward, her earlier fear now past. "It'll only take a few minutes, but I think you'll find that what I have to say is to both our advantages."

"You scratch my back, I'll scratch yours?" Steele said sarcastically.

"Exactly," Norris said smugly.

"Not interested," Steele said flatly. He took Taylor's arm and turned toward the apartment.

"Are you convinced of Mr. Barrett's innocence?" Norris yelled at his retreating back.

Steele stopped. He looked straight at the reporter. "Absolutely. Mr. Barrett was not in any way involved in his wife's death. Any attempt to claim otherwise is a gross miscarriage of justice. You can quote me on that. Now, if you'll excuse us..."

"Is it true he's just a hair's breadth from being indicted?" Norris pressed, dodging in front of them, blocking the doorway of the apartment.

"No comment," Steele said, pushing Norris aside.

But the reporter was not to be deterred. "Wait!" Norris cried. "What would you say if I told you that I'd come into possession of information that could help exonerate Mr. Barrett?"

Steele paused, crossed his arms over his chest. "Start talking."

Norris's mouth curved into a smile, a supremely confident smile. "I'd rather not talk in the hallway. Why don't we all go inside and have ourselves a nice little chat?"

"I don't think you have anything to say that the whole world couldn't hear," Steele said coldly.

"That's where you're wrong," Norris said, but her confident smile seemed to have slipped slightly.

"Then let's hear it." There was steel in his voice.

"I'll tell you this much," Norris hedged. "I have information that indicates Ms. Barrett was blackmailing someone."

Taylor's heart began to pound as excitement coursed through her. So they were right! "Do you know the identity of the person she was blackmailing?" Taylor asked, keeping her voice neutral.

"I've got an idea," Norris said smugly.

"Okay," Steele said, "you've got our attention. What do you want?"

"Tsk, tsk, tsk." Norris smiled. "Don't be so cynical. I'm a business person just like you. I think it only fair that I get something for the fruits of my labor." Clearly Norris was really enjoying this cat-and-mouse game.

"What do you want?" Steele repeated.

"An exclusive interview with Barrett."

"After he's exonerated," Steele offered.

Norris shook her head. "Not good enough. I want it now."

"Forget it," Steele said, stepping inside the apartment and closing the door.

Norris was right up against the door, one foot thrust in the doorway to keep it open. "You're making a big mistake. I can—"

"Unless you want to lose it," Steele said quietly, "move it."

Norris hesitated for a moment before deciding he was serious. With a muttered expletive she stepped back. Her eyes took on a faintly predatory gleam. "If I can't go with that story, how about this one—Barrett's attorneys are engaged in a hot, heavy affair."

Steele opened the door and looked at the reporter. "There will be hell to pay if I see or hear anything of that nature on your talk show or in the papers," Steele said. Taylor had never heard such coldness in his voice before.

But Norris was not so easily deterred. "Are you threatening me?" the reporter shot back.

"It's no threat. It's a promise," Steele replied, then slammed the door. He looked at Taylor, then let out a long breath. "That woman's a real pain in the butt," he muttered. He plopped down on the sofa and laid his head back.

She shivered, thinking again of the fear she'd felt at the sight of his gun. "Do most criminal attorneys carry a gun?"

"I don't know. I do because of the kind of cases I handle. Over the years I've had a few people threaten my life. You have to take things like that seriously."

His words were chilling, not just in content but because of the matter-of-fact manner in which he said them, and it brought her back to their immediate problem.

"Steele," she said, dropping down next to him on the sofa, "I didn't want to say anything in front of Norris, but why not take her up on her offer? We can't be any worse off than we are now?''

He looked at her surprised. "You can't be—"

She held up a hand, halting his words. "Wait! Hear me out. We believe Allison was blackmailing someone. Perhaps Denning or Daniel Ridgeway. Maybe even Ted Larson. But after three weeks of running down leads, we have absolutely nothing to corroborate that belief. There's no guarantee that we'll ever find Betsy Boyd or Lamden's files. You know as well as I do that we don't have an unlimited amount of time to establish the fact that someone other than Craig may have killed Allison. If an exclusive interview is the only way we can get that information, then I say we go for it. It would be a small price to pay."

Steele shook his head. "It could also place a noose around Craig's neck." He gave her a hard look. "What if the information doesn't vindicate him? I don't want Craig pleading his case to anyone but a jury."

"Yeah, and at the rate we're going, that's exactly where he's going to be pleading it," she said angrily.

Hazel eyes darkened. "It's too risky."

"I don't agree. Craig is an experienced talk-show host. He can handle Norris. And I think we can coach him enough to minimize any potential risk of entrapment."

"No." The way he said it, she knew he considered the matter closed, and that angered her even more.

"Am I or am I not a part of this defense team?" she challenged. "If I am," she continued without waiting for his answer, "then I should have some say in how this investigation should proceed."

"You do have some say," he replied. He raked a hand over his hair in frustration. "I've not only listened to you but taken most of your suggestions. But this is just one instance where we don't agree." At her stormy face, he added, "Craig is in no condition to handle the kind of badgering Norris would subject him to. Besides, I don't think Norris knows anything."

Taylor shook her head. "Yes, she does! You, Hawk and I are the only people that had an idea that she might be blackmailing someone and we haven't said anything to anyone. But Norris knows about it."

"Okay," Steele admitted reluctantly. "I grant you, she may know something, but whatever it is, it's sketchy or she wouldn't be trying to cut a deal with us. She'd be blabbering it all over network television. She's only interested in ratings, not justice."

"I know that!" she snapped. The man could try a saint. "But because she's interested in ratings, she wants to milk this story for all it's worth. Working with us would give her greater mileage with any story."

"We don't need Norris. We're perfectly capable of figuring out the identity of Allison's blackmail victim all by ourselves."

"I wish I had your faith."

"Faith has nothing to do with it. It's the only logical thing to do. We have no way of knowing where Norris got her information. Her producers are known for paying for information and they don't care how it's obtained, either. We are not only Craig's attorneys but officers of the court. We can't compound a felony or put Craig at risk by using stolen information."

Everything he said was true. But...if Norris really did know something, it meant that someone other than Craig was probably the killer; that knowledge alone would certainly give her some peace of mind. It also meant that she wouldn't have to worry about the police or some reporter getting wind of the family's medical history.

But she couldn't go against Steele's wishes. Then it hit her. She could stake out the reporter's house and the television station—follow her around. Maybe Norris would lead her to her source. Steele didn't have to know. And if she was right, then she could get the information without having to deal directly with Norris. If she was wrong, then she wouldn't have compromised the case in any way.

Steele must have construed her silence as acceptance. He looked at her and smiled. "Let's not talk about Norris anymore," he said.

He was right, she thought. There was no point in discussing the matter further. She knew what she was going to do, but now that was behind them, she didn't know what to talk about. She felt a little self-conscious sitting so close to him on the sofa. "I think I'll make some coffee," she said.

But before she could move, Steele took her by the shoulders and turned her to face him.

"Coffee is not what I want," he said smoothly, trapping her eyes with his so she was unable to look away.

Her heart began to beat erratically as she tried to think of something to say to ease the sexual tension—but her mind was totally blank. The way he was looking at her...those hazel eyes of his...that soft, seductive voice...Taylor felt heat rippling through her, which, paradoxically, made her shiver.

"I've a better idea," he said. His voice was low and husky. "Why don't we continue where we left off before we were interrupted?" He looked into her eyes and smiled. "I think I had my arms around your waist like this."

Taylor felt all her body hairs stand erect as his arms slid around her waist, drawing her close.

"And you had your arms around my neck." As if her body had a mind of its own, she placed her arms around his neck. "Good." He smiled. "And I was kissing you...like this." His lips lowered onto hers, and she felt his tongue lightly probing. His left hand tangled in the hair that cascaded down her back and anchored her lips to his in a ravenous kiss that left her breathless, wanting more.

She could only draw in a quick, unsteady breath, then give herself up to the pleasure that coursed through her. Tremors shook her body as his lips left hers and moved down the length of her slim neck and into the hollow of her throat.

"You taste so good," he whispered raggedly into her throat. "Sweet. Just like honey."

"Oh, Steele," she moaned. "I don't think this is a good idea."

"Why not?" he whispered, dropping a series of slow, shivery kisses along her neck. "Don't you like the way I make you feel?"

"Yes...but maybe..." She struggled to make the words come out, but none came. She was lost in a world of pleasurable sensations.

"No maybe." His breath was hot and sweet on her neck as he blazed a path of kisses toward her ear. Then he began to nibble on her earlobe, and shivers of delight swept through her. Gently he eased her down onto the sofa, then removed his jacket and dropped it to the floor. He pulled her back into his arms and took her mouth again.

"Steele," she moaned. She was breathing heavily, panting and gripping him tightly, her fingers running up and down his back, caressing the nape of his neck and stroking the thick black hair. "Please don't stop."

The hard thrust of his tongue between her teeth cut off her pleas. His tongue thrust deeply into her mouth, finding and caressing hers. His mouth was hot and intoxicatingly sweet. She returned his kiss fiercely, and the kiss went on and on.

Finally he lifted his head and pulled her arms from around his neck to slide them down his chest. "Touch me," he said, looking into her eyes. Her hands sliding up and down his chest made his erect flesh strain even more tightly against the confinement of his slacks. He ignored the harsh urgency of his sex, knowing that things were moving too quickly. But he was powerless to call a halt to their lovemaking.

"Oh, God, I want you," he said, his voice deep and husky. As he spoke, he drew her closer to him, molding her soft body to his. She could feel his arousal against her lower body and pulled back.

But he misinterpreted her action. "Yes, baby, I know," he said in a voice husky with desire, shifting his position and sitting up. "Let's go into the bedroom." He clasped her hand in his, interlocking their fingers in a possessive lover's gesture.

"Steele, no." Taylor pulled her hand away, a mixture of anxiety and anticipation bubbling within her. He wanted her and she wanted him. But it wasn't that simple. She wasn't free to give in to her feelings, fall in love like other people. God, she would dearly love to pretend she was a normal woman and lose herself in the pleasure of his arms. But no matter how she might wish it, she thought sadly, it could never be and she might as well accept it.

"No," she repeated with conviction. She squared her shoulders and sat up straighter, forcing herself to meet his passion-filled eyes. "What happened was a mistake," she said, struggling to keep her voice steady. "I like you, Steele, but I want you as a friend, not as a lover. I'm not interested in anything more."

Steele raked a hand over his hair. "I want to be friends with you, too, Taylor. But I see no reason to place artificial barriers around our feelings. We're strongly attracted to each other. Why deny those feelings? If we have the makings for something more than friendship, then I say we go for it."

"But I don't want more, Steele. All I want is to be friends, okay?"

No, it wasn't okay, Steele thought. He'd been with enough women to know she wanted him as much as he wanted her. But for some reason she was putting up walls to prevent any meaningful relationship from breaking through. He had news for her, though—he wasn't about to settle for just friendship.

But he didn't want to scare her away, either, so he decided to back off—for now. "I'm sorry. I didn't mean to come on so strong."

He stood and walked over to the bar in the corner, poured himself a drink and downed it in one swallow. He turned to Taylor. "Want one?"

"Yeah. I think that would be a good idea." She came over and took the offered glass. Then she crossed the carpeted living room and continued out onto the balcony, looking out on the city. The night was warm and balmy.

A slight sound alerted her, and she turned to see Steele cross the balcony to stand behind her. He slipped his arm around her waist and pulled her back against him. For a long time neither of them said anything. Surprisingly, though, it was a comfortable silence.

Finally he turned her to face him. He looked into her eyes and smiled. "We'll play it your way for now, but I'm not giving up. I guess if you aren't going to let me make love to you, then we might as well get some work done. C'mon, let's talk about what we need to do tomorrow."

STEELE GLANCED at his watch again. Where the hell was Taylor? It wasn't like her to be late. He frowned. Maybe she was upset about last night. But as quickly as the idea crossed his mind, he was discarding it. He'd come on strong, but she had assured him she wasn't angry with him and they'd ended the evening on a pleasant note. No, that wasn't it. She'd probably gotten tied up in court.

He thought back to the night before. They probably should take it slow. He was just learning to trust his instincts and he sensed she was, too. But God, he wanted her. He wanted to scream in frustration. Every time he thought about her, looked at her, touched her, his body gave him hell.

He sighed and picked up Hawk's investigative report, which detailed the work to date. He quickly skimmed the portion relating to Harold Lamden's suicide, then turned to the section on the senator. Denning was reputed to be in the pocket of several corporate supporters. Whether this rumour was just partisan politics or actual fact only some heavy-duty investigating would determine. Hawk indicated he'd asked a friend to check it out. On the issue of an affair, he'd gotten O'Rourke and another former staffer to admit that a couple of years back Denning had had an affair with Allison. He'd also found a motel clerk in a little town outside Chicago who was willing to swear that he'd seen Denning with a woman matching Allison's description. But that was the only good news. Hawk had found nothing to connect the money in Allison's account to Denning or, for that matter, to Daniel Ridgeway.

From all accounts, Ridgeway was a quiet churchgoing man, well-liked and respected by people in the community. At the time of the murder, he claimed he was driving back to Chicago from a business meeting in Detroit. Hawk was in the process of verifying Ridgeway's, as well as Denning's alibis.

The next section of the report was devoted to Ted Larson. Hawk had been able to trace him back about three years, when he'd changed his name from Gary Lewis to Ted Larson. He'd also changed his birthdate and social-security number. However, Hawk had been able to find his former birthdate and social-security number, but those numbers proved to be false, as well. No doubt Gary Lewis was also an alias. What the hell was Larson hiding? Steele wondered.

But Hawk was one of the best P.I.'s in the business. If there was anything there, he'd find it. For now all Steele could do was focus on building Craig's legal defense, which from all accounts was not going to be easy. The prosecution had a mountain of circumstantial evidence against him.

His thoughts were interrupted by the jingling of the phone, and he reached for it with reluctance. "Yes," he said wearily.

"It's Senator Denning," his secretary said. "He'd like to talk to you."

Denning? He didn't believe in coincidence; maybe Hawk was on to something. "Put him through." He waited until he heard a click, then said with as much heartiness as he could muster, "Senator. What can I do for you?" Steele rummaged through the pile of papers in front of him till he found a legal pad with some empty pages.

"I was wondering if you could meet with me this morning. Say elevenish at the Maryland Café? I have some information about Craig Barrett that may have some bearing on his wife's murder."

First Norris, now Denning. Suddenly everyone had information about the case, he thought, but aloud he said, "The Maryland Café is fine. Elevenish."

"Good. I'll see you there, Mr. Steele."

He stared at the phone. Now what kind of information could Denning have about Craig? If he thought it was important, it couldn't be good news.

He picked up the phone and called Taylor's office again, only to be told she still wasn't back. He lowered the receiver back in the cradle and frowned. Where the hell was she?

"TAYLOR, MR. STEELE has been trying to reach you all morning," Brenda said, following her into the office. "Should I tell him you're back?"

Taylor stared at the piles of work on her desk. Damn! She'd hoped to have time to at least go through that morning's correspondence before meeting with Steele. She'd spent the morning shadowing Norris, but hadn't learned anything.

"Tell him I'll be down shortly," she said absently. She'd already started going through her correspondence, deciding what she needed to act on and what could wait.

"George Avery called again," her secretary said. "He said he really would like to talk to you."

She sighed. She didn't have time for this. "Tell Matt to call him. Then I want you to pull the Patterson file—"

A knock on the opened door had both women staring at the man in the doorway.

"I hope I haven't come at a bad time," Detective Donaldson said as he sauntered into the room.

Taylor looked again at the mountain of work of her desk and issued a silent groan. "I can spare you a few minutes." She pointed to the chair in front of her desk, then sat down herself.

"I'm here because I want to lay my cards on the table," Donaldson began.

Taylor leaned back in her chair and studied the detective. "What is this? A variation of 'you show me yours. I'll show you mine'?"

He threw her a sour look. "Cute. Look, Ms. Quinlan, you strike me as a reasonable person."

"Thanks, I think."

"Why don't we save ourselves, not to mention the taxpayers, a lot of hassle. If Barrett would just admit he killed his wife, I think I can get the prosecutor to accept a murder-two plea. I'll even recommend that he be sent to one of our less violent state prisons. Hell, with good behavior, he'll be eligible for parole before I collect my pension."

She laughed. "That's in about ten, fifteen years?"

He nodded.

"That doesn't sound like much of a deal to me, especially when you consider Craig is innocent."

Donaldson shook his head. "Come on, Ms. Quinlan, there's just you and me here now. Barrett is guilty as sin, and you know it."

Taylor's heart nearly jumped in her throat. He knew! No! No! He couldn't know. *Don't lose it,* she admonished herself. She schooled her features to look calm as he continued to speak and when he did, she knew she'd overreacted.

"Maybe if you hadn't been around that Michael Steele so long, you'd see reason. I'm willing—"

"Did I hear my name?" Steele asked, stepping into the room. "Detective Donaldson, you're looking well. How nice of you to drop by to see us."

"Cut the crap!" Donaldson snarled.

Steele's eyes widened in mock surprise. "This isn't a social visit?"

"He came to offer us a deal," Taylor explained calmly. She took a moment to outline his proposal. "Murder two for a guilty plea."

"Better take it now," the detective said coldly. "I'm not going to be such a nice guy after I nail Barrett's butt."

"You don't have anything," Steele challenged, leaning against the corner of Taylor's desk.

Donaldson stood. "Maybe not enough now, but soon. And when I arrest Barrett, no amount of money is going to get him out of this. You can count on it."

As soon as he was out of the room, Taylor turned to Steele. "What was that about?"

Steele shrugged offhandedly. "He's fishing, trying to determine what chinks exist in our case and intimidate us. But if he's playing that kind of game, his case against Craig can't be that strong."

"That may be," Taylor sighed. "But I bet it's stronger than ours."

DENNING WAS LATE. Steele and Taylor sat in a booth in the back of the Maryland Café sipping coffee.

"You think he got cold feet?" Taylor asked, glancing about the diner.

"I don't know, but we'll give him five minutes more, then we're out of here." The two women sitting across from them looked as if they'd just gotten in from the night before—working girls, he thought. Farther down from them was an older man who was talking to himself.

Steele swore under his breath.

"It's not that bad." Taylor laughed. "I can think of a lot worse places he could have asked us to meet him."

"Okay." He smiled, looking at Taylor sitting across from him. All his displeasure at Denning's tardiness faded at the sight of her smiling face. God, she was lovely.

"I guess I'm just a little on edge." He rubbed the back of his neck. "I reviewed Hawk's latest investigative report. We have a number of suspects and a theory, but nothing that exonerates Craig." He looked at her and smiled. "The only bright spot in the day thus far is the fact that I've got you to help me handle this meeting. Though for a while there, I thought I might have to come alone. Where were you?"

"Oh, I had a few things to do," she said vaguely. "What do you think Denning wants to talk about?"

Steele shrugged. "He claims he has some information about Craig. Somehow I don't see him as the magnanimous type, so it can't be good."

"We're about to find out," she said, looking at something behind him. He turned and saw Denning coming toward them.

Steele's eyes narrowed as he took in the senator's attire. He was wearing a jogging suit and sweatband and carrying a backpack. No doubt, his idea of a disguise. Denning gave them both toothpaste smiles as he squeezed in the booth next to Taylor. Steele looked him over. He looked smug. He was up to something.

"I'm glad you could see me." He propped his arms on the table. "We'll have to make this quick, I have a League of Women Voters luncheon in a little over an hour."

Steele gave him a sour look.

"You said you had information regarding Allison's murder," Taylor prompted.

Denning nodded once, then leaned forward and spoke in a quiet tone. "Before I say anything, I want your word that you'll call off your private investigator."

"You have nothing to be afraid of if you're clean."

"That's beside the point," Denning hissed. "I have political enemies who will say anything to stop my bid for governor. I'm afraid your P.I. won't be able to separate the truth from the lies. He's also making some of my supporters nervous. I want you to call him off—stop this witch-hunt."

Several people looked at their table. Denning glanced nervously about the room, then lowered his voice. "You know what I mean."

Steele speared him with a hard look. "Senator, you know what you have to do to stop it."

"Okay," Denning said, then issued a frustrated sigh. "Allison and I had an affair. Is that what you want to hear? I admit it, but it's been over for more than two years."

"Is that why you let her stay in your condo? Because she was blackmailing you?"

"Of course not!" he sputtered. "I was just trying to help an old friend."

That Steele found hard to believe.

Denning set his backpack on the table. "I've got the videotape from the surveillance camera outside Allison's condo from the night of the murder. It shows a tall black man entering then leaving the condo about the time the murder is supposed to have occurred." Denning zipped opened the backpack, pulled out a large manila folder and handed it to Steele.

Steele opened the folder and took out a videotape and several photographs. He skimmed the pictures, but as far as he could see, they didn't identify anyone or tell them anything they didn't already know. He handed them to Taylor, then looked at Denning and shrugged. "I assume there's a point to this."

Denning looked at him as if he were the village idiot. "These pictures were taken the night of the murder," he said. Then he moved his finger along the bottom of the photos. "The time the pictures were taken is listed on each frame." He tapped one particular photo. "This is the man that killed Allison."

Steele read the time listed at the bottom of the picture. According to this, it had been taken at eleven twenty-seven.

"I thought we could make a deal," Denning whispered. "You don't say anything about uh, me and Allison, and I'll give you the tape and the pictures. You can do whatever you like with them."

"Why would I want them?" Steele asked coolly.

Denning looked as if he was going to have a stroke. "Because that's your client in those photographs!"

"You think that's Craig?" he asked lazily.

Denning's blue eyes narrowed. "I don't need to say it, Mr. Steele. The pictures speak for themselves."

"Yes, they do," Steele said calmly. He leaned back against the booth. "You know, the police have been looking for this tape. I would advise you to turn it in as soon as possible, and you'd better have a good reason for having it in your possession."

"Now, look!" Denning glanced over his shoulder, then lowered his voice to a conspiratorial whisper. "I don't know what kind of game you're playing, but I'm not bluffing."

Steele stared him down. "Neither am I," he said coldly. "I would also advise you to tell them about the affair. If we uncovered it, so will the police and the press."

The senator stood. "I'm sorry you feel that way." He scooped up the tape and pictures and stomped away.

The moment Denning was out of hearing range, Taylor looked at him, frowning. "Why didn't you take them? We could have made copies, then taken them to the police."

"It could have been a setup. Also it seems to me that if he admitted that readily to an affair, if Allison was blackmailing him, the basis for the blackmail may have been something entirely different."

Surprised, Taylor looked at him. "Like what?"

Steele shrugged. "I don't know, but Hawk must be on to something. Denning's scared stiff. I thought for a moment there he was going to have a stroke."

Taylor nodded. "Speaking of strokes," she said. "If I don't get some food soon, I just might have one myself.'' She'd wanted to get an early start on tailing Norris and hadn't had time for breakfast.

Steele grinned. ''So where do you want to go?''

''What's wrong with here?'' she asked, glancing about the diner. ''The food looks pretty good.'' Steele gave her a skeptical look but didn't say anything.

They had finished lunch and were chatting over coffee when Taylor noticed a very determined woman headed their way.

''Oh, no,'' Taylor groaned, ''Vanessa Norris. How did she know we were here?''

He shrugged. ''She must have been in the office when you called to tell Brenda where we were. I wouldn't—'' He broke off as the woman in question came within earshot.

''Mr. Steele. Ms. Quinlan. I was hoping to run into the two of you.''

Steele crossed his arms over his chest. ''I thought I made it clear last night, we're not interesting in anything you have to say.''

Norris ignored the remark. ''Just give me five minutes, that's all I ask,'' she said, sliding in the booth next to him.

''Save your breath,'' Steele said coolly. ''I don't think you've got anything, and if you did, I would question the veracity of the information.''

''I'll have you know I'm a first-rate investigative reporter,'' Norris said heatedly. ''I was ferreting out information long before I became a talk-show host.'' She lowered her voice and leaned forward. ''So what if we occasionally pay for information? As long as the information is good, what's the harm? I'm not saying that's how I came across the information about Allison Barrett. Let's just say I got lucky.'' She glanced over her shoulder then back to them. ''Let's talk turkey. Allison Barrett had over three hundred thousand dollars in her savings account.''

She scanned their faces. ''Don't bother to deny it. I know it's true. I also know she didn't get that money based on her sparkling personality." She gave them an expectant look. When they didn't say anything, she said, "Look, if we pool our efforts, I think we can all benefit."

Steele gave her a cool look. "Okay, you've had your say. Now we'd like to get back to our lunch."

Norris looked into his set face and must have decided it was useless to argue with him. She shrugged her shoulders, but instead of leaving, she leaned over and whispered, "Look, to show you that I really do want to help, I'll give you a clue."

She made a show of looking over her shoulder before whispering, "Look for the sheep in wolf's clothing, and you'll find your killer."

Chapter Nine

Norris's cryptic comment haunted Taylor. Steele had shrugged it off as simply a ploy to make them think she really knew something. He'd even pointed out that Norris hadn't correctly stated the old adage, which was, A Wolf In Sheep's Clothing.

Taylor didn't agree but knew it would be fruitless to argue. His mind was made up and so was hers. She'd quickly made up an excuse about a meeting with a client that she'd forgotten about and scurried out of the diner. She was going to stick with Norris and find out if the reporter really was on to anything.

But as the hours ticked by with no movement from Norris since she'd gone inside the television station, her resolve began to waver. *What am I doing here?* she wondered. Maybe Steele was right. Maybe Norris didn't know anything. She hadn't offered one shred of evidence to support her claim. Was she simply grasping at straws? Perhaps she was willing to accept someone lacking in credibility like Norris because it meant she didn't have to confront her real fears—that Craig was guilty or that she would have to tell Steele about her family's medical history. She hadn't thought so, but the mind could play tricks on you. She thought back to the night before. Hadn't she almost convinced herself that she could have a relationship with Steele?

She sighed and thought about Steele. No doubt he was on his way to see Larson right now. God, she ought to be with him, not wasting time on some wild-goose chase. She glanced at her watch. If she hurried, she could still participate in the interview. She turned on the ignition, but instead of pulling away she sat still. What if Norris did know something? an inner voice whispered. She leaned back against the seat rest, torn. Should she go or should she stay?

As if her troubled thoughts had conjured up the woman in question, Norris walked out of the station. Taylor's heart began to pump as she watched the reporter climb into her Mazda, pull out of the parking lot and head south. From years of watching cop shows on television, she knew the trick was to stay close to the quarry, but not too close. She timed her progress to ensure that she wouldn't get stuck at a red light while the Mazda cruised on down the street. Once or twice she let another vehicle slip in between her Toyota and Norris's Mazda.

She was certain she had not revealed herself. Norris made no attempt to shake her pursuit, no sudden stops or unsignaled turns.

The Mazda hooked south onto Cermack and turned onto the Dan Ryan Expressway. She drove for about thirty minutes. The Southtown Shopping Mall was just ahead.

Norris guided her car into the mall parking lot and pulled in next to a maroon sedan. Taylor drove passed slowly, risking a sidelong glance just as Norris was opening the car door.

Could this be Norris's informant? she wondered as she found a parking space in the opposite lane.

She watched Norris in the rearview mirror as she got into the maroon car. The driver was a man, but his back was to her so she couldn't see his face. Even though the car windows were down, they were too far away for her to hear what was being said, but she could tell from the man's body language that he was upset. They talked for about five minutes, then Norris abruptly climbed out and got back into her car.

Taylor watched as Norris pulled out of the lot; the maroon sedan followed. She was about to join the procession when she saw Hawk Longtree's Jeep cruising the lane. She ducked down. God, she hoped he hadn't seen her. When she looked up again, he was gone, but so were Norris and the maroon car.

Where could they have gone? she wondered. Wherever it was, it wouldn't be a place where they would be readily observed. They'd want privacy. Meeting in a parking lot was a good indication of that. She chewed her lower lip as a million places sprang to mind, but driving aimlessly around was pointless. She sighed. She might as well head back to the television station. She'd wait there an hour. If Norris didn't return, she'd call it quits.

STEELE LEANED against the doorframe of the weight-training room of the Lake Shore Country Club watching Larson put a cute little blonde through a weight lifting program. She was lying on a bench with a small barbell in each hand. Larson stood behind her, ready to help if she got into trouble. However, it seemed to Steele that he went out of his way to touch or brush up against the blonde. It was probably just as well Taylor hadn't come with him, he thought. Larson would flirt outrageously with her, and he wasn't sure he would be able to contain himself this time.

He frowned, thinking again of Taylor's behavior. He couldn't believe she'd passed up the opportunity to question Larson, not when she'd been so adamant about questioning him again. It didn't make sense. Her behavior was totally out of character, or at least what he knew of her. Again he wondered if his behavior the night before had upset her and again he found himself dismissing it.

Just then Larson spotted him and came over.

"I'd hoped I'd seen the last of you," he said, his voice surly. "Now, that pretty co-counsel of yours can bother me anytime."

Steele held his temper when all he wanted to do was smash his fist into the younger man's face. "Is there some place we can talk?"

Larson's eyebrows drew downward in a frown. "Why are you hounding me? I've told you everything I know." Without waiting for an answer, he walked over to a soft-drink machine in the corner, inserted some coins, then made his selection.

"I guess I was mistaken," Steele said coolly. "I thought you really cared about Allison."

Larson's head whipped around. "Don't try to lay a guilt trip on me."

"I wouldn't dare. But I must admit, you had me going there for a while. You almost had me convinced that you and Allison were friends, but I guess she was just another client to you after all."

For a moment Larson seemed to waver, and Steele took advantage of that moment of indecision. "You know," he said, "what's sad about all this is Allison herself. She's the victim. But she has no one to make sure she isn't forgotten. The police are focusing all their time and money on Craig. It may take a little while, but I'm going to clear him. By then the trail is going to be so cold, the police will never find Allison's murderer." He gave Larson a hard look. "I don't know how you can sleep at night knowing that you didn't lift a finger to help apprehend her killer." Steele turned and was about to walk away.

"Wait," Larson said. "We can talk in the lounge."

When they were seated, Steele got right to it. "I believe you and Allison were close," he began. "You seem to have known her longer and better than anyone else. During all that time, she must have confided in you, told you about the blackmail."

Larson gulped his drink and looked everywhere but at Steele.

"You don't have to answer. I can tell from your reaction you knew."

Larson's gaze shifted guiltily away. "I don't know what you're talking about," he mumbled.

"You were always around," Steele continued. "Everyone thought it was because the two of you were having an affair, but I think there was more to it than that." It was just a hunch, but from Larson's reaction, he knew he'd hit the mark.

"I don't know what you mean," Larson said, but Steele noticed the tiny bead of sweat on his upper lip.

"Then let me see if I can clarify it for you. Isn't it true that the two of you were always together because you were plotting your blackmail scheme?"

"Of course not!" Larson spluttered. "I wasn't blackmailing anyone!"

"Maybe not." Steele shrugged. "But you're implicated up to your neck in Allison's blackmail scheme. By the time our investigating is concluded we'll have enough evidence to present to the police for you to be charged as an accessory in Allison's crime. If you want to deal now is the time."

For a long time Larson didn't say anything. "Okay." He sighed finally. "I knew about the blackmail but I didn't have anything to do with it. I tried to talk her out of it, but she wouldn't listen." He slumped back in his seat. "She didn't need to go that route. We already had a good thing going." At Steele's look of inquiry, he said, "She was an attractive woman. There are a lot of men who will pay for a pretty woman's time."

Steele nodded. "What was your role in all this?"

"I'd find the mark, find out as much as I could about him, then pass the information on to Allison. She'd use it to approach and hook him. We'd split the money, fifty-fifty." He threw Steele a quick look. "The guy's ego was flattered, and we were a little richer. No one was hurt, and there was certainly nothing illegal about what we did."

Perhaps not technically, Steele thought, but it was certainly immoral.

"It started about three years ago," Larson continued. "There were several men before Denning, but he was our first big score. After him there were a couple of other businessmen, and then we targeted Barrett. With him, though, she changed the rules."

Steele nodded. "She married him."

"I tried to talk her out of it, but she wouldn't listen. She said that as Mrs. Craig Barrett, she could get her hands on more money than we'd ever seen." His voice broke. "It was only supposed to last a few months."

"And then she was to move on to Gordon Ridgeway?" Steele prompted.

Larson nodded, then looked at Steele, his expression bleak. "Allison was beautiful. She didn't have to resort to blackmail to get what she wanted from a man."

"But," Steele interrupted, "she got greedy and began to blackmail the men she'd been involved with."

Larson nodded again. "She went after Denning. I told her he was trouble, but she wouldn't listen."

"What did she have on him?"

He ran a hand over his face. "During some pillow talk, he made an off-the-cuff comment about one of his campaign contributors, a poultry company. It wasn't much, but it stuck in the back of her mind. About six months ago, I did some digging and found a couple of transactions between the senator and the owner of Caravan Foods that could be considered kickbacks and political bribes."

Steele whistled. No wonder the senator was willing to admit to an affair; that was the least of his problems. Even if there was no proof of wrongdoing, the mere hint of it could be enough to destroy his career. And if it was true, then the senator was not just facing political ruin but some serious jail time. He certainly had reason for wanting Allison dead.

"BLACKMAIL!"

Senator Denning gave a loud guffaw but without any

amusement. "That's not a very nice word."

"But it's a great motive for murder," Steele said calmly. "Ted Larson says Allison was blackmailing you, that she had information that suggested you were taking kickbacks from Caravan Foods in exchange for your power and influence on legislation regulating the poultry industry."

"The man's a liar!" Denning said with sudden heat, his face deepening in color.

"Why would Larson lie?" Steele asked.

"How should I know why he's lying? He just is." Anger and fear were seeping out of every pore of the senator's face.

"Even if it is a lie, we both know the press and your opponent would have a field day with it," Steele said calmly. "You couldn't afford Allison and now Larson to go public with that kind of allegation."

"He's going public?" Senator Denning stood abruptly. He strode up and down, agitated. "You've got to stop him! He can't say anything." He paused in his pacing and gave Steele a pleading look. "None of what she claimed is true."

"Convince me, Senator. You have my word, if your alibi holds up, I'll do everything in my power to keep your name out of this."

Denning slumped wearily into a nearby chair. "I guess I have to trust you are a man of your word." All the anger had gone out of him.

"Allison was rotten to the core," he said. "Whenever I think of her, I think of a black widow spider. Beautiful and charming on the outside, but inside she was actually a cold, calculating woman, a scheming bitch who didn't care who she hurt to get what she wanted."

"And what did she want?"

"Money," he said bluntly. "Lots of it."

"Go on," Steele said.

"Allison had the most horrible pair of ears in the world. She heard everything and she forgot nothing. She would encourage you to talk, get you to tell her about your thoughts, your feelings, your background. I thought she was the most attentive, sympathetic listener in the world, but what she was really doing was collecting information she could use against me later.

"She'd pick up every piece of gossip, every little thing from lots of different people and then she'd start correlating them, putting them all together, fitting them into a pattern until gradually she knew more about you than you could possibly realize." He paused, then ran his hand over his face. "She accused me of political wrongdoing. I'd done nothing wrong, but she didn't care. She threatened to go to the press. I had no choice but to pay her off."

"How much did she want for her silence?"

"A half million. But I couldn't get my hands on that kind of money, so I gave her the condo. We agreed that I'd sign it over to her after her divorce was final. For a while she left me alone, then a few weeks before the murder, her demands for money started all over again. She said this would be the last time. I had to believe her." He sighed. "I began to quietly liquidate certain assets. When I got the money together, I sent her that note you found at her condo. I didn't want her calling me, so we agreed the note would be the signal that—"

"Wait a minute," Steele interrupted. "That note didn't arrive until after she was murdered. Are you telling me you didn't make the payoff?"

Denning nodded. "That's right. She was murdered the day before I was to deliver the money to her."

Steele's eyes widened. If the money in Allison's account hadn't come from Denning, then who had given it to her?

DARKNESS HAD DESCENDED by the time Taylor pulled up in front of the television station. Her heart leapt when she saw the red Mazda and the maroon sedan parked out front. She smiled wryly; while she'd been racking her brain, trying to figure out where they had gone, Norris and her visitor had gone back to the station.

Now what? she wondered. She couldn't sit out here indefinitely. First because the area wasn't all that safe. Second, and more important, she needed to see what Norris and the mysterious man were up to. Maybe even get a look at him. But she couldn't just march into the station. No doubt there was a security guard in the lobby.

As she sat there trying to decide what to do, a van bearing the station's name pulled up and parked in front of her. She watched as two men and a woman walked around to the back, opened the rear hatch and began unloading camera equipment. *That's it!* she thought. When the reporter and camera crew walked into the station, she'd walk in with them. With any luck, the guard would assume she was with them.

She gave them a moment's head start, then she was out of her car, hurrying after them. She drew a deep breath and entered the building on the heels of the trio. She wasn't sure what she'd have said to the security guard if he had stopped her, but luckily he didn't. When she was a few feet from the guard's station, she separated from the group. Glancing over her shoulder, she walked quickly over to the building directory, located Norris's office number, then stepped into an elevator.

The elevator came to a stop and opened with a quiet *swoosh* on the fifth floor. Taylor stepped off and moved cautiously through a set of double doors leading into a suite of offices. She listened for the sound of voices but heard nothing. The place looked deserted, but that couldn't be. There were people still working in some of these offices, so she had to be careful not to let anyone see her.

She moved cautiously down the corridor, looking for Norris's office. About midway down, she came to a smoked-glass door. Next to the door was a small wooden nameplate, proclaiming this to be Vanessa Norris's office. She pressed her ear as close to the door as possible, listening for sounds inside. Either they were whispering or there was no one inside. Taylor knocked once on the glass door. When she received no answer, she turned the knob and stuck her head inside. "Ms. Norris?"

She was greeted with silence. She slipped into the room, pulling the door closed behind her. Her eyes quickly swept the room, noticing a number of file cabinets, a desk, a chair and a narrow band of light coming from an open doorway in one corner of the room. From where she stood, the room looked vacant. She ran over to the file cabinets and began rummaging through, looking for anything that remotely resembled information on Allison's murder. There was nothing. She crossed the room to Norris's desk. It was littered with papers as if she'd been working on a story and had been called away. Taylor took a few minutes to go through them before moving on to the desk drawers, all the while keeping one eye trained on the door. Again there was nothing. She was just about to leave when she noticed Norris's computer was on.

The screen was blank, but the cursor was blinking. She wondered if Norris had been called away after deleting the document she'd been working on. If she'd been in a rush, then maybe she'd used the Delete key, which meant if she hadn't touched the computer after she'd deleted the document, it could be retrieved. She closed her eyes and said a silent prayer as she pressed the Redo button. When she opened them, the screen was filled with text. In the second line, the name Harold Lamden jumped out at her!

There was no time to read. She looked quickly toward the door. Norris might return any moment. She sent the document to print, then deleted it from the computer's memory.

She ran over to the printer. Her heart pounded fiercely as first one page then the next came out of the printer, her eyes all the while darting from the door to the printer. As soon as the last page printed, she stuffed the pages in her shoulder bag.

She was just about to leave when she heard someone moving about in the corridor outside and saw the outline of a person on the other side of the door. Norris!

Panic clawed at her. She quickly shut off the printer and tried to think of a plausible explanation for being in the reporter's office.

Her heart raced as she waited for the door to open, but nothing happened. Norris just stood there, saying nothing, as if she was staring in. But Taylor knew you couldn't see through the smoked-glass door.

"Ms. Norris?" she called. She took a step toward the door, then something made her stop. "Ms. Norris? Is that you?" She frowned. Why was Norris acting so strangely? Then she realized the figure was too tall and bulky to be the reporter's. To someone with an overactive imagination, it seemed huge and black and menacing.

Taylor began to back away. Suddenly two long arms went up, and the hands splayed out against the glass. Taylor's heart thudded in her chest. *Stop it!* she chided herself. *It's just your imagination. You're scaring yourself to death.* She shook her head, clearing the frightening images from her mind.

"Ms. Norris?" she called again.

There was the faintest creak in answer. Taylor looked down just in time to see the doorknob turn. The door was slowly moving inward!

A layer of cold sweat beaded on her skin as panic assailed her. *Hide!* an inner voice screamed. Taylor backed up fast, bumping into a chair, stumbling as her eyes darted around the room. She turned and ran toward the room with the light, slamming the door behind her. It was a bathroom, and there was no lock on the door. She bit back a sob as her eyes swept the tiny room. There was just the sink, a stall and a tiny window. But the window was too high for someone of her small stature to reach. There was only one place to hide in the room . . . a stupid, useless place, a dead end. She went to it anyway, pushing at the stall door. She pushed harder, but it wouldn't budge.

The heavy footsteps came closer.

Using the strength adrenaline was pumping into her veins, Taylor pulled the door toward her instead of backward. She knew she was saying Steele's name over and over again, like a mantra, a prayer. Suddenly the stall door jerked open. But instead of running forward, Taylor froze in terror.

Vanessa Norris was sitting upright on the toilet, her knees together, her hands folded primly on her lap, like a little girl dressed in her Sunday best whose mother had told her to sit quietly. She was wearing a short navy skirt, matching jacket and a white ruffled blouse. The faint scent of her expensive, spicy perfume mingled with the stronger, mordant smell of blood. Her throat had been cut from ear to ear.

"Taylor," a male voice said from behind her.

She whirled around, fighting the scream that rose in her throat.

Chapter Ten

Taylor opened her mouth to scream again before a familiar voice penetrated her subconscious.

Strong hands grabbed both her arms. "Taylor, it's me! Steele!"

"Oh, God," she cried, falling into his arms. She had never been so glad to see anyone in her life. "It's Norris. She's dead."

Steele released her to inspect the body. She kept her back turned, not wanting to see, but over her shoulder she could see he was careful not to touch anything. When he was done, he took her into his arms.

She pressed her head against his shoulder, but she couldn't get the ghastly sight of Norris out of her mind. She felt lightheaded. *Oh, Lord,* Taylor thought as black spots flashed before her eyes and she felt both hot and cold chills rack her body. As if from a great distance, she heard him say, "Let's get out of here and call the police."

Everything after that was a blur: Steele's quick search of the room, the call to the police and their subsequent arrival. After a while the fog that had engulfed her mind began to lift.

"Better?" Steele asked, rubbing her back. He'd taken her into Norris's office and held her close, all the while whispering words of comfort.

Taylor nodded from within the safety of his embrace, and looked about the office. Every light in the place was on, and several uniformed officers were already swarming about in a methodical search for clues. She watched as Detective Donaldson walked toward them. He pulled up a chair next to the sofa.

"Ms. Quinlan, you feel like making a statement?" he asked. Even though his request was formed in the nature of a question, she knew she didn't have much choice.

She closed her eyes and drew a deep, ragged breath. "I think so."

She felt Steele's arm tighten around her. "Donaldson, Ms. Quinlan has been subjected to quite a shock," he said. "Can't this wait until tomorrow?"

"No, it can't wait," Donaldson growled.

The two men squared off like prizefighters.

She placed her hand on Steele's arm. He looked at her, his expression one of concern. She gave him a reassuring smile. "It's okay." She drew another deep breath. "Frankly I'd like to get this over with."

Donaldson pulled out a notepad and pen. "Why don't we begin with your telling me what you were doing here?"

Taylor shifted slightly under his steady gaze and decided it was best to stick as close to the truth as possible. She'd tell him everything except about following Norris and finding the document. She dared not look at Steele as she briefly explained that she'd stopped by in response to a call from the reporter. She could tell by the tension in his body that later she was going to have a lot of questions to answer.

"Did she give you any indication of what she wanted to talk about?"

"She said she had information about Allison's murder that would exonerate Craig."

Donaldson gave her a sour look. "Did you see anyone when you arrived?"

Taylor shook her head. "No, but someone was here. While I was waiting in here for Norris, I heard someone moving about in the corridor. At first I thought it was Ms. Norris, but the person's behavior was so bizarre, I got frightened and was looking for a place to hide when I stumbled onto the body.''

''But you didn't see who it was?''

She shook her head again. ''I'm sorry, but at the time I was too busy trying not to let him see me.'' She shuddered, remembering the terror she'd felt. Steele's arm tightened.

''When I drove up,'' he said, ''I saw a man run from the building and get into a maroon sedan and drive away.'' He glanced at Taylor, then back at Donaldson. ''It looked like Daniel Ridgeway.''

Taylor sucked in her breath. Had it been Ridgeway that Norris had met in the mall parking lot?

''Interesting.'' The detective leaned back in his chair and regarded Steele steadily. ''Now, why don't you tell me what *you* were doing here?''

''A friend of mine spotted Ms. Quinlan's car parked out front and called me. He didn't think it wise for her to be in this part of town alone this time of night.''

For a moment Donaldson didn't say anything. She was sure he was trying to decide if he believed them or not. Then the detective sighed and glanced at a uniformed officer who was waiting to talk with him.

Steele stood, pulling Taylor up with him. ''Donaldson, if you don't have any further questions, we'd like to go.''

At Donaldson's grunt, Steele wrapped his arm around her shoulders, tucking her securely against his side. Her pulse rate began to beat double time. She didn't know which was more unsettling—his nearness or the overwhelming horror she'd felt within these walls.

Steele led her outside to his car. ''I'll have Hawk drive your car to your place.'' Instead of starting the engine, he draped his arm over the back of the seat and turned toward her. ''You've had a shock, so I'm not going to yell at you for that stunt you pulled, but it's a good thing

Hawk spotted you at the Southtown Mall parking lot and called me."

"What was Hawk doing there?"

"He was tailing Daniel Ridgeway." He paused and gave her a pointed look. "I had a good idea what you were up to and knew you would eventually end up here. I sent Hawk to talk to Mr. Jasper and came over here."

"You think Ridgeway killed Norris?" she asked.

"I don't know but I would like to know why he was meeting with her." Steele sighed. "There have been some developments since this afternoon that you should know about." He gave her a brief rundown of his meetings with Larson and Denning. "Allison may have been blackmailing Denning," he said, "but it doesn't look as if he killed her."

"We only have his word that he didn't make the pay-off," Taylor contended.

Steele nodded. "I know, but that's not the only reason I'm excluding him. Hawk was finally able to talk to the night watchman. He confirms the senator's story that he was in his office the night of the murder." He sighed again. "We're running out of suspects."

A cold shiver shook her. No, she thought, they were not out of suspects. They were back to Craig.

Steele must have misread her reaction. He threw her a concerned look. "I'd better get you home."

He was about to put the key in the ignition when she remembered the documents. "Wait," she said. She pulled the papers out of her bag and laid them on the seat between them. "This was in Norris's computer."

Steele looked from the pages to her. "Do you know what this is?" he asked. "It's a copy of the police report on Harold Lamden's suicide."

TAYLOR LEANED BACK against the sofa and looked at Steele. "I've read that report a half-dozen times, as well as studied the police photographs, but I still don't see what it is that Norris saw," she said. They were in her living room, drinking coffee and discussing the events of the evening.

Steele looked up from the notes he'd taken. "It's a pretty standard police report," he said. "There's the usual write-up of the case and investigative photographs—a picture of Harold Lamden's body slumped over the steering wheel of his car, photos of the interior rooms of his house. Yet there must be something in this document or the photographs that led Norris to conclude Craig couldn't have killed Allison."

"Do you think she located his files?"

Steele shook his head. "I don't think so. She wouldn't have approached us if she had. I think she had a hunch."

Taylor sighed. "I followed her around all day, and other than the meeting with Ridgeway, I didn't observe her doing anything else connected with Allison's murder. And I did a fairly thorough search of her office, and that report is the only thing I found."

Steele gave her a thoughtful look. "She may not have written down what she'd gleaned from these documents or what she knew about Allison't murder. But she apparently tipped her hand to the killer. It's the only plausible explanation for her murder."

"I think you're right."

"I'll have Hawk try and retrace her steps for the last week or so," he said. "Maybe if we can find out where she went, who she saw, we can identify our killer. In the meantime, let's go through the report again. This time let's compare Hawk's report on Lamden with Norris's."

They spent several hours studying the two reports until it was late. Taylor was about ready to call it quits when Steele grabbed her arm.

"You know," he said slowly, "we may have been looking at this all wrong. We've assumed that because of Norris's murder, she must have been on to something. But Norris was an ambitious reporter, looking for a sensational story. But a story that related to Allison's murder. There have been all kinds of allegations appearing in the media that are nothing more than pure conjecture. I don't think it would have been too great a stretch for Norris to make the leap that Lamden hadn't committed suicide but was murdered."

"There's no evidence to support that claim," she said, looking into his handsome face.

"A suicide can be mistaken for murder and vice versa, especially when the victim dies in this manner." Steele laid the photographs on the cocktail table. "According to the police report, Lamden dropped a sleeping pill in a glass of wine before he climbed into his car."

Taylor nodded. "That's right."

"But there is no mention of a wine bottle being found in the car or inside the house. And there's no bottles in any of the photos. Also there's a bruise on Lamden's right ankle that couldn't be explained, as well as a small grease spot on the back of his shirt, just above the waistband of his slacks." He pursed his lips. "I think Norris was working on the theory that Lamden was the first murder victim."

Taylor's eyes widened as his words sank in. "What if she was right?"

"Then we'd better find those documents. Our killer may have already killed three people."

She shook her head. "But Ridgeway couldn't have killed Lamden. From all accounts, Allison didn't meet his father until after she separated from Craig."

Steele issued a frustrated sigh. "I feel as if I'm running around in circles. Nothing in this case is what it appears. We'll question Ridgeway in the morning. By then the police should have finished their questioning. Maybe Hawk will also have some information for us."

She shivered. "It gives me goose bumps just thinking about being in that office with him. I've never been so scared in my life."

Steele had been staring at her. Now he put his cup down and said, "Whoever the killer is, he's a very desperate man. He kills very easily. Probably whenever he feels threatened. I don't want you going off and doing any more investigating on your own."

She didn't want to argue with him, but there was no way she would let him talk to her like a two-year-old kid. "You don't own me, Steele. I can do whatever I want, whenever I want."

"No, you can't," he snapped. He ran his hand over his hair and looked her straight in the eyes. "In case you've forgotten, burglary is a felony, punishable in this state by up to twenty years in prison." His words were hard and sharp, like a knife. "I told you that I didn't want to deal with Norris. Yet you went behind my back. Why?" His demeanor was that of defense attorney questioning a hostile witness. From the expression on his face, she knew he was not going to be satisfied until he got an answer to his question.

Tell him, an inner voice whispered. For a moment she considered telling him, but then decided now was not the right time. Not after this most recent incident. She'd tell him tomorrow.

"It was wrong to go behind your back, but you left me no other choice," she said. "You were positive she didn't know anything."

"Okay, I was wrong." He ran a hand over his hair in frustration. "But what you did was stupid and dangerous...." His words trailed off, and he reached out to take her arms, then abruptly pulled her against him, his arms closing tightly around her. "My God, Taylor, when I think of you alone in there..."

She closed her eyes, fighting the images that flashed in her mind's eye. "I had to do something. Tailing Norris was the only thing I could think of doing. And after what's happened, I'm more convinced than ever that those documents Allison left with Lamden will identity our blackmail victim—and maybe our killer."

Steele shook his head. "Maybe. Or maybe someone wants us to *think* Allison was killed by her blackmail victim. I'm not so sure anymore. If Lamden was murdered, it puts a whole different slant on things."

Taylor looked at him curiously. "How so?"

He shrugged his shoulders in an offhanded way. "Just a hunch."

"I don't believe it. *You* have hunches?"

"You're real cute." He gave her a wry smile. "All defense attorneys play hunches. But our hunches are grounded in years of experience in defense work, not some harebrained idea."

Harebrained! Taylor's temper flared. "If you think I'm a harebrain, why are you here?"

The look he gave her could have melted steel. "You know the answer to that," he said in a husky voice.

Taylor didn't know what to say.

"Taylor," he said in that same husky voice, "you have to promise me you won't take any more chances like you did tonight."

"I don't know...." Her voice broke.

He came closer and placed his hands on her shoulders, pulling her around to face him despite her resistance. He waited until she looked at him. "Let Hawk do the investigating, sweetheart. He does that quite well. I promise to be more open-minded. I don't want any secrets between us."

Tell him, that inner voice urged again, but the words stuck in her throat. She didn't want to spoil the moment.

She dropped her head, and he slid his hand up under her throat, lifting her chin. His fingertips were warm on her skin, and Taylor stiffened, resisting not the warmth, but the way it made her feel.

Everything inside her tensed at the look in his eyes. Before she could move, Steele gripped her upper arms and dragged her against his hard body.

"I don't want to fight anymore, Taylor," he whispered before his mouth covered hers in a passionate kiss.

She knew she ought to push him away, not make love while this secret lay between them. But the slow stroking of his tongue touched a need deep in her being, and she could no longer deny the realization that she had feelings for this man. Strong feelings. And she responded with a passion that shocked her. Hot and hungry, his mouth captured hers, mingling desire with something nameless.

Minutes passed, and nothing else existed beyond their mutual desire and exploration of each other. Finally Steele dragged his mouth away. He looked down at her with eyes that were dark with passion.

"There's so much you don't know about me," she began.

Steele smiled and gazed down at her. "I know everything I need to know about you. You're warm and kind and intelligent."

"Steele," she began. "We need to talk—" He cut off her words with a finger on her lips.

"No more talking," he said huskily. "I want to make love to you."

Common sense told her to call a halt to their lovemaking before it was too late. But it was already too late. She wanted to make love with him—wanted it more than anything she'd ever wanted in her life. It felt so right.

For now she would push her fears aside and pretend she was a normal woman engaged in a relationship. She smiled up at him as she traced his lips with a feather-like finger. "I think we'd be more comfortable in the bedroom," she said softly.

He gave her a joyous laugh, swung her up into his arms, carried her to the bedroom and laid her on the bed.

Afterward he was never sure how he'd extracted Taylor from her skirt and blouse or when he'd stripped off his shirt and trousers. What he did remember with aching clarity was the first sight of her naked body lying beside him, the slender legs, the narrow waist, the full, satiny breasts.

"You're more beautiful than I could have imagined," he said, looking down at her until she was trembling with need, longing to be joined with him. He quickly took a small packet out of the back pocket of his trousers and slipped it on.

"Now we're ready," he said in a passionate whisper. Then he gently lowered himself onto her and gathered her close, letting her feel every plane and angle of him.

She caught her breath as she felt his strong thighs nudge hers apart and his hardness poised on the brink of her feminine core. He hesitated long enough to make sure she could accept him without discomfort. That consideration, even in the face of overwhelming need, touched her deeply. Then he slowly entered her and paused, deep inside.

After a moment he began to move. Slowly at first. Then harder, faster, deeper as her body instinctively matched his rhythm. She felt the impact of him throughout her body... hot, demanding, deliciously overpowering. He was like a flame burning into her. She gasped and couldn't stop to catch her breath, the feelings were so intense.

She ached to speak the words of her heart, but sensed he was not ready to hear them and she wasn't ready to say them. Instead, she held him close, stroking his head, his back.

When the electricity coursed through her body, warning of the impending climax, she heard herself cry out his name and heard his answering cry as if from a distance. Totally spent, he raised his head and kissed her, then he laid his head on her breasts. "That was heaven," he sighed.

"I never knew it could be so wonderful," she whispered softly, stroking his back.

"It will always be wonderful between us," he promised, knowing he would never tire of her. He rolled off her body and pulled her into his arms.

Tell him, that inner voice whispered, but a stronger, more powerful voice whispered, *Tell him later. Why spoil this magic moment?* She contented herself with curling up into his strong, protective arms. She sighed as she thought again of the joy they'd shared. She felt an overwhelming sense of happiness and completion.

She was just nodding off when she was startled awake by the jangle of the telephone. She felt Steele lean over to answer it. Then she heard the receiver being lifted and Steele's quiet voice.

She kept her eyes closed, not wanting the magic to fade.

"No apologies necessary," Steele said after a moment. "I agree this may put a whole new slant on the investigation."

Taylor's eyes flew open at that last statement, and all vestiges of sleep left her as her heart began pounding. She turned to look at Steele, who sat on the other side of the bed with his back to her.

"We'll question him in the morning," Steele said. He returned the receiver to its cradle, then ran a hand over his face and swore under his breath.

"Steele?" she said softly. "What is it?"

He turned to look at her. "That was Hawk. We got a problem. Norris located Betsy Boyd."

"How?" she asked.

"Through one of the secretaries at Jasper and Kline. Norris was able to jog her memory with the offer of a huge sum of money. That was about a week ago. Mr. Jasper heard about it earlier today and called Hawk." He gave her a wry smile. "That was the bad news—now for the good news. We now know what Allison was holding over Daniel Ridgeway's head."

She held her breath as she waited for him to continue.

He paused for a moment and shook his head, almost as if he had difficulty believing it himself. Then he sighed and said, "Daniel Ridgeway was having an affair with Allison."

STEELE AND TAYLOR SAT on the couch in the Ridgeway mansion and watched an agitated Daniel Ridgeway pace back and forth.

"We're sorry to barge in on you like this," Steele said. "Especially since you were probably up late answering questions for the police about what you were doing at Vanessa Norris's office last night.''

Ridgeway lit a cigarette and inhaled deeply. ''Not that it's any business of yours, but I went there to discuss an article she wanted to do on my father.''

Ridgeway's hand shook. The poor man was almost a basket case, Steele noted.

''That's what you were talking about in the parking lot of the Southtown Mall, then later at her office last night?''

Fear, stark and vivid, glittered in his eyes. ''I—I don't know what you're talking about.''

Steele shook his head slowly. ''That's a lie! You were observed by at least three people—Ms. Quinlan and my investigator saw you meeting with her in the mall parking lot, and I saw you running from the television station right before the body was discovered.''

Ridgeway nibbled on his lower lip, troubled eyes finally resting on Steele's. ''You're mistaken. I left earlier....''

''You may think you've fooled Donaldson, but he's not going to just take your word for why you were there. He's going to check out your claim and when he does, he's going to find that you lied. Things will go a lot easier for you if you tell the truth now.''

''Oh, God,'' he moaned, slumping into a nearby chair and dropping his head in his hands. ''I didn't kill her,'' he moaned. ''She was dead when I got there.''

For a moment no one said anything. Then Taylor said slowly, ''Tell us what you were doing there.''

He drew a deep, ragged breath. ''Norris called me. She said she wanted to talk to me about Allison. I could tell from the way she sounded, sort of smug, that she knew.''

''About your affair with Allison?''

Ridgeway's head snapped up. ''Yes, but you can't tell my father any of this.'' He stood and began pacing back and forth again. ''It would kill him.'' He paused and looked at them with the eyes of a man who'd been to hell and back.

"Donaldson is going to do a thorough investigation and he's bound to find out," Steele said. "I think before he does, you should tell your father."

"I didn't mean for any of this to happen," Ridgeway moaned. "I knew what she was like, but she was so beautiful and she made me ..." His voice trailed off.

"How long did the affair last?" Steele asked.

Ridgeway gave a bitter little laugh. "I'm not sure you could even call it an affair. It was more a series of one-night stands over a two-month period." He clutched his hands together. "I didn't mean for it to happen. I went to see her to tell her to lay off Dad and instead I ended up betraying him." He looked at them. "I broke it off."

"But it wasn't that easy, was it?" Steele asked.

Ridgeway shook his head. "No, it wasn't. She threatened to tell Dad about us if I did anything to interfere with their coming marriage."

"Like insisting that she sign a prenuptial agreement?" Taylor prompted.

He gave her a bleak look and nodded. "Yes."

"Did she ask for any money?"

Ridgeway shook his head. "I wish she had," he said bitterly. "I offered it, but she just laughed and said she was going to have plenty when she married Dad." He stared at his hands. "I'm not proud of it but I did back off at first. When I saw how she was using Dad. Laughing behind his back with her lover. I couldn't do it. I went to her house the day of the murder and—"

"Don't say another word," a voice barked. They were so engrossed in Daniel Ridgeway's narrative, no one had heard Gordon Ridgeway enter the room. He crossed the room and stood next to his son.

Daniel Ridgeway cringed. "How long have you been there?" he asked his father.

"Long enough. I heard everything."

Daniel's mouth worked, and at first no words came out as his emotions welled up within him. "Dad, I'm sorry." He covered his face with his hands.

Gordon placed a hand on his son's shoulder. "Mr. Steele, my son's no killer. He didn't kill Allison or that reporter. If he's guilty of anything, it's of caring too much about a foolish old man."

"You knew about the affair, didn't you?" Steele asked.

Gordon nodded. He took a seat on the sofa. "I must admit when I first met Allison, I was smitten, but as time went by, I began to have second thoughts about marrying her. I guess she thought I was a doddering old fool, that I'd turn a blind eye on her unfaithfulness." He sighed. "I knew something had happened between her and my son."

"You sure she didn't want you to know?"

He shook his head. "I'm sorry to say, she simply thought I was not smart enough to notice. But I did and I hired a private investigator. First to find out what, if anything, was going on between them. And second to get something I could use against her when I broke off our engagement. I knew she'd kick up a fuss if I tried to break things off. I needed some ammunition to protect myself and my son from her wrath." He handed Steele a large manila folder. "I think the information in there will show you that Allison had quite a history of romancing older men for the sole purpose of relieving them of their money."

Steele glanced briefly at the documents inside. "Why didn't you take this to the police?" he asked.

Gordon cleared his throat. "Allison was dead. I didn't want to have to answer a lot of embarrassing questions about how or why I acquired the information."

Steele turned to the son. "You were saying the day of the murder, you talked to Allison."

"Mr. Steele, my son didn't kill Allison." Gordon Ridgeway pointed to the documents in Steele's hand. "My private investigator tracked my son's every movement during the period Allison was murdered. His report supports my son's alibi claim."

Steele quickly scanned the report and had to agree. Daniel Ridgeway couldn't have killed Allison. In the last twenty-four hours, they'd excluded both Denning and Ridgeway. That only left Ted Larson. But Larson had an airtight alibi. Steele ran his hand over his hair in frustration, then turned again to the son. "How did she react when you told her you wouldn't keep quiet anymore?"

Daniel frowned. "That's the strange part. I was prepared for her to be angry, and she was, but not to the extent she should have been." He thought for a moment. "She seemed preoccupied and rushed me out. She said something about hooking a big one."

Steele frowned. That was the same thing she'd said to Trebeck the day of the murder. It had meant something to Allison, but what?

"THINK, HEATHER," Taylor said. "You and Allison went shopping the day of the murder. Are you sure she didn't say anything to you about 'hooking a big one'?"

"I don't think so." Heather looked totally bewildered, and Taylor couldn't blame her. They'd left the Ridgeways and gone straight to the McCalls. Heather had been one of the last people to see Allison alive the day of the murder. Allison must have said something to her. She just prayed Heather would remember it and the context in which it had been said. Heather remembered with amazing clarity the stores they had frequented, where they'd lunched, even what they'd purchased, but when it came to any actual conversation, she drew a total blank.

"I don't understand any of this," Heather whined. Matt put his arms around her.

"Do you think there's some connection between Vanessa Norris's murder and Allison?" Matt asked.

Taylor nodded. "There appears to be."

Craig sighed. "Well, the cops can't pin that one on me. I was right here. Matt can vouch for me."

"It's actually to your advantage for them to connect the cases," Matt noted. "If they do, surely you'd be excluded. You—"

Before he could finish the sentence, Donaldson barged into the room, two uniformed officers on either side of him.

Matt was on his feet immediately. "What is the meaning of this?"

"Sit down, Counselor," Donaldson growled. He turned toward Steele, and his mouth curved into what might have passed for a grin. "Good, I'm glad you're here. I wouldn't want you to miss the show."

The hair on the back of Taylor's neck stood up at the tone of his voice.

"Cut the crap," Steele said. "What do you want?"

"Mind if I sit down?" Donaldson said, though Taylor noticed he didn't bother to wait for an answer before plopping into the chair next to the sofa. "I'm here to arrest your client."

Craig's eyes grew as round as saucers. "But I didn't kill anyone!"

"Don't say another word!" Steele cautioned. He turned to Donaldson. "What are the charges?"

"First-degree murder in the death of Allison Jane Barrett."

"But he didn't kill anyone," Matt insisted, coming to his friend's defense. "Craig wouldn't hurt a fly."

"Oh, we've got plenty of evidence to the contrary," Donaldson replied. "Not to mention the security folks at Allison's condo located the tape from the surveillance camera outside her condo from the night of the murder. It showed a man that roughly matches Barrett's description leaving the condo the night of the murder. Then there is the undisputed fact that he doesn't have an alibi."

Steele shook his head. "Donaldson, I'm surprised at you. There is no way State Attorney Marshall is going to bring an indictment against Craig on such flimsy circumstantial evidence. He'll be laughed out of court."

Donaldson slapped his forehead in mock surprise. "Oh, didn't I tell you? We found the murder weapon. It was a fireplace poker, just like we suspected."

Taylor sucked in her breath and waited for the next shoe to drop.

"We got an anonymous call a few hours ago that suggested we search Barrett's house and Mrs. Barrett's condo again. We found the poker at Barrett's house during our search." He grinned. "It had been wiped clean, but forensic was able to detect traces of the deceased's blood and hair on the poker."

"That's impossible!" Craig yelled, his head swiveling from Steele's to Donaldson's. "I didn't kill Allison!"

"It's a plant," Steele insisted. "Don't you recognize a frame-up when you see it?"

Donaldson shook his head. "Maybe. But that wouldn't explain the tape we also found during the second search of the condo." He nodded to one of the uniforms who pulled out a tape recorder and placed it on the cocktail table and pressed the Play button. A female voice punctured the silence. "If you're listening to this tape," the woman said, "then I'm dead. I have lived in fear for my life since I left my husband, Craig Barrett. He has sworn to kill me and I know he will. If I had known of his violent past, I never would have married him...."

"It's a lie!" Craig yelled, jumping to his feet. "None of that stuff she's saying is true. You've got to believe me!"

Donaldson clicked off the tape recorder. "Craig Barrett, we're arresting you for the murder of your wife, Allison Barrett."

Taylor watched, horrified, as Craig was handcuffed and read his *Miranda* rights. "You have the right to remain silent. If you give up that right, anything you say can and will be used against you in a court of law...."

Chapter Eleven

"There is no way in hell that's Allison on that tape," Steele said. He paced back and forth, agitated. They'd accompanied Craig to the police station and begun the procedural steps to get him released on bail, although the likelihood of that happening was slim to none. The prosecutor was opposing bail on the grounds that Craig was likely to flee the country. Now they were back at Taylor's apartment, laying out strategy for the coming preliminary hearing. "We need to get a copy of that tape so we can perform a voice analysis. Talk to Craig and Matt, see if you can find an audio of Allison's voice."

Taylor looked up at him. "What about her answering-machine tape?"

Steele nodded approvingly. "That should do it." He paused in his pacing. "I knew Donaldson was itching to arrest Craig, but I never thought he'd rush to judgment like this and do such a sloppy job of investigating the murder. There's as much evidence pointing to his innocence as there is to his guilt. And that drivel about an anonymous caller is a crock. Donaldson has been on the force long enough to recognize a setup."

"You don't believe they just overlooked the poker and tape during the first search?"

Steele gave her a hard look. "I don't believe in coincidences. The police get an anonymous phone call and as a result go back and search Craig's house and the condo.

This time they not only find the murder weapon but that tape, as well." He shook his head. "That evidence was planted. I'd stake my life on it."

"But proving it isn't going to be easy," Taylor added. "The grounds at Craig's house are secure. It would have been next to impossible for anyone to have gotten in and out of there undetected. And we doubled the security at the condo after the break-in."

He nodded. "I know, but somehow the killer got in both places. I refuse to believe that Craig had anything to do with Allison's murder or the other murders, for that matter."

Tell him, an inner voice whispered. She closed her eyes, trying to think of a way to broach the subject.

"And now we've got that damn tape to worry about," Steele continued. "It's a powerful piece of evidence in the prosecutor's arsenal. Symbolically you've got the murder victim reaching out from the grave, naming her killer. There's no way a jury hearing that tape will render anything but a guilty verdict." He issued a weary sigh and sat next to her. "We're dealing with a very cunning killer, but he slipped up when he added that garbage about Craig's alleged history of violence. I'm going to take that point and drive a truck through this frame-up."

Tell him. Things had gone too far. She couldn't let him continue believing a lie, couldn't allow him to step into a courtroom with a distorted picture of the facts. No matter what happened, she had to tell him the whole story.

In a voice filled with equal parts of pain and hope, she said, "Maybe it isn't a lie."

He sighed and pulled her close to his side. "It has to be," he said, rubbing her back. "Craig doesn't have a history of violence. You said yourself that other than that instance of juvenile behavior more than a decade ago, he has no history of violence, right?"

It was time to come clean. Past time. She shook her head. "No, it's not."

She felt the change in him immediately. One minute he was stroking her back, then in the next, he'd gone rigid.

He took her by the shoulders and turned her so that she was facing him. "What did you say?" The words were spoken softly, but she could hear the force behind them.

"I said he does have a history of violence." She drew a deep breath and looked at Steele. Her eyes pleaded for understanding. "As you know, Craig has a reputation for being quick-tempered and impulsive. Before Allison's murder, people chalked his behavior up to an artistic temperament."

He nodded, his mouth a grim, straight line.

"But what was dismissed as artistic temperament may have been in fact evidence of an unstable personality." Taylor swallowed as she began the more difficult part of what she had to tell him. "You know Craig's father committed suicide," she continued. "What you don't know is that his father was mentally ill. As a result of the disease, there were several violent episodes during his marriage. Culminating with him trying to kill his wife before taking his own life."

Steele sat perfectly still, but his hazel eyes conveyed his mounting fury. "There's nothing like that in the official police report."

"Aunt Ida didn't tell anyone what really happened— not the police and certainly not Craig."

"Then how do you know?" Steele asked, his tone challenging.

The way he was looking at her made her want to jump up and run out of the room, but she remained seated. She licked her lips. "I guess that kind of secret is too much for anyone to bear. She had to tell someone."

Steele shook his head, trying to take it in. "That doesn't make sense. She told you but didn't tell her own son. What does he think happened?"

"As far as Craig knows, his parents separated. Uncle Bob wanted a reconciliation and, when Aunt Ida refused to take him back, he took his life. You have to understand, Craig adored his father and blamed his mother for the separation. Then when his father took his life...well, he was devastated. There was no way Aunt

Ida was going to tell him what really happened, that what Uncle Bob had planned was a murder-suicide." Her voice shook with the force of her emotions, and she prayed he would understand and forgive her for not telling him the whole story earlier.

"Aunt Ida covered for him for years. Behavior the family thought of as eccentric and impulsive was really symptomatic of—of mental illness." Now came the difficult part. She swallowed hard. "Aunt Ida never told Craig, but there's a good chance he may have inherited this mental condition from his dad."

For a moment Steele didn't say anything, but his eyes spoke volumes. He looked at her as if he'd never seen her before. "Let me get this straight," he said in a voice taut with anger. "You're telling me Craig may be mentally ill and as a result violent? Yet his own mother never told him or sought any medical treatment for him?"

Taylor shifted uncomfortably under his intense scrutiny. "She thought she was doing what was right. I'm not sure he would have even believed her if she'd told him. For a long time after Uncle Bob died, they weren't close. It's only been in recent years that they have been able to put the past behind them and forge any kind of relationship. I'm sure from her perspective, she didn't see any need to say anything since there weren't any signs of mental illness." She paused and looked at him, her eyes pleading for understanding. "I'm sorry I didn't tell you the whole story before, but I couldn't betray my aunt's confidence."

Steele turned a disparaging smile on her. "What were you going to do? Let me go on indefinitely believing there was no history of violence in Craig's background?"

"No! No. I was going to tell you—"

"When?" His voice was hard and cold. "When we were confronted with the evidence at trial?"

"No, of course not. I—I tried to tell you a couple of times. Remember last night? I told you we needed to talk."

"But you didn't try very hard, did you?"

"No," she admitted shamefully, dropping her head.

There was a long pause before he spoke again, and when he did his voice was colder, harsher, more distant than she had ever heard before. "You've had weeks to tell me, but suddenly you were going to come clean and tell me the truth? Why should I believe you?"

Her head snapped up. "Because it's the truth. I care a great deal about you and I knew we needed to get this behind us."

He closed his eyes, shutting off the image of the pain he saw in her eyes. He wouldn't let her tears touch him. He hardened his heart. "You lied before. Why should I believe you now?"

"I never lied," she protested.

"No," he agreed coldly. "You just conveniently decided to withhold certain information, didn't you?"

On his lips it sounded so calculating, so deceitful. "Yes," she whispered.

"You know how important trust is to me, and you still didn't come clean, did you?"

"I wanted to but I was afraid."

"Afraid?" He gave her a skeptical look.

"Of how you might react. Afraid of what you would think of me...." She looked at him then. "My mother and Craig's father were twins. And according to Aunt Ida, my mother..." She swallowed the lump in her throat. "The car accident that killed my parents was no accident. My mother deliberately drove the car off the road."

She heard his quick indrawn breath, and something flickered in the back of his eyes—sympathy, understanding, concern? She couldn't be sure. The only thing she was sure of was that he was fighting an inner battle. Hope soared inside her, but when he spoke she knew she'd lost. "You thought I would reject you because your mother was mentally ill? You don't think much of me, do you?" His eyes were hard and cold.

Incredulously his lips drew back in something that could have been a smile, but only if the observer was generous. "The woman I thought of as honest to a fault. The woman I would have bet my life would never lie, is a liar."

"Steele . . . please. I know you're hurt and angry. I can see it in your eyes, but please, please . . . don't take your feelings for me out on Craig. He didn't know—"

"How dare you even *think* I would do such a thing!" he barked. "I took this case because I believe Craig is innocent. And I still believe it. I'm not going to abandon him now because you withheld information vital to his defense. Do you think I would walk away from him because his cousin is a consummate liar?" He raked a hand over his hair and looked away as though he couldn't stand the sight of her right then. When his gaze came back to her, he looked even angrier than before. "I'mv going to get Craig off, and you're going to help me. And after that, I never want to see you again." He stormed out of the apartment.

TAYLOR HAD NO IDEA how long she stood in the middle of her living room, staring at the door Steele had slammed so hard it rattled the hinges. She had no idea how long she would have to remain there until the numbness faded, until she could pick up the pieces of her heart, not to go on living but merely to go on to the next minute, the next necessary heartbeat. But even if she could find all the broken pieces of her heart, which she doubted was possible, even if she could move to the next instant, how did she deal with the pain?

She swallowed a lump that had formed in her throat and bit back tears. She'd known trust was an issue with him but she really hoped he'd understand why she hadn't said anything and forgive her. But he'd reacted just as she feared. Her eyes filled with tears. She hadn't meant to hurt him. She really cared about Steele and she thought he cared about her, too.

God, she'd really made a mess of things. It was over between them. A glazed look of despair began to spread over her face at the thought of never seeing him again, of never being held by him. She shuddered inwardly and told herself she would have to go on with her life, but she knew she was lying to herself. In the brief time she'd known him, she'd come to depend on him, to care about him. She wrapped her arms around herself and stared blindly around the room.

Haltingly she took a step, but she couldn't have said whether it was forward or backward. She didn't want to sit, but she didn't want to stand. She didn't want to cry, but neither did she think she could stand this gut-wrenching pain. She didn't want to stay in the apartment, but couldn't bear to leave. She wanted . . . she wanted . . .

To run. To scream. To raise her fists at God or fate, whoever or whatever was controlling her destiny. She had tried to do the right thing, and it had blown up in her face. Steele was never going to forgive her. It was over between them. One tear fell, then another and another. Once the floodgates were opened, she couldn't stop. She sank slowly to the floor, rocking back and forth as she yielded to the compulsive sobs that shook her small frame. Just twenty-four hours ago, she'd been on top of the world. Now that same world had been torn asunder. How was she going to live with the pain?

AFTER STEELE LEFT Taylor's, he'd driven around for a while until he'd cooled down, then he'd called Hawk on the car phone. He'd outlined the situation to him.

He'd been surprised when Hawk had sided with Taylor. It was easy for Hawk to take this self-righteous attitude about forgiving and forgetting. It wasn't him that she had betrayed. *Betrayed* was a good word for it. He'd let his guard down, opened up his heart to her, and she'd trampled all over it. What other things hadn't she told him? he thought bitterly.

God, she'd really fooled him. The man who swore he would never be taken in again by a pretty face had been deceived. He'd thought her sweet and innocent and honest. An image of Taylor telling him about her parents flashed before him. He closed his eyes, blocking out the way she'd looked, her pain. He didn't want to feel sympathy or be understanding, and forced himself to think only of her deception.

She could tell herself that she'd withheld the information from him to protect her aunt and her parents' memory, but the reason really didn't matter. The bottom line was she'd withheld information that, if true, would be the final piece in the prosecutor's case.

He couldn't see how he was going to keep it out of the case. He could argue that it was irrelevant and inflammatory, but the prosecution was going to fight like mad to get it in. Hell, he'd do the same thing in their place. It was a powerful bit of information. The prosecution would use it to show the kind of violent environment Craig had grown up in and how that environment had influenced his later behavior. It went to motive—bolstering the prosecutor's theory that Craig had a propensity for violence. He'd point out to the jury that Craig's violence toward Allison was like the violence his father had inflicted on his mother. Once he sold them on that point, he'd bring out the murder-suicide angle. The jury would be led to infer: like father, like son.

Damn Taylor for withholding such damaging information, and damn him for missing it. He ran a hand over his hair in frustration. How the hell had he missed it? Well, what was done was done. What he needed to do was lay out a strategy for addressing it as soon as possible. He was going to have to explain it or discredit it, and there was only one way that he could effectively do that. He immediately thought of Taylor. What he had in mind, she wasn't going to like.

THE TENSION in the room was so thick you could cut it with a knife, Taylor thought, glancing about the brightly lit parlor. But the only outward sign Aunt Ida had given that she was aware of the trouble between her and Steele was a slight tremor in her hand when she'd passed the coffee cups.

"More tea?" Ida Barrett asked. Her nut brown face and sharp, dark eyes looked curiously from Taylor to Steele.

Taylor shook her head and wondered what her aunt was thinking. She would have had to be as thick as a brick not to notice that the two of them only spoke to each other when absolutely necessary.

It had been like that for the past week. She'd hoped that once he'd calmed down, they could talk. But he'd rebuffed all of her attempts to talk, and with each passing day, the gulf between them seemed to grow wider. She'd made a mistake but she wasn't going to beg. If he couldn't forgive her, she was just going to have to accept that it was over. Pain ripped through her at the thought and she was almost overwhelmed by grief. She swallowed hard and bit back tears as she tried to focus on the drama that was about to unfold.

When Steele had told her of his plans to question her aunt, she'd been adamant about sitting in. It was all right for him to be angry with her, but she wasn't about to let him badger her aunt and she'd told him just that. He'd reluctantly agreed to let her sit in on the interview.

"I'm sorry to bother you, Mrs. Barrett," Steele said from his seat on the love seat opposite them. "I know the past few days have been especially difficult for you, but there are several items that I need your help in clarifying."

"I'd do whatever I can," Mrs. Barrett replied.

Steele gave her a reassuring smile. "As you know, the prosecution is making much of that tape they found at Allison's house."

Mrs. Barrett nodded quickly. "It's terrible the things she said about him. It's not true, but people are bound to believe it."

"I'd have thought we didn't have to worry on that score, but now I'm not so sure." He glanced over at Taylor and he felt a twinge of conscience at what he was about to do. There was no easy way to say it, so he plunged right in. "It's come to my attention that Craig's father suffered from mental illness and as a result tried to kill you before taking his own life.''

Mrs. Barrett stood, her back to Steele and Taylor. ''I don't know where you got your information, but someone is pulling your leg.''

Steele sighed. He'd hoped she wouldn't make things any more difficult than they were already. ''Mrs. Barrett,'' he said gently, ''does your son suffer from mental illness?''

She whirled around like an angry tigress protecting her cub. ''Of course not! And I won't have you say such terrible things about him,'' she snapped.

Taylor rushed over to the visibly shaken woman and put an arm around her. ''It's okay, Aunt Ida,'' she said, trying to calm her. ''Steele knows. I had to tell him about Craig.''

She shook off Taylor's arms and pinned her with a pained look. ''How could you?'' she cried before turning on Steele. ''There's nothing wrong with Craig. He's a little temperamental and headstrong, but there's nothing wrong with that.''

Steele looked at Taylor, then back at her aunt. ''Are you saying it isn't true?''

''Of course it's not true!''

Taylor stared at her, shocked.

''If it isn't true, why did you tell Taylor that it was?'' Steele asked, frowning.

She ran a hand wearily across her forehead. ''Now isn't a good time to talk about this. I'm not feeling very well.''

''Mrs. Barrett, I know this is hard, but you're going to have to answer my questions. Either here or in a courtroom. The police have a tape, purportedly made by Allison, in which she not only accuses Craig of having a history of violent behavior but names him as her killer. The prosecution is going to use that tape to convict your son. You're the only person who knows the truth. I'll ask you again, did your husband suffer from mental illness?''

"That's none of your business!" Mrs. Barrett snapped.

Steele stared at her for a moment, and when he spoke, his voice was deadly calm. "None of my business? Your daughter-in-law has been murdered. Your son stands accused. I have to build a legal defense for your son, and if that means I ask questions about your personal life that you find embarrassing, so be it. *Everything* related to this case is my business." Steele gave Mrs. Barrett time for his words to sink in, then he went on. "You told Taylor that your husband was mentally ill and had a history of violence."

Mrs. Barrett closed her eyes and nodded faintly. "That's correct," she whispered.

"Did your husband tell you about his mental illness or was it the doctor?"

"The doctor."

Steele nodded. Now they were getting somewhere. "What was his name?"

"It was a long time ago," Mrs. Barrett replied vaguely. "I don't remember."

He gave her a skeptical look but didn't press. "What's the name of the hospital or clinic that he worked out of?"

"I don't remember that, either."

"Was it the same doctor that told you that there was a genetic basis to the disorder?"

"I don't know. It could have been. It was a long time ago."

Steele's eyes narrowed. "Give me a specific instance of a violent act that Craig committed that you witnessed."

She give him a bewildered look. "A violent act, uh, I don't remember."

Steele put his pen down and glared at her. "You don't remember a lot about something that has shaped your life and Taylor's, do you?" he said. He did nothing to hide his sarcasm.

"Steele, please," Taylor said.

"Taylor, stay out of this," he warned.

"Now, look," Taylor said, "I'm sorry I didn't tell you about our medical history, but I'm not going to let you browbeat my aunt." Her eyes flashed with anger, and he thought she'd never looked more beautiful.

His hazel eyes softened. "I'm only trying to get to the truth."

Mrs. Barrett wrapped her arms around her middle and began to rock back and forth.

"Okay," Steele said. "Let's start again. You said your husband tried to kill you. How did he do it?"

"I don't want to talk about it."

"Did he use a gun, a knife? How did he try to kill you?"

Mrs. Barrett turned pleading eyes to Taylor. "Make him stop!"

He could see the pain in Taylor's eyes as she tried to comfort the older woman. "Aunt Ida, we're not trying to be mean," she said gently. "We need to know what we're up against."

"She can't tell us because it never happened. Your husband did not try to kill you."

"It is true!" Mrs. Barrett's head swiveled from Steele to Taylor. "Bob tried to kill me."

"Then why is there no record anywhere to support your claim?" Steele challenged. "And before you say anything else, you should know I reviewed his military records, and there is no indication of mental illness. I also talked to Craig. He was seventeen when your husband died. Unlike Taylor, he was old enough to remember what happened. He says his father never laid a hand on you, that it was your possessiveness that drove him away."

Mrs. Barrett didn't respond.

Taylor's head swiveled from Steele to her aunt. "Aunt Ida, tell him!"

"Yes, Mrs. Barrett, tell me," Steele urged. "Tell us both what happened."

"I don't care what you think," Mrs. Barrett cried, jumping to her feet. "I know what happened. I was there." She looked like a caged animal. "My husband and my son..." Her voice broke and she turned her head to the side.

"Mrs. Barrett, don't you think there's been enough lies in this family? Isn't it time for the truth to come out?"

Mrs. Barrett didn't say anything.

"If you care anything about your son, you'll tell me the truth."

"I have," she moaned. "How many times do I have to say it?"

"Until I believe it," Steele went on. He waited until she'd regained a measure of control and then began again. "Mrs. Barrett," he said gently, "I know this is hard, but you've got to tell me what really happened. Your son's life may depend upon it. I can't build a defense based on lies and half truths. I need to know what happened all those years ago." He looked at Taylor. "No matter what."

There was a long pause before Ida Barrett finally spoke. "Everyone I loved left. First Bob, then Craig. After Bob died, I was lost. I couldn't talk to Craig. I had no one and then you came." She looked at Taylor and smiled through her tears. "Your parents were dead. You needed me. For the first time in a long time I had someone who needed me." She paused for a moment and when she began again, her voice had a pleading, desperate quality. "I loved you and wanted to keep you safe. But as you got older, I could see the same things happening with you that happened with Bob and Craig."

"What was that?" Steele asked gently.

She gave Taylor a sad look. "That you were drifting away. Soon you wouldn't need me anymore. I had to do something." Her eyes locked with Taylor's, pleading for understanding. "At the time it seemed the only way..."

Taylor looked at her horrified. "W-what are you saying?"

Steele slid an arm around her, but nothing could lessen the impact of Ida Barrett's words when they came.

"I made the whole thing up."

IT HAD ALL BEEN A LIE! Hours later Taylor was still reeling from the shock. Steele had driven her home but hadn't questioned her about her aunt's revelation. He wanted to give her time to absorb the shock.

She'd been sitting on the living room sofa for the past hour, not saying a word since he'd brought her home. It was beginning to trouble him. She'd just experienced a devastating loss—the trust of one of the people she loved most in the world. He knew personally how painful that could be and that it was probably best to talk about it. Yet she was holding everything inside, probably the way she'd always done.

"Do you want me to make you something to eat?" he asked. He sat in one of the leather armchairs across from her, fighting the urge to pull her into his arms.

"No," she said, wrapping her arms around her, staring off into space.

He knew she was hurting and he wanted to chase away the pain, tell her it would be all right—that she should talk about it, not hold the pain inside to fester and grow.

Yet he didn't have the right to make her open up to him. Not when he'd told her he didn't want to have anything to do with her once the case was over. Not when he still couldn't say the things he knew she wanted to hear. But as he examined her ashen face, she looked as if she'd shatter if she moved too fast. She needed to get it all out so she could move on.

His eyes followed her as she stood and walked to the window, staring out.

"Taylor, for God's sake, stop it!"

She didn't respond, just continued to stare blindly out the window.

"You've got to talk to someone about what happened. It might as well be me."

When she still didn't reply, he forced himself to continue. "You've had a shock. You need to talk about it—get it out." He paused, then continued. "You have every right to be hurt and angry. What your aunt did was wrong. I don't know what kind of relationship the two of you will have in the future. Maybe none. Now you're thinking only of the hurt and pain her lie has caused you, but don't forget the good times and that she loves you very much. And remember this—her lie was prompted out of her love for you." Even as he spoke the words, he could see the irony of the situation. Here he was trying to get Taylor to understand her aunt's motivtion, when he hadn't extended the same courtesy to her. He felt deeply ashamed.

For a long time Taylor didn't say anything. "How could she have lied like that?" she said, finally. Her voice sounded as hurt and bewildered as a small child's. "I questioned Craig's innocence because of her."

Steele let out the breath he'd been holding. "What did you say the other day? She did the best she knew how. Mrs. Barrett loves you very much and she made a mistake."

"But she lied," Taylor said in a low, tortured voice, "not just about Craig and Uncle Bob but about my mother. She made me afraid to love my own mother."

Levering himself out of the chair, he crossed to where she stood and folded her into his arms. For a moment she stiffened. Then, with a tiny sound that was half sigh, half sob, she turned and slumped against him.

She pressed her head against his chest, and he could feel the beat of his heart thumping against her cheek. After a while he lifted her up in his arms and sat down again with her in his lap, cradling her protectively. But he didn't press her to talk.

Long moments later she began on her own.

He didn't say anything. Just let her talk. She told him about all the things she'd given up: dating, best girl-friends, the junior and senior prom, all the things that a young girl generally did. The words were fierce, but he held her tenderly, rocking her in his arms, kissing her hair and her forehead, giving her all the comfort he could. When the words stopped, the tears began. He blinked back his own tears and held her close, trying to absorb her pain.

After a few moments she stopped crying, but she kept her face hidden against his chest. He wished he could say that they could pick up where they'd left off a week before, but he couldn't. While he could forgive her, he didn't think he could forget.

Chapter Twelve

Steele surveyed the crowded courtroom, then leaned over to engage in a hurried conference with Taylor.

"Ben Marshall, the State's Attorney, is going to take charge of the preliminary hearing," he whispered. "That means the state is pulling out its big guns to ensure an indictment—not that it's going to be all that difficult to get. At this hearing, all they have to show is that a crime was committed and that there is probable cause to believe that Craig committed it. I can't see—"

"All rise for the Honorable Edwin Werner," cried the bailiff's deep male voice.

The door from the judge's chambers opened, and Judge Werner walked into the courtroom and took his place on the bench. Werner, in his early forties, had dark hair flecked with gray, a strong nose, drawn cheeks and huge bags beneath his eyes. He was a slight man even encumbered in the black robe of his office.

"The matter before the court," the judge said, "is a preliminary hearing in file 1373, entitled *State of Illinois versus Craig Thomas Barrett*. The record should reflect the defendant is represented by counsel, Michael Steele and Taylor Quinlan. The state is represented by State's Attorneys Benjamin Marshall and Richard Deaver. I am Judge Edwin Werner. Is the state ready to proceed?"

State Attorney Marshall exchanged a glance with his co-counsel, who was seated beside him at the prosecution table. On the defense side, Steele sat nearest the prosecutors, with Taylor next to him and Craig on the far side. Matt sat a row behind, ready to assist.

Benjamin Marshall stood. "Your Honor, the people are ready."

"Is the defense ready?" Judge Werner asked.

Steele was on his feet immediately, his manner cool, controlled, confident. "The defense is ready to proceed, Your Honor."

Judge Werner nodded, then looked out on the crowded room, focusing on the reporters and camera crew that jammed the back and one side of the room. "Before we begin, I want to state that there has been a lot of newspaper and television coverage of this case, about the facts and about the people involved. I want to caution the spectators that this is not a show, this is not a debate, this is not entertainment. This is a court of law. The spectators will conduct themselves accordingly—otherwise, the court will take steps to ensure proper decorum." He paused, then looked about the courtroom. "Mr. Marshall, please call your first witness."

"Thank you, Your Honor. The State calls Deputy Coroner James Kingsley to the stand."

Dr. Kingsley identified himself as the deputy coroner for the city of Chicago. Marshall then walked him through the night of Allison's murder. He explained what he observed at the crime scene, stated the time and cause of death and outlined the autopsy results. His testimony was consistent with the testimony he'd given at the coroner's inquest. Then it was time for the defense to cross-examine the witness.

"Dr. Kingsley," Steele said, taking his place at the podium. "You testified at the coroner's inquest and here today that Allison Barrett was killed between ten-thirty and eleven-thirty. Is that when death actually occurred, or is that an estimated time of death?"

Taylor knew where Steele was headed. Establishing the time of death was critical in any murder case, doubly so in this one. If they could get the coroner to admit that the murder could have occurred closer to eleven-thirty, the prosecution would have a harder time proving that Craig had the opportunity to kill Allison. Pam Olsen would testify he was with her at midnight.

Dr. Kingsley peered over his bifocals at Steele. "It's an approximation." He leaned back in his chair. "It's impossible to establish the exact time of death of any murder victim unless that murder is actually witnessed. Otherwise, only a reasonable estimation can be made, usually within a range of hours or days at best."

Steele nodded, then walked toward the witness box. "Please tell the court how you arrived at your estimation."

Dr. Kingsley leaned forward slightly. "The police found the body at eleven forty-five. A neighbor indicated that the victim was alive at ten-thirty. He was certain of the time because of a television program he was watching. So death would have had to have occurred between ten-thirty and eleven-thirty. But since the neighbor heard a struggle around ten-thirty, I believe death occurred shortly thereafter."

"So in other words," Steele said smoothly, "you arrived at the time of death based on when a TV program was on?"

There was a slight tittering in the courtroom that Judge Werner pounded to silence. Taylor smiled. Steele was making the county coroner look incompetent.

Dr. Kingsley coughed and shifted uncomfortably in his chair. "Ah, but under the circumstances, I believe—"

"Just answer yes or no."

"Yes," Dr. Kingsley admitted grudgingly.

Steele then got the coroner to admit he'd failed to conduct several tests that would have provided a scientific basis for approximating the time of death.

"So, Dr. Kingsley," Steele continued, "the death could have occurred at eleven?"

"That's correct."

"Or as late as eleven-thirty?"

"Yes," the coroner replied. He took a handkerchief out of his pocket and mopped his brow.

"Thank you, Dr. Kingsley." Steele smiled. "No further questions."

Taylor looked at Steele as he resumed his seat. He'd just gotten the coroner to admit that death could have occurred at a time more advantageous for the defense, but they were still a long way from exonerating Craig.

Next to testify was the patrol officer who had testified at the coroner's inquest. Marshall led him through virtually the same testimony he'd given earlier: how he'd found the body and secured the crime scene.

Judge Werner looked toward the defense table. "Does the defense wish to cross-examine?"

Cross-examination at this time wouldn't be worth the effort required to ask the questions, Taylor knew, and waited for Steele to waive.

Steele appeared to study a few tidbits he'd jotted down on a legal pad, but Taylor knew it was all for show. She had learned enough about him in the past eight weeks to know he had a nearly photographic memory and could recall every word the cop had said as easily as if he'd had a tape recorder. Steele's pretended study of his inconsequential notes was designed to create a brief period of silence, to make the judge, the prosecution and the spectators wonder what was coming next.

"No questions," Steele said finally.

Marshall threw Steele a sour look before calling Lee Trebeck to the stand.

Taylor wasn't sure who was more nervous, herself or Trebeck. She would be doing his cross-examination. *Surprised* was an understatement of how she'd felt when Steele had asked her. It was so out of character. He'd never let any co-counsel question witnesses before. Try as she might, she couldn't help but believe that it was a crack in the wall he'd erected around his emotions.

Trebeck looked like a nervous rabbit as he took the stand and was sworn in. He slowly began to relax as he told the court about hearing a loud argument coming from Allison's condo, becoming concerned, calling the police, then seeing the man as he looked out the window.

Marshall folded his arms and appeared to be thinking about his next question. "What was the man doing?"

"He looked like he was running away from Allison's condo, uh, I mean Mrs. Barrett."

Taylor was on her feet immediately. "Objection. Speculation."

"Sustained."

Marshall frowned. "How far away was the man you saw?"

"Not very far. Just at the end of the street. About seventy-five feet."

"Could you see the man clearly?"

Trebeck's head bobbed up and down. "He was near the streetlight, so I could see him pretty good."

"Please describe the man you saw for the court."

Trebeck shifted in his seat and folded his hands across his middle. "He was tall, about six feet with a lean, muscular build. I could tell he was young by the way he moved—real fast."

"This man. Was he about the same height and build as anyone you are now looking at?"

"Objection," Taylor said. "Leading and suggestive."

"Objection sustained."

"Well, how would you describe him?" Marshall asked.

"Objection," Taylor said again. "Already asked and answered."

"Sustained."

"Had you ever seen the man before?"

"Yes, sir," Trebeck said, his head swiveling in the direction of the defense table. "It was the defendant, Craig Barrett."

Taylor threw Steele a grim look. Trebeck's memory had undergone a drastic improvement.

There was a buzz throughout the courtroom, and Judge Werner pounded it to silence.

"No further questions, Your Honor," Ben Marshall said. A smile played around his lips as he walked back to the prosecution table. "Your witness."

Taylor stood and walked over to the witness box. "Mr. Trebeck, you testified at the coroner's inquest that you couldn't identify the man you saw, but today you claim the man you saw was the defendant?"

Trebeck looked nervous, but his voice was strong when he spoke. "I always thought it was Mr. Barrett that I saw. I didn't say so before because I wanted to be sure. Now I am."

"And just what makes you so sure?" Taylor said sarcastically.

"Objection," Marshall boomed. "Counsel is badgering the witness."

"I withdraw the question," Taylor said calmly. "Now, Mr. Trebeck, was the man you saw standing directly under the streetlight or some distance away?"

"He was a few feet away."

"So he was sort of in the shadows?"

"That's right."

"You testified a moment ago the man appeared to be running away. Is that correct?"

Trebeck's head bobbed up and down. "Y-yes."

"If the man you saw wasn't standing directly in the light and he was moving quickly away from you, how do you know that it was the defendant that you saw?"

"Because he had on the same kind of jogging clothes that Mr. Barrett often wore when he came over."

"In other words, the man you saw that night was a man of about the same height and build as the defendant, and wearing the same kind of garments you'd previously seen Mr. Barrett wear?"

"That's right."

"But you didn't see the man's face, did you?"

"Yes—no." Trebeck threw Marshall a look of desperation.

"Which is it?" Taylor fired back. "And remember you're under oath."

Trebeck looked at his hands. "No," he mumbled, his voice little more than a whisper.

"I'm sorry. What did you say?"

"I guess I didn't see his face."

"No further questions," Taylor said. Her heart did a flip-flop at the smile Steele threw her.

Judge Werner broke for lunch, but Taylor was too keyed up to eat. Not just about the case, but because Steele's attitude seemed to have warmed toward her. Sitting next to him in the cramped space made her heart flitter.

After lunch the state called Detective Donaldson. Marshall began by asking a number of preliminary questions: the detective's full name, his years on the force, concluding with his dispatch to Allison Barrett's residence. "On your arrival at the condo on the night in question, what did you find?"

"It was a crime scene. Officers Gonzales and Meeker had cordoned off the area. The lab techs were dusting for prints. I don't think the coroner had arrived. There was a body lying on the floor that was identified as Allison Barrett. Her head had been bashed in with a fireplace poker, which we subsequently recovered."

There was a rattling of papers as Marshall dug into his file. He stood holding a large photo, walked around to the front of the defense table and handed the picture to Steele. Marshall stood by and brushed imaginary lint from his sleeve while giving the defense a second to look over the photo.

Steele held the picture so Taylor and Craig could see. It was a picture of Allison as she lay dead on the floor of her condo. Her face was turned unnaturally to one side. Her purple lounge pajama top and the surrounding carpet were soaked in blood. Craig covered his face. Wordlessly Steele returned the photo to Marshall. Taylor cringed inwardly as she pictured the impact that photo would have on jurors when it turned up at the trial.

Marshall then took the photo and strolled up to the witness box, his gait leisurely and thoughtful, his manner confident.

"I show you," Marshall said, "what has been marked state's exhibit number ten and ask if you can identify it."

"It's a photograph of the crime scene." Donaldson's mild brown-eyed gaze flickered briefly at Steele, then darted quickly away.

Marshall nodded, retrieved the picture from the witness and took a step forward and handed the photo to Judge Werner.

The judge looked dispassionately at the picture, then at the defense table. "Any objection?"

Steele and Taylor looked at each other. It would be pointless to object. "No objection," Steele said.

"So admitted." Judge Werner gave the picture back to the State's Attorney, then leaned back.

Marshall gave the picture to the court reporter, who filed it away. Taylor knew Marshall was through with the photo for now. He had it into evidence that a brutal crime had been committed. He had revealed nothing that hadn't already been in the paper, and hadn't tipped any of his trump cards. Ben Marshall, Taylor thought grudgingly, was one hell of an attorney.

Marshall turned and faced the witness. "Detective, did you and your men check the condo for signs of a break-in?"

Donaldson nodded his head. "We checked, but there were no real signs."

Marshall crossed his arms over his chest. "Detective, isn't there an alarm system in that house?"

"Yes, sir, there is."

"And on the night in question, was the alarm system activated?"

Donaldson nodded again. "Yes, sir. The patrol officers had to break a window to get inside."

"So, then," Marshall said, "it would be safe to say that no one could have entered the premises undetected without knowing the code to deactivate the alarm, wouldn't it?''

"I'd say so," Donaldson said. "Unless someone was hiding in the house when the system was turned on, but I think that's unlikely. He'd have to know the code to re-arm it."

Marshall nodded. "How many people knew the security code?"

"Just Mrs. Barrett and the defendant."

"Were there things missing from the house? Valuables?"

"The killer tried to make it look like a break-in, but burglary was ruled out," Donaldson said. "Like I said before, there was no sign of a break-in. No money was taken. At my request, Mr. Barrett did a complete inventory of his wife's jewelry, and every piece was present and accounted for."

"So whoever killed Allison Barrett came into the house with one purpose and one purpose alone—to kill Allison Barrett?"

Donaldson nodded. "I believe so."

"At the start of the investigation, Detective, did you have any leads or suspects whatsoever?"

"No, sir. Not one."

Marshall flipped over a page in his file. "Did that situation later change?"

"It certainly did."

"And how was that?"

Donaldson recounted how they'd found Craig's prints at the crime scene, his lack of an alibi, the recovery of the surveillance tape and Craig's threats to kill Allison. He then related a conversation with the bartender at the Lake Shore Country Club, where Craig and Allison both had memberships.

"And if you would, Detective, please relate Mr. Clark's story."

Steele was on his feet immediately. "Objection. Hearsay."

"Overruled," said Judge Werner. "The witness may answer."

Donaldson folded his arms and leaned back. "Mr. Clark told us the day before the murder he saw Craig Barrett grab his wife and shake her while yelling that she'd played him for a fool but he'd kill her before she got another red cent."

"Detective, did you later find out what that cryptic comment meant?"

Donaldson now looked toward Craig. His intense expression was rehearsed, of course, just as all his answers had been. The theatrics were fooling no one, Taylor thought, except maybe Judge Werner, whose opinion was the only one that mattered. "Yes, sir," Donaldson said. "Mr. Barrett told us."

"And what did he say?" Marshall asked, his voice an octave lower. Taylor sensed the witness was about to drop a bombshell.

Donaldson's gaze remained riveted on Craig and never wavered. "He said that he'd had a prenuptial agreement with Mrs. Barrett, but after they reconciled, he'd torn it up. But when the reconciliation didn't work out, he thought he'd been used."

"Detective Donaldson," Marshall said, "did you then place Mr. Barrett under arrest?"

"No, sir. We had a lot of circumstantial evidence but we didn't want to go off half-cocked."

Taylor almost gagged. "Give me a break," she mumbled.

"It wasn't until we recovered the murder weapon from his home that he was taken into custody."

"Did you find anything else that implicated Mr. Barrett in his wife's murder?"

"Yes, sir. We also found a tape that Mrs. Barrett had made naming him as her killer."

"Objection," Steele said. "Speculation. Detective Donaldson doesn't know if that tape was in fact made by Mrs. Barrett."

Judge Werner nodded. "Sustained. Rephrase the question."

"Detective, during a second search of Mrs. Barrett's condo, did you find a tape?"

"Yes, sir. It was in an envelope hidden inside the pocket of a mink coat in the master-bedroom closet. The outside of the envelope read, 'To be opened in the event of my untimely death.'"

Marshall folded his arms across his chest. "Did you listen to the tape?"

Detective Donaldson looked at Steele and nodded. "Yes, I did. On the tape a woman identifying herself as Allison Barrett stated that she was afraid of her husband, Craig Barrett. Apparently he had quite a history of violent behavior. She said she was afraid he was going to kill her."

"Thank you, Detective Donaldson. No further questions." Marshall all but skipped back to the prosecution table. *And why shouldn't he feel good?* Taylor thought bleakly. They'd made their case against Craig. They'd established that he had motive, means and opportunity.

She saw no point in cross-examining Donaldson. He'd been a great witness and would be an even better one at dodging difficult questions. But she knew Steele had to try to punch holes in his testimony.

"Detective Donaldson," Steele said, smiling, "did you question Mrs. Barrett's neighbors to see if anyone might have seen or heard anything unusual the night of the murder?"

"Yes, sir."

"What about a Ned Kramer? Did you question him?"

"Yes, sir."

Taylor could tell from the stiffening of Donaldson's body that he knew what was coming and didn't like it one bit.

"Then you know that Mr. Kramer saw Allison arguing with a man around eleven o'clock on the night of the murder. And that man didn't fit Mr. Barrett's description, did he?"

"No, sir, he didn't."

"Did you follow up on that lead?"

Donaldson frowned and looked at Marshall. He cleared his throat. "There was nothing to follow up on."

"Nothing to follow up on?" Steele repeated. "How did you arrive at that conclusion?"

Donaldson threw Marshall a helpless look. "It would have only been a waste of time. Mr. Kramer is not a credible witness. He'd had quite a bit to drink the night of the murder. Besides, we knew who killed Mrs. Barrett."

"So once you determined that Mr. Barrett was the killer, you didn't follow up on any other leads?"

"There was no reason to," the detective said. His tone was angry and defensive.

Steele nodded. "That's what I thought." He looked at his notes, then back at the witness. "Let's go back to the night of the murder. You said the crime scene had been staged to make it look like a burglary but nothing of value had been taken. Isn't it possible that what was taken was only of value to Allison and the killer?"

"Anything is possible," Donaldson hedged.

"Isn't it true, Detective, that Allison Barrett was blackmailing someone?"

Donaldson threw Steele an angry look. "I don't know," he mumbled. "We don't have any evidence pointing to that."

"Then how do you explain the presence of over three hundred thousand dollars in Allison Barrett's savings account?"

"Objection, Your Honor. Irrelevant."

Judge Werner nodded. "Sustained."

"Detective, have you considered the possibility that there is a connection between Allison Barrett's murder and those of Harold Lamden and Vanessa Norris?"

Marshall was on his feet immediately. "Objection. Irrelevant. Your Honor, those deaths have no bearing on this case. And for the record, Harold Lamden's was a suicide."

"Sustained."

Steele threw Marshall a disgusted look. "Okay, let's go back to the murder weapon and tape you found. Isn't it true you found those items during a second search of the defendant's and his wife's respective premises? A search prompted by an anonymous call that occurred six weeks after the first search?"

Donaldson shifted. "Uh, that's correct."

"Plenty of time for someone to have planted the murder weapon and the tape there?"

Donaldson shook his head. "No, that's impossible."

Steele gave him a hard look. "Is it?" He turned and walked back to the defense table. "No further questions."

Taylor's lips curved into a smile of admiration. They'd made a number of dents in the prosecution's case: they'd pointed out that the time of death could have been later, that there were other suspects and that it was possible that Craig was being framed. Whether it was enough for the judge to find that the prosecution had not established that there was probable cause to believe that Craig had killed Allison, she didn't know.

"WE ALL KNEW it was a long shot," Matt said, "but I really thought . . ." His voice broke and he looked away.

Taylor leaned over and gave his hand a reassuring squeeze. "I know. But the war isn't over yet."

Heather threw Steele and Taylor a helpless look, then put an arm around Matt. "Darling, you're tired. Let's go home. We'll see you later."

She watched Heather lead him out of the room. When the door closed, she looked over at Steele. There was a strained silence. Taylor coughed, trying to relieve the tension. They needed to talk about their relationship, but she was afraid to broach the topic. So instead of speaking what was in her heart, she launched into a discussion of the case. "You know, no matter how you look at it, this case doesn't make sense. Whoever heard of a killer who continues planting evidence against the accused?

He's made anonymous calls to the police, followed us. Why?''

Steele shrugged. "Maybe to feel powerful. He certainly doesn't seem to have much fear of being caught." He sighed. "And maybe he shouldn't, he's gotten away with killing three people thus far, and we don't have a clue to his identity."

"I still think Ted Larson could be our killer," she said. "Everything always comes back to him. He knew about the blackmail, so he would have known about the documents Allison left with Lamden. He's also probably the only person besides Craig that she would have given her security code. He could also have learned enough from her about Craig's security to be able to get in and out of Craig's house undetected."

Steele nodded. "You may be right, but it's going to be hell proving it." He issued a frustrated sigh. "God, our luck has got to change."

"It just did," Hawk said from the doorway. "I found Betsy Boyd."

Chapter Thirteen

Another dead end! Taylor dropped the accordion folder she'd just perused and glanced about the warehouse. When Hawk had burst into Steele's office two weeks ago and announced he'd found Betsy Boyd, Taylor had not appreciated the monumental task that still lay ahead of them in locating Allison's missing documents.

The secretary had confirmed that she'd talked to Norris but claimed only to have told her the address of the warehouse and the floor of the building that she'd sent Lamden's files to. Boyd maintained that she'd only remembered that bit of information because that's where she'd sent all her documents while she had been with Jasper and Kline.

Technically that information should have been enough for Hawk to locate Allison's documents, which were supposedly filed in alphabetical order by client name. However, a quick search of the B's turned up nothing. Since Taylor hadn't come across them when she'd searched the reporter's office, they'd had to consider the possibility that the documents were missing because they'd been misfiled, rather than Norris having taken them. Though it would have been an easy enough task for the reporter to slip in and out of the old warehouse undetected. Building security was almost nonexistent.

Operating under both theories, they'd obtained a warrant to search the reporter's apartment and the television station. Hawk, along with four paralegals from the law firm, had been given that task. Steele and Taylor had headed for the warehouse.

But the moment they'd stepped through the set of double doors on the third floor of the old warehouse, Taylor's heart had sunk. The room was large and musky and contained rows and rows of floor-to-ceiling bins filled with papers. As far as the eye could see, there was nothing but paper.

Taylor knew instinctively that a random search would be fruitless. She shared a dismayed look with Steele and, as if by tacit agreement, they plopped down on a large, wooden packing crate and began trying to formulate a plan of action. They'd tossed various ideas back and forth before deciding they'd have to work under the supposition that Norris had located the files and had hidden them in the safest place possible—in the warehouse. That's where Norris's clue might fit in.

The reporter had said, *"Look for the sheep in wolf's clothing and you'll find your killer."* Norris could have been referring to a personality type or an actual person. Maybe Denning, Larson or Daniel Ridgeway? None of the men were what they seemed. If Norris had hidden the files in the warehouse, perhaps she'd placed them under the first letter of the last name of one of these men. It was a shot in the dark, but it was all they had to go on. The search of Norris's office and apartment had turned up nothing.

Even using their methodology, there were still thousands of documents that had to be examined. Taylor didn't even want to contemplate the possibility that the clue had simply been a red herring.

She issued a weary sigh and picked up another file. They'd been at the warehouse a week and even with the help of four paralegals, Hawk, Matt and Heather, they were just started on the *L*'s. It would probably take another week to finish up completely. If they hadn't found Allison's documents by then, she thought it unlikely they ever would.

She glanced over at Steele and Heather. This afternoon it was just the three of them. The paralegals were needed at the office, and Hawk was running down a lead he'd gotten on Ted Larson. Matt had a late afternoon meeting and had left earlier. Heather had walked him to the door. They'd been whispering and smooching like newlyweds.

Watching them brought a lump to Taylor's throat. She longed for that kind of unconditional love. She glanced at Steele. On several occasions he'd looked as if he wanted to say something, but each time he'd frozen up. He may have forgiven her, but she wondered if he would ever trust her enough to ever open his heart to her again. Her eyes filled with tears.

"Is something wrong?"

She looked up and found Steele studying her. "Oh, no," she said, blinking the tears away. "I guess I'm just a little tired."

"We'll finish up this batch, then call it a day," he said, then added, "I swear, I can't believe the helter-skelter manner in which these documents are filed."

"It's a mess, all right," Heather agreed. "I guess that Betsy Boyd wasn't the only employee guilty of mislabeling documents. By the way, how did Hawk locate her?"

"He got Ms. Boyd's social-security number and birthdate from Jasper and Kline," Steele explained. "Once he had those two items, he was able to come up with an address in Rock Island, Illinois. Unfortunately, after Norris's murder, she made herself scarce for a while."

Heather giggled. "Too bad Hawk wasn't able to come up with some quick and easy way for us to go through these documents."

"Well, it could be worse," Taylor said dryly. "Imagine having to go through *all* of them. With our method, we only have to look at a fraction of the documents."

Heather looked at her curiously. "What are you going to do if we don't find them?"

"We still have a few cards up our sleeve," Steele answered. "That's one of the reasons we didn't put on a defense at the preliminary hearing. I had to consider that Craig would be bound over for trial, and I didn't want to tip the prosecution to the strategy we'll use at that point."

Steele sounded a lot more confident than Taylor felt. The prosecution had an awfully strong case against Craig, and that tape had just been the final nail in his coffin. Thinking about the tape made her think of Aunt Ida. Maybe in time they could have some kind of relationship, but not now. Aunt Ida had caused her so much pain, had caused her to lose Steele. She was so lost in this thought that she almost missed the file.

She did a double take when she saw the names on the outside of a slightly tattered folder: Allison and Craig Barrett. "Steele," she said excitedly. "I found it!"

He was instantly by her side. "Let's see if there are any more." It took another hour before Steele was satisfied they had all the folders relating to Allison and Craig's separation agreement. There were three in all. They each took one and began leafing through the documents, but it was slow going. Harold Lamden had been a very meticulous man, and there was quite a lot of material to go through.

"Look, Taylor," Steele said after a few minutes of searching. "It's Lamden's appointment book for this calendar year." He handed it to her. "Why don't you go through it while Heather and I continue looking for Allison's documents?"

"Sounds good," she said. She turned to the day of the murder and quickly skimmed the page.

"Anything?" Heather asked.

She shook her head. "Lamden only had two appointments that day. One with Matt, probably to go over the separation agreement, and the other with another accountant."

Her disappointment must have shown, because Steele leaned over and gave her arm an affectionate squeeze.

"Hey, we're just getting started," he said. The way he looked at her made her feel all warm inside.

"Looks like we're going to be here a while," Heather said. She glanced at her watch. "I'd better call my cook and tell her to hold dinner. I don't want to desert you at this point."

Taylor smiled her thanks. Heather really had been a lot of help. She'd been there every day, pitching in.

Heather stood, looking about the large room. "Did either of you see a phone?"

"There's one on the first floor by the rest rooms," Steele said absently.

After Heather left, a quiet descended on the two that neither knew how to break. She was very much aware of Steele sitting next to her. She wanted to reach out, to tear the wall down that he'd built around his emotions, but she didn't know how. So once again, instead of speaking what was in her heart, she began to talk about Ted Larson and her certainty of his guilt.

Steele nodded. "Hawk has found a hole in his alibi, but we need more than that to connect him to Allison. Let's hope we find it in Allison's documents."

Taylor was no longer listening. The pain she'd kept at bay the past few weeks suddenly burst free—rushing over her. Tears welled up in her eyes. She had to get out of this room, away from Steele before she embarrassed herself.

"I'm going to get some fresh air," she said. She rose from her makeshift seat, crossed the expanse of the third floor, stepped through the double set of doors and walked over to the railing and looked over the side to the floors below.

Her heart jumped in her throat at the sight that greeted her. A thick gray curtain of smoke poured from the lower floor and floated up. It only took her a moment to see that the second floor was engulfed in flames. "Steele!" she screamed. "The building is on fire!"

He was at her side immediately. "We've got to get out of here," he said, his eyes scanning the area. "Come on! There's no time to lose."

Heather! Her eyes widened in horror. "No," she said when he tried to pull her back into the warehouse. "Heather's down there. We've got to find her." She headed toward the door marked Exit.

Steele reached her just as her hand was about on the knob. He turned her to face him. "There's no way we can reach her," he said. "The fire is on the second floor. I'm sure Heather saw it and got out, which is what we're going to do. Come on!" he said, turning toward the room they'd just come from.

"What about this stairwell?" she asked, pointing to the exit door next to the elevator.

Steele shook his head. "It's probably full of smoke, and I don't know how fast that fire is moving. There should be another exit on the other side of the warehouse. We'll take that." He took her hand and ran back into the room they'd just exited. "Try the windows while I look for a door," Steele shouted as he ran to the opposite side of the room.

Taylor tore to the windows. She tried the first one. She pulled with all her might, but it wouldn't budge. She tried the next window. It was the same. She checked the sill to determine what was holding it in place. It had been nailed shut! Probably to keep vandals out, but in this case it might cost them their lives. She looked wildly about the room. There had to be a way out!

"Taylor, over here!" Steele shouted. "I found a door."

She raced to the back wall where Steele was pulling boxes down, trying to clear a path to the door he'd found. The stack of boxes looked like a small mountain. Sweat poured down her brow as the odor of smoke slowly seeped into the room. The fire was getting closer. They worked quickly, uncovering the door. Steele grabbed the doorknob and turned. It wouldn't budge. He put his shoulder to the door, but still it didn't budge. "It's blocked from the other side," he said finally, taking her hand. "C'mon, we'll take the other stairwell."

Her eyes widened in alarm. "But you said it was probably full of smoke."

"I know, but it's our only chance," he said, his face grim. "We'll go up, not down. When we enter the stairwell, try not to breathe. Here," he said, tearing a strip of cloth from his shirt and covering her nose and mouth. Then he followed suit.

He sprinted out into the hallway with Taylor in tow and entered the stairwell. It was like stepping into a roaring furnace. A thick gray curtain of smoke greeted them, and below flames flickered, but the third-floor stairwell was free of fire. Smoke filled her lungs. Her throat spasming and her eyes burning, she followed Steele up the stairs. Trying not to breathe, they made their way through the smoky fog until they reached the next floor, which opened onto the roof. She stood back as Steele pressed the iron bar to open the door. It didn't open and he pressed again.

She glanced over her shoulder. The smoke was getting thicker, and breathing was becoming increasingly difficult. Just when she began to think they might not make it, the door gave. A gush of fresh air hit her in the face as she followed Steele out on the rooftop.

The moment she was outside, Taylor tore the make-shift mask from her lower face and breathed in great gulps of fresh air. In the distance she could hear the sirens of a fire engine.

"Thank God," she panted. "Heather must have made it out and called the fire department. They should be here any moment."

"I don't think we can wait for the fire department," he said, glancing at the smoke that poured out on the rooftop from the open doorway. "That fire is moving a little too fast for me." He turned and looked at her and smiled. "Don't look so worried," he said, kissing her forehead with unexpected warmth. "I won't let anything happen to you."

Taylor felt a warm glow as she scampered after him, her feet silent and just a tiny bit slippery on the tarred rooftop. She frowned. "What are you looking for?"

"A fire escape. A ladder or some kind of bridge that connects this building to one over there." He pointed to a building to the right of the warehouse.

After a few moments it was clear there was none.

"It's not that far away," Steele said. "We'll have to jump."

She looked at him with shock and disbelief, but he just shrugged his shoulders. "Don't think about it," he advised. "Do it before you have time to be frightened." He gave her shoulder a reassuring squeeze.

The second building was about two feet shorter than the one they stood on, but that wasn't what terrified her. It was the yawning abyss between the two buildings. A vast chasm of perhaps five feet. Her heart pounded. She couldn't do it. If that same space was flat on the sidewalk, she would have made it with inches to spare, but this was different. If she tried to jump those sixty inches, four stories above the street, she would miss and fall to her death. It was just that simple.

Steele jumped first, making it look ridiculously easy—a child's hopscotch game. He stood on the other building waiting for her. "Come on, Taylor," he coached. "You can do it."

"I can't," she said.

He gave her a reassuring smile. "Do it for me. C'mon, I'll catch you," he said, then he held out his arms—waiting.

It was rotten and unfair of him, and it left her no choice whatsoever. She took a deep breath and, with her eyes trained on Steele, she leapt.

Of course he caught her. Not that she'd ever have had any doubt about it. They tumbled onto the rough surface, his arms locked so tightly around her that she couldn't breathe. She didn't think she wanted to, anyway, and she hugged him back, closing her eyes and savoring the feel of his arms.

"You're safe," he cooed in her ear. "You're safe."
There was no way she could answer, first because the arms crushing her didn't give her enough breath to do so,

then because his mouth came down over hers, stopping any effort at speech.

His kiss was wonderful and told her everything words couldn't say: how much he needed her, wanted her. It wiped away all the pain and loneliness of the past few weeks. When he released her and smiled, she knew everything would be all right. Below she could hear the sound of fire engines.

"We need to talk," he said, hugging her to him again briefly. "But not now. Later."

Taylor refused to get her hopes up too high and simply nodded. "Heather is probably worried sick."

They'd shouted and waved for about five minutes before a fireman noticed and sent someone inside the building to unlock the outside roof door. By the time they made it to the ground floor and outside, several fire engines and a dozen fire and police personnel swarmed the area. Streams of water from hoses pelted the warehouse from various directions, but the efforts appeared useless against the viciousness of the flames.

Heather was sitting in the doorway of the ambulance being checked out by a paramedic. The moment she saw them, she tore the oxygen mask from her face and rushed over to them.

"Thank God you're all right," Heather breathed, wrapping her arms around Taylor. "I was so scared. I didn't know what to do." Taylor could hear the note of relief in her voice.

"You did fine," she said, giving Heather a wan smile. "You got out and called the fire department."

"But if I had gotten out sooner," Heather wailed, "the fire department would have gotten here sooner and maybe you'd have been able to save the files. They did burn, didn't they?"

Taylor looked from Steele's grim face back to Heather's. She nodded slowly. "Yeah, but don't worry about it." She tried to sound upbeat, confident, but she knew the task of trying to clear Craig had just gotten harder. At Heather's skeptical look, she gave her hand a little squeeze. "We'll just have to work around it, right, Steele?"

"Oh, yes," he replied vaguely as he watched Taylor hover over the distraught woman.

Fifteen minutes later the fire chief came over to question them. By the time he was done, their terrifying afternoon had taken its toll on Heather. She was almost a basket case.

"Steele, call Matt and tell him what happened. I'll take Heather home and stay with her until he arrives."

Steele nodded but she could tell his mind was elsewhere; that fact was confirmed by his question to the fire chief. "How do you think the fire started?"

The fire chief scratched his head. "I can't say for sure until we've completed our investigation. But it looks like it might have been arson. That fire was moving too quickly for it to be anything else. Several people also noticed a suspicious-looking man hanging around the building a few minutes before the fire started."

"Were you able to get a description?" Steele asked.

"They said he was black, in his late twenties, tall, slender and was wearing a leather jacket with a patchwork design forming a lightning bolt on the back."

Heather's knees buckled, and if Taylor hadn't been holding her, she'd have fallen to the ground. She looked from Taylor to Steele, her eyes filled with horror. "Oh, my God," she whispered. "Allison bought a jacket just like that for Ted Larson!"

"I DON'T KNOW what you're talking about," Larson snarled. He was leaning against the doorway of his Lincoln Park apartment. His stance was calm, but every muscle in his body was tense, alert. "I was nowhere near any warehouse."

"Don't give me that," Steele said, pushing his way inside the apartment. Hawk followed and closed the door.

"Hey! You can't barge in here like that," Larson yelled, but his voice wobbled slightly, as if he were frightened.

Steele ignored his words as he glanced about the apartment. "A man fitting your description was spotted running from that warehouse right before the fire started. He was said to be wearing a very distinctive black leather jacket, which Heather McCall thought sounded like one you owned."

Larson smiled. "Heather McCall is the last person you ought to be listening to. The woman's a flake." His grin slipped as Hawk walked over and sniffed the air around him.

"You a smoker?" Hawk asked.

Larson ran his arm over his forehead, wiping his brow. "Of course not."

Hawk nodded. "Then how come you smell like smoke?"

"I—I—" Larson spluttered.

"Give it up," Steele said. "You might as well tell us the truth—we're going to find out. The fire department will conduct a thorough investigation. Trust me, there are any number of people that can place you at the warehouse."

"All right," he said, his tone defiant. "I was there but I didn't start that fire. It was me who called the fire department."

Steele's eyes narrowed. "If you had nothing to hide, why did you run away? Why didn't you wait for the police and the fire department?"

"I—I didn't want the cops asking me a lot of questions, all right?" Larson said, his eyes wide as they darted from Hawk's to Steele's.

"Like what you were doing there, for starters?" Steele asked dryly.

"Yeah," Larson admitted. He hesitated then said, "I—I've been following you and Ms. Quinlan." He licked his lips. "I wanted to know if you'd found Lamden's files." At the look Steele threw him, he added, "From something Allison said, I surmised he still had her documents. I also knew the identity of the person she was blackmailing had to be in those documents because he'd signed over some assets to her. I'd thought Craig was the killer but after Norris's murder—''

Steele's head snapped up. Suddenly it all clicked into place. "You were the one who told her about Allison's blackmail scheme and Lamden's files. You were her source. But you couldn't find the files. Once she located them, you killed her, didn't you? What were you going to do, pick up where Allison left off?''

"Of course not!" Larson snarled. Tiny beads of sweat dotted Larson's brow. "I told Norris about the blackmail and the documents but I certainly didn't kill her." His eyes shifted from Steele's to the floor. "Look, I was trying to help. I want to find Allison's killer just as badly as you do, but I can't get involved in the investigation.''

"Tell me another one," Steele barked. "You didn't say anything about what you knew for the same reason you didn't tell the police about your relationship with Allison or that you were at her condo the night she was murdered—''

"I was at a club," Larson cried. "Remember? The cops checked me out. I sent you the pictures. They verify I was there.''

Steele nodded. "You were there, all right, but not all evening. We took a look at those pictures you put so much faith in to establish your alibi. In the photo taken at nine-thirty, you're wearing a clean white shirt. In the second photo taken at 10:15, you have a small red spot on the lower right-hand side of that shirt. It looks like a wine stain. In the last photo taken at midnight that spot isn't there anymore.''

"I—I don't know what you're trying to pull," Larson spluttered.

Steele continued as if he hadn't spoken. "You left the club sometime around eleven and went to Allison's. Her apartment is only ten minutes from the club. You could easily have made that trip to her house, killed her, run by your apartment to change and gotten back to the club before midnight.''

"That's ridiculous!"

"What happened?" Steele pressed. "Did you get blood on your shirt so you had to go home and change?"

"No! I didn't kill Allison. You said yourself the killer was someone she was blackmailing."

"Maybe that's just what *you* wanted us to think."

"Now, look, I'm getting sick and tired of your accusations. I tried to be cooperative but I don't have to take this crap. I don't even have to talk to you."

Steele speared Larson with a hard look. "You're right. You don't have to talk to us but you will have to talk to the police." He nodded at Hawk. "Call 'em."

"Wait!" Larson pleaded. "Look, I didn't kill her. She was already—" He caught himself.

Steele pounced on his words. "She was already what?"

Larson sagged back into the sofa. "Oh, hell!"

"She was already what?" Steele repeated.

Larson looked like a cornered animal. His eyes were wild as they darted from one man to the other. "Nothing. You just confused me," he stammered.

Neither Steele nor Hawk said anything.

Larson was sweating like a pig. "Look, I didn't kill Allison! If Barrett didn't do it, then it must have been Denning." When he saw they weren't buying it, he moaned. "Oh, hell. Now you're gonna try to pin her murder on me. Look," he said, licking his lips, "I loved Allison. I would never have harmed her." As if to emphasize his words, he gave his head a little shake. "I wouldn't have."

"I find that hard to believe," Steele said coolly.

Larson's eyes filled with tears, and he looked at Steele, his expression bleak. "I wouldn't have harmed Allison. Never in a million years." His eyes pleaded for understanding as he said, "She was my sister!"

TAYLOR PACED back and forth in the living room of the McCall residence, alternating between worrying about how things had gone with Larson and what she would say to Steele now that the case was almost over. Heather had taken a sedative and was upstairs sleeping. What was keeping Steele? It was after seven o'clock. He and Hawk had been gone almost two hours. She hadn't thought it would take this long to get a confession. They had Larson dead to rights. By his own admission, he'd known about the blackmail, and they could place him at the crime scene the night of the murder, as well as at the warehouse today. He'd killed Allison—probably out of greed—Lamden and Norris because they'd stumbled on to the blackmail scheme. Maybe even to his involvement in it. She sighed.

A part of her was glad it was all over, but another part was afraid of where that left her and Steele. When they'd been trapped on that rooftop, he'd let his guard down. Any doubt that he still had feelings for her had been removed the moment he kissed her. His kiss had told her how much he cared for her, how much he wanted her. Hope filled her despite her resolve to not read too much into his words. The fact that he'd said they should talk had to be a positive sign.

She sighed, again. She was driving herself crazy. She wouldn't think about it anymore. She'd just have to wait for Steele to arrive, then they could talk it all out. She crossed to the window and stared at the setting sun. It was getting late. Matt would be home soon.

"Ms. Quinlan," the housekeeper said, breaking into her thoughts. "Your office is calling."

"Thanks," she said, picking up the phone.

"I'm sorry to bother you, Taylor," she heard Brenda say, "but George Avery has been trying to reach you all day. He says it's imperative that you call him immediately." She jotted down the number.

George Avery? She frowned, turning the name over in her mind. Oh, yes, the brokerage house. Her frown deepened. She'd given the message to Matt and asked him to return the broker's call. She sighed. With everything on his mind, he'd apparently forgotten.

She let out a long breath as she dialed the number and waited.

"I'm sorry to bother you," Mr. Avery said, "but as the holder of Mr. Barrett's power of attorney, I thought I should check with you on Matt McCall's request to transfer another fifty thousand shares of Appleton stock to Whiteseals Industries."

It sounded like a pretty routine financial transaction. "Thanks for telling me," she said. "Is there anything else?"

"No, I just thought I should give you this information." He spoke slowly, as though making a decision about something. Then he said quickly, "Well, there is something else. We also received a request to liquidate close to two hundred thousand dollars and transfer the funds to a bank in the Cayman Islands. I wouldn't have thought much of Mr. McCall's request, but this is the third such transfer to the Cayman account in the last six months. It's most irregular. I thought as the holder of Mr. Barrett's power of attorney, you ought to know."

"Of course. Thank you." Taylor lowered the receiver into the cradle thoughtfully.

Why would Craig need that kind of money? Unless— unless he and Matt had planned to use the money to get out of the country. But Craig was in jail and had been for the past three weeks. She frowned. Whiteseal Industries. She turned the name over in her mind. As many times as she'd read the separation agreement, she was pretty familiar with Craig's investments. But that name didn't sound familiar.

She flipped opened her briefcase and pulled out the separation agreement. As she'd suspected, there was no Whiteseal Industries listed among Craig's reported assets. It could be that it was a recent acquisition or... As quickly as the thought occurred to her, she was rejecting it. Matt was Craig's best friend. He wouldn't do anything like that. But still she couldn't shake the feeling and she knew she would have no peace until she checked out her suspicion. Heather was upstairs asleep, and Matt wouldn't be home for another fifteen, twenty minutes. He'd told her his computer password when she'd com-

pleted a brief for him a few weeks back. If she just could
remember what it was, she could access his office files
from the computer in the study. She could take a peek at
Craig's portfolio. Set her mind at rest. No one would ever
know.

She headed to Matt's office. At the door she quickly
checked the corridor to make sure it was vacant, then
slipped inside. *"Now what was that code?"* she mumbled. It had been numbers, of that she was sure. A birthdate? But whose? She typed in Heather's. That wasn't it.
Then she tried Matt's, then Craig's and then her own.
She sighed, then tried Matt's. Still no luck. Maybe it
hadn't been a birthdate but a date of equal importance to
him. Of course, his wedding date! It took her three more
tries to get the right date, and then she was in.

A moment later, she was pulling up Craig's file.
"Matt, please forgive me," she whispered, then took a
quick breath and began to read.

She swallowed hard, hand shaking slightly as she regarded the information on the screen. "It can't be," she
whispered, but the truth was staring her right there in the
face. It was a complicated financial process, but the bottom line was Matt had set up several offshore dummy
corporations for the sole purpose of transferring monies
from Craig's account into his. Matt was stealing from
Craig! Had been for about six months... Her hand flew
to her mouth. It hadn't been Allison's assets that Lamden questioned but Craig's! He must have discovered that
Matt was embezzling from Craig; that's why he'd wanted
to meet with Matt—to confront him, and Matt had killed
him. "Oh, my God," she whispered.

"I'm sorry you found that," a man's voice said.

Taylor's eyes flew to the doorway.

Matt stood in the doorway, a sad expression on his face
and a gun in his hand, pointed straight at her heart.

STEELE WATCHED as Larson slumped back into the sofa.
"We know you're Edward Garrison, Allison's brother,"
he said. At Larson's look of surprise, Steele added,

"Hawk got the lowdown on you right before we came over here. We also know about the contract that the loan shark you scammed four years ago has out on you. We know you've changed your name several times because of that. But why did you and Allison pretend not to be related?"

Larson ran a weary hand over his face. "We had different fathers. Allison was sensitive about people knowing her background—that she was illegitimate and that she grew up dirt poor. So we agreed not to broadcast our relationship."

Steele nodded. "It also gave you the perfect cover for your little extortion scams. It wouldn't help to let the marks know you were the one collecting the information on them?"

"No," he said, his voice little more than a whisper. He looked at Steele, his expression bleak. "I was going to come forward once this was all over."

"I'm sure you were," Steele said dryly. "Allison left her entire estate to you. But for now let's focus on the murder. Why did you go to Allison's that night?"

"She called and asked me to come over. Whoever she was blackmailing was giving her trouble. She said she wanted me to hold something for her, but she didn't say what. When I got there…" Larson swallowed. "She was dead."

"About what time was that?"

He shrugged. "Around eleven-twenty."

Steele's eyes narrowed as realization dawned. It *had* been Larson that Trebeck saw running from the condo. "She must have given you some clue to what it was she had on the person or who she was blackmailing," he said. "Try to remember. What did she say about the person she was blackmailing?"

Larson shook his head. "Not much. Just that she was really enjoying putting the screws to Red." His looked at Steele. "Yeah, that's it. She called him Red."

"Red?" Steele pounced on the name. "Is that a given or nickname?"

Larson shrugged. "She just said Red."

"Red." Steele turned the name over in his mind. The person Ned Kramer saw had red hair. There couldn't be that many men in Allison's circle of friends with red hair. He frowned. Something tickled at the back of his mind. A conversation? A memory? He shook his head.

"Does it sound familiar?" Hawk asked.

"Yeah, it rings a bell, but I can't say why." He turned back to Larson. "Tell us everything Allison said about this particular blackmail."

Larson was slowly recounting various conversations he'd had with his sister, when a name and face suddenly flashed in Steele's mind's eye. Red! Of course! He remembered the name. Not from the present but from the past, but the memory had been triggered by a recent conversation. His eyes widened in horror. Oh, my God, Taylor! "Come on," he yelled, tearing out the door. "We need to get to the McCalls' right away."

He drove like a bat out of hell. Praying he'd get to Taylor in time. The car came to a screeching halt in front of the McCall residence, and he jumped out. Hawk was right behind him. He didn't bother ringing the doorbell, but pounded on the door until it was opened by a frightened maid. One look at her face told him they were too late. She said Matt, Heather and Taylor had left ten minutes before. They hadn't said where they were going, but from an overheard conversation, she thought they were headed for the marina.

TAYLOR STARED at Matt in numb horror. "Why?" she whispered. "Why did you do it?" It was still hard for her to imagine that he would steal from Craig, let alone kill anyone.

She took a step back as he moved toward her. He paused and a flash of pain appeared in his eyes at her action.

"Don't be afraid," he said. "I won't hurt you."

That comment coming from a man who had already killed three people did nothing to reassure her. "Steele..." she managed to croak.

"Can't help you," Heather said from her seat on the cabin bunk. "He and Hawk are probably still questioning Larson." While Matt held the gun on her, Heather had driven the car to the marina. Once on board, she'd lost no time setting sail.

"Why couldn't you have left well enough alone?" Matt asked.

"You know I couldn't do that," she said. She looked at him. "Why, Matt? Why did you do it?"

With his free hand, Matt rubbed his forehead. "Money," he said succinctly. "Paying for the wedding, the honeymoon, I couldn't make the down payment on the house."

"Why didn't you just ask Craig to loan you the money?"

"Two hundred thousand dollars? I couldn't." He hesitated, then looked away. "I'm not proud of what I did, but I thought I could replace it without anyone ever being the wiser. But after..."

He couldn't say it, she thought. But killing Lamden changed everything.

"This isn't the way I wanted it, but everything is going to come out. Craig is going to..." His voice broke and his face looked bleak. "We have to leave."

"What are you going to do with me?"

He gave her a wry smile. "I'm not going to hurt you. We're sailing to Michigan. I'll leave you tied up on the boat at Benton Harbor. From there, we'll take a plane out of the country. Once we're safely in the air, I'll call Steele and tell him where you are."

"Don't lie to me, Matt. I know you're going to kill me. Just like you killed the others." She was being deliberately dramatic. She was hoping her words would propel Heather into helping her.

"Oh, no, you got it all wrong," he said. "I'm not going to hurt you."

"Oh, come off it, Matt. You're not going to leave me alive so I can testify against you later."

"Taylor, you're like a sister," Matt said with a puzzled expression. "I'd never hurt you."

Heather looked at her nails and sighed heavily. "Taylor is right, you know. *You do have to kill her.*"

STEELE PRESSED the accelerator—pushing it past ninety. Red lights, green lights, they were all the same. His teeth were clenched and his mind was racing. A cold sweat beaded on his forehead. He had to get to the marina before the McCalls set sail. Once they were under way, it would be doubly hard to find them. He made it to the marina in record time. They reached the McCalls' boat bin in time to see the faint outline of their boat in the distance. They were too late! "No!" he screamed, falling to his knees. "No!"

MATT'S MOUTH DROPPED OPEN. "*What* did you say?"

Heather continued to study her nails. "I said you have to kill her—but do it outside—then throw the body overboard." She looked up, only then seeming to sense Matt's astonishment. "What's the matter?"

"I—I'm...not going to *kill* Taylor," Matt stammered.

"Why not?" Heather asked him curiously.

"Dear God, Heather...you don't kill people. "

Taylor's hand flew to her mouth as realization dawned. Matt might have stolen from Craig, but he was no killer. She turned toward Heather. "It was you. You killed Allison."

"No!" Matt said, looking at her incredulously. "No! You can't seriously think something like that."

"I'm afraid she's very serious," Heather said calmly. "And that's why you have to kill her."

Matt's head swiveled from Taylor to Heather. "B-but...you didn't kill Allison."

Heather looked at her husband and shrugged. "Oh, but I did."

Matt flinched as if he'd been struck.

"She didn't leave me any choice," Heather continued. "I had to do it. And now you have to kill Taylor. It's the only way to stop her from going to the police."

Taylor stood there listening to her, hardly able to believe her ears. But it all fit. Heather was familiar with the residence and grounds of Allison's condo and Craig's house. It would have been easy for her to slip out of the condo after killing Allison, as well as for her to get back inside later to plant evidence against Craig. No doubt it had been Heather who she and Steele had encountered at the condo and who had planted the murder weapon at Craig's. She'd killed Lamden and Norris...and now she was going to kill her. She had to stall for time. By now, Steele had to know she was missing and looking for her.

"If you let me go, I won't go to the police," Taylor said. "Besides, what can I tell them? I only know about the embezzlement, nothing else."

"Don't underestimate yourself." Heather's voice was bland and the smile that touched her lips was not reflected in her eyes. "You know everything. You just haven't put it together, yet."

Taylor looked at her puzzled.

"I knew Allison had found something," Heather said. "But before I could really search the place, I heard Ted Larson coming. Later, when I went back to the condo, I ran into you and Steele. But I thought I was safe until the night of the dinner party, when Steele started teasing you. Matt thought his story was funny, but I was terrified."

It took a moment for Heather's words to sink in. Steele had teased her about... Taylor's heart jumped in her throat as realization dawned. The true crime studies. Heather was the young girl who had killed her foster parents!

Once Heather was certain Taylor had made the connection, she picked up the narrative. "I made the mistake of telling Allison that I lived in Philadelphia with a foster family for a while, and that they called me Red. I don't think she'd thought too much of what I'd said until that nosy Mrs. Kent started filling her head with a lot of nonsense about not trusting me, that I wasn't what I seemed. Then, when Mrs. Kent died, she became suspicious. Somehow she found out about my past. She threatened to tell the police that I'd killed Mrs. Kent if I didn't give her three-hundred-thousand dollars.''

''Why didn't you tell me?'' Matt's voice was strangled, and his face was drained of any color. ''Whatever you did was in the past. But killing Allison? There had to be some other way.''

''Really, Matt, there was no other way,'' she snapped. ''If you must know, I did kill Mrs. Kent.''

''Oh, God, no!'' Matt moaned. ''No!''

''Don't you understand,'' she said angrily. ''I had to kill Allison. There would have been no end to her blackmail.''

Taylor looked at Matt. He appeared to be in shock. Keep her talking, an inner voice screamed. At the same time, she prayed that Steele had figured out where she was and would arrive at any moment.

''I know why you killed Allison,'' she said. ''But why Harold Lamden?''

Heather raised her hand in a gesture of dismissal. ''Lamden uncovered the embezzlement.'' At Matt's look of surprise, she added, ''Not yours, though, like Taylor he did think you were the culprit. But it was me. I knew where you'd gotten the money for the down payment. And I knew you were eaten up with guilt and distracted, not managing his portfolio that way you should. I took the money from Craig's account and paid off Allison.'' She threw Taylor a cold smile. ''I'm not as dumb as you and Matt's friends thought, am I? Anyway, Lamden called the house. He wanted to give Matt the opportunity to make restitution. I told him Matt was out of town and persuaded him to let me come by his house that evening to resolve the matter. When he wasn't looking, I slipped a sleeping pill in his drink. You know the rest.''

Her words were spoken calmly, matter of factly, with no remorse whatsoever. Taylor knew then that Heather was totally without a conscience—a sociopath—and, as such, could not be reasoned with or appealed to for mercy.

"Is that why you killed Norris? Because she figured out that Lamden hadn't committed suicide?" Taylor tried to hold in her fear.

"Something like that," Heather said, turning to rummage in her shoulder bag. "She was asking entirely too many questions. I couldn't take the chance of her putting the pieces together."

She pinned Matt with a pained look. "This is getting very tiresome. Get on with it."

"Why can't we just leave her on the boat at Benton Harbor like we planned?" Matt asked, lowering the barrel of the gun.

Heather sighed heavily. "Because I don't want to leave any loose ends." She produced a gun from her shoulder bag. "If you can't do it, I'll do it myself," she said petulantly. "You know, Matt, I am very disappointed. I thought I could *count* on you."

Matt looked at her, horrified. "Not for...murder."

"Obviously not," Heather said, and sighed again in exasperation. She gestured with the gun. "Okay, Taylor, out on deck."

"No!" Matt said, blocking the doorway. "I'm not going to let you do this!"

"That's too bad," Heather said, and fired at point-blank range. Matt grabbed his chest and fell to the floor.

"Matt!" Taylor screamed. She stared at Matt's lifeless body.

"Move," Heather said, jamming the barrel of the gun into her side for emphasis.

Taylor swallowed, trying to hang on to her panic. She tried to steady her nerves, but her fear kept getting the best of her. Steele would get here in time. She knew he would.

Out on the deck, she looked around her, at the gleaming mahogany of the deck where she would soon lie bleeding. *What a stupid place to die,* she thought. She closed her eyes against the pain of never seeing Steele again, of never telling him she loved him. When she opened them, she blinked twice, not sure if her mind was playing tricks on her. Over Heather's right shoulder, off in the distance she could just make out a boat. Her heart jumped in her throat. Steele!

"You'll never get away with this," she said, stalling for time. "How are you going to explain Matt's and my deaths?"

Heather chuckled. "I'm going to tell the authorities that you discovered that Matt killed Allison and the others. He then shot you and tried to killed me. It was self-defense."

Keep her talking, her mind screamed. "From all accounts, Allison was a shrewd cookie—how did you outsmart her?"

"Oh, that was easy." Heather laughed, then launched into a narrative of how she'd lured Allison into thinking she was going along with the blackmail. "Well, Taylor, this is where—"

Suddenly, out of the night, a light caught Heather and Taylor in its beam. "This is the United States Coast Guard," a deep male voice boomed. "Drop your gun and prepare to be boarded."

Heather whirled around, giving Taylor a chance to put some distance between them. Out of the corner of her eye, she saw Heather swivel back and take aim. A bullet whizzed past as she ducked down.

"Drop the gun and put your hands up in the air," the voice boomed again.

Heather ignored the command and charged toward her. Taylor jumped up, but before she could take more than a step, excruciating pain shot through her scalp. She screamed as her head was snapped back brutally by a vicious yank on her hair. She turned, clawing at the other woman's face.

Over Heather's left shoulder she saw that the coast guard cutter had drawn up alongside the boat and Steele was jumping on deck. He grabbed the first thing he saw, a fire extinguisher. "Heather!" he shouted. Startled, Heather spun toward the voice, and he sprayed her full in the face before she could bring the gun around.

The icy breath of the CO_2 extinguisher spilled over Taylor's face as she tried to grab the gun from Heather's hand. "Damn it! Let go!" Heather screamed out, choking on the gas that momentarily blinded her as she turned the gun toward Steele. But Taylor pushed her arm up just as she fired, sending the bullet flying through the night air. Heather twisted, spinning Taylor away.

At that precise moment, the deck tilted and Heather fell against her, still swearing and struggling. Taylor felt the rail hit the back of her knees, and then she was arcing through the air. She hit the water on her back, and the impact knocked the wind from her lungs.

She seemed to go down forever, but she never reached the bottom. Then she began to rise, but it also took forever. Her lungs were in agony, and the darkness of the air and water were one, so she didn't know she was near the surface until she broke through it.

The McCall yacht was about a hundred yards from her and moving away. She could see Heather firing aimlessly at Steele as he searched the water for her.

How long before Steele could subdue Heather and be able to look for her? she wondered, trying to fight her mounting panic. She was miles from any land, and she was not a strong swimmer.

"Oh, Steele . . ." she whispered, and went on whispering in a litany of pleading until a wave filled her mouth with water and she choked.

All Taylor's life, her worst fear had been to drown. Time and again, through childhood and beyond, she'd jerk awake from dreams in which she'd seen herself drowning. Horrified, she suddenly knew that they had not been nightmares but premonitions. She *was* going to drown.

As if to confirm her destiny, as a promise of things to come, something cold and slimy passed by in the blackness beneath her, brushing lightly against her right leg.

Taylor screamed and kept on screaming until the water filled her mouth.

STEELE'S HEART STOPPED when he saw Taylor go overboard. He threw the fire extinguisher at Heather, then ran around the side of the boat he'd seen her go over. He didn't see anything.

"Taylor! Taylor!" he shouted, then ducked back down as he dodged another shot.

Steele's next action was not premeditated. He only knew he had to subdue Heather before he could help Taylor. He picked up the first thing he saw, a life preserver, and flung it at her.

Heather shrieked, whether at seeing an object being hurled at her or at the actual contact, Steele never knew. As Heather ducked to avoid the life preserver, Steele leapt forward.

It was a simple matter to wrench the gun from Heather's fingers and grab her right arm and pull it behind her back. He wrapped his left arm around her throat. Heather twisted and turned, but to no avail.

"Are you all right?" Hawk asked, stepping aboard the boat. Three coast guard officers followed, their guns drawn.

"Here," he said, pushing a defiant Heather toward Hawk. "Taylor's overboard!" He frantically searched the water, calling her name. "Get a light in the water and have someone turn this boat around."

It seemed like hours, but in reality it probably took only a few minutes for them to spot her, and then he was in the water.

He dragged a moaning and limp Taylor from the water and onto the boat. Hawk dropped a blanket for him and Taylor.

"Taylor? Can you hear me? Can you open your eyes?"

Taylor's eyelids fluttered and slowly opened, then closed on a moan.

Relief swelled in Steele's chest and filled his heart. He knelt down and took her in his arms. "Taylor," he murmured, hugging her fiercely to his chest. He'd come so close to losing her. If he lived to be a hundred, he knew he'd never get the image of her falling overboard out of his mind. If he'd been just a few minutes later, she would have—

He shoved the disturbing thoughts aside. She was safe. She was with him. And he was never going to let her go.

"Don't worry about anything," he said. "I'll take care of everything."

She nestled into his shoulder. "I never had any doubt."

The false bravado in her voice struck all the right chords in his heart. She was tough about the right things. And soft about the right things, too. He kissed her forehead.

"How do you feel?" he asked.

She sighed and burrowed closer. "Numb, I think. I would never have guessed in a million years Heather was the killer." She twisted in his arms. "Remember the case studies from that true-crime book I found at Allison's? The one about the young girl? That was Heather!"

"I know," he said. He caressed her cheek and cradled her head. "Larson said Allison called the blackmailer Red. I'd heard that nickname before in the context of the case and remembered it was a reference to the girl's hair color. And the only female connected with this case with red hair was Heather. I'd always thought she wasn't what she seemed. Plus she lied about calling the fire department and she was awfully interested in knowing if Allison's documents burned. She had to be the killer. She's a real psycho—this time she's going to be put away for life."

"Oh, Steele…" She trembled in his arms, and he held her tight. Her face darkened as another memory came coursing back. "Matt—Matt's dead. Heather shot him." She closed her eyes and shuddered.

Steele pulled her closer. "Hawk said he's lost a lot of blood, but he's going to be all right."

Taylor's head rose from his shoulder. "Thank God," she whispered. Then in a rush of words, she told him about the confrontation between Matt and Heather.

"What's going to happen to him?" she asked.

He covered her hand with his. "I don't know. He did embezzle money from Craig, but he had nothing to do with the murders and he tried to help you. That should go a long way if any criminal charges are filed against him, but I'm not sure what's going to happen between him and Craig."

She shivered again, and Steele brought her back to his side. He held her there for several minutes until he could feel her heart slowing and matching the beats of his own. He felt so good now that the terror was finally over. That she was safe by his side. "It's all over now," he said, hugging her close.

He felt her grow still, and there was a catch in her voice as she said, "Well, I guess you'll be heading back to Washington soon."

He traced a heart across her open palm with his index finger. "Yeah, but I'd like for you to go with me."

She lifted her eyes slowly to look into his, and he saw the tears swimming in the deep brown of her eyes. "Steele, are you sure?"

"Taylor, I've never been so sure of anything in my life." He drew a deep breath, then released it in a long sigh. He exhaled a lifetime of loneliness in his next words and he knew it. "Taylor, I love you very much and I want to share my life with you."

Her face broke into a brilliant smile. "Oh, Steele, I love you, too."

She loved him. Warmth expanded in his chest, trickled out into his shoulders and arms, rushed down through his legs. It made him feel strong, weak, invincible, vulnerable, full and empty all at the same time. And very happy.

Steele took her into his arms. His last thought as his mouth covered hers was of how much he loved her. She was his life. He was happier than he'd ever thought he could be. His life was complete.